M000296260

Daisy Doyle

Madonna Ball

Abuzz Press

Copyright © 2018 Madonna Ball

ISBN: 978-1-63263-893-9

All rights reserved. No part of this publication may be reproduced, stored in a retrieval system, or transmitted in any form or by any means, electronic, mechanical, recording or otherwise, without the prior written permission of the author.

Published by Abuzz Press, St. Petersburg, Florida.

Printed on acid-free paper.

The characters and events in this book are fictitious. Any similarity to real persons, living or dead, is coincidental and not intended by the author.

Abuzz Press
2018

First Edition

Library of Congress Cataloguing in Publication Data
Ball, Madonna
Daisy Doyle by Madonna Ball
Fiction: General | Fiction: Young Adult| Family and Relationships
Library of Congress Control Number: 2018955027

Dedication

For my mother, Ann Franklin and all mothers who teach their daughters how to love.

Table of Contents

Part One

1
Where's Denny?
Late Fall 1983

The silence that marked my brother's absence from the dinner table wasn't cause for concern—not at first anyway. Denny was dead, but we didn't know it at the time.

"Emily Post would turn over in her grave," Mom said, placing the still steaming pot of broccoli on a trivet in the center of the table instead of transferring it to a serving bowl, "but I'm too exhausted to make another trip back to the kitchen."

"Who's Emily Post?" asked Daniel.

"Never mind," said David. "You're such an imbecile. You don't know anything. Just shut up so we can eat. I'm starving."

Mom shot David a cautionary look before addressing Daniel's question. "Emily Post was a writer. I think she wrote a few novels, but she's mostly known for her books on etiquette—" she stopped mid-sentence. Neither Daniel nor David were listening to her explanation. They were too busy kicking each other under the table.

Dad also observed my brothers screwing around, so he reached over and swatted David in the back of his head. "You're both imbeciles! Now stop playing footsies under the table, sit up and listen to your mother!" he snapped, but Mom didn't bother to elaborate. She gave the table another once-over and removed the lid from the pot.

"Yuck! Gross!" yelled Daniel, holding his nose. "Put the lid back on. That broccoli smells like farts."

"If I leave the lid on, the broccoli will continue cooking and then it won't be any good," Mom said, ignoring his crude comment.

"Here she goes again," Daniel complained. "You can't die from eating overcooked broccoli, so what's the big deal?"

To our mother, a self-proclaimed health guru who was always experimenting with new foods and diets, it was a very big deal. Her dietary regime *du jour* consisted of serving one green, lightly steamed or raw vegetable at every meal—even at breakfast.

"Don't be ridiculous." she said. "You're not going to die, but overcooked vegetables have little to no nutritional value. Raw vegetables with their skins left on and dark, leafy green vegetables are really the way to go. Count your blessings that I'm not serving you a plate full of kale or raw zucchini spears." David scrunched up his nose and Daniel stuck out his tongue. "Stop with the faces and smear a little butter on the broccoli if you must, but either way, the two of you are eating it. It's good for you." To appease my persnickety brothers, Mom placed the lid back on the pot and took her seat at the table. Only then did she notice the empty chair next to mine. "Where's your brother?" she asked. Denny was frequently a no-show at the dinner table, so none of us bothered to answer.

"Can't we just say grace and eat?" David asked. "I'm hungry."

"No, but someone can tell me where Denny is. I'm quite certain I told one of you to call him in for dinner. Where is he?"

The three of us looked down at our empty plates in response to Mom's question.

"C'mon guys," Dad said, unfolding his napkin and placing it in his lap. "Your mother asked a question. Don't just sit there like a bunch of deaf mutes."

Accusatory glances bounced from person to person, but in the end, her inquiry was met with shrugged shoulders and blank expressions, which fueled her and Dad's aggravation even more. Thoroughly disgusted, Dad pushed his chair away from the table, threw his napkin down onto his plate and announced that he'd go track Denny down. "I'll go get him. You kids don't listen worth a darn and it's getting old."

I didn't want to be at the table in the first place, so I jumped up and offered to go look for him. "I'll go find him. You don't have to go."

With an angry stare, he ordered me to sit down. "Never mind! It's too late for that, Daisy. Maybe you should've worried about doing as you were told the first time around. I expect more from you. You're the oldest! You need to start acting like it."

"But she didn't ask me," I insisted.

Nobody said as much, but we all assumed that Denny was somewhere outside still playing and not giving a second thought to how dark or late it was getting. My little brother was stubborn and rarely came in the first time he was called. He'd beg for just a few more precious minutes of playtime. With him it was always, "Why can't I eat later when I'm actually hungry?" Or, "Let me do x, y, and z first and then I'll come in." Like the rest of us, he was pretty good at pretending not to hear. Only when Mom or Dad threw down the gauntlet and threatened to spank him did he comply.

Dad always complained about Denny's poor listening skills, but deep down we all knew that Denny was his favorite, and that he secretly admired his tenaciousness. He was forever saying things like, "Denny's his own man," or "He'll make a fine litigator some day because he doesn't take no for an answer." As for the rest of us, excluding Mom, we viewed our youngest brother's inability to ever do what he was told as a sign that he was an overindulged little brat. Mom coddled him because he was her baby and made the lamest excuses ever for his bad behavior. She fawned all over him, and so had I in the beginning, but the older he got, the more annoying he became. He was a spaz and literally didn't stop moving or talking until he passed out at the end of the day from exhaustion. More nights than not, he was found asleep on his bedroom floor with puzzle pieces or Lego bricks mushed into one side of his face. My parents often argued over whose turn it was to wake him, but in the end, it usually took both to get him into the bed after several minutes of gentle coaxing and sweet-talking on Mom's part. "C'mon sweetie, get up and get in your bed." He'd semi-waken, but act like a total space cadet. Once when Dad was steering him to his bed, Denny stopped in front of his toy box, pulled down his pants and started peeing all over his toys. Only when he was super tired or not feeling well did he go to sleep willingly, but it was never in his own bed. Instead, he'd crawl up on Mom or Dad's lap or grab his ratty *Bert and Ernie* blanket and snuggle next to Gus on the oversized dog bed and fall asleep. Getting Denny to follow any kind of schedule was like pulling teeth for my parents especially once Denny started school. He began kindergarten the same year I entered middle school. I left in the morning long before my other two brothers even dreamed of getting out of bed, so it was just Denny and I in our bathroom. Denny played in the tub while I did my hair and make-up for an hour or so in front of the mirror. Mom fixed breakfast and packed our lunches. Denny loved taking baths and played in the tepid bathwater until his fingers and toes resembled shriveled up prunes. I wouldn't admit it at the time, but he looked so cute splashing around in the tub surrounded by mountainous piles of frothy bubbles and bath toys. He looked like a miniature figurine in a swirling snow globe. Overall, Denny was a pretty happy-go-lucky kid, just as long as he was doing exactly what he wanted to do, which included eating when he was hungry and not at a fixed time. The night he went missing was no exception.

"He knows how important Sunday dinner is to me. It's the only time we ever eat in the dining room. Everything will be ice cold by the time he gets in and washes up and nobody will want to eat the fish then," Mom complained as she eyeballed the platter of fried smelt and hand cut French-fries. The smelt were a gift from one of Dad's work associates and our freezer was full of the pint-sized fish, even though not even Dad really cared for them. The tiny fish were tolerable only fresh from the deep fryer when their golden-floured skins were still crispy. Soggy, cold smelt and smelt-flavored French fries—it never occurred to Mom to change the oil after frying the fish—were disgusting. Frustrated, Mom released a long deep sigh. "I guess it doesn't matter to Denny if dinner's ruined. He's not going to eat what I've fixed anyhow. If it was up to him, he'd eat a fried bologna and cheese sandwich for every meal."

We waited at the table for Dad to return with his prodigal son. After several minutes, Dad came in from outside, but Denny wasn't with him.

"John, where's Denny?" Mom demanded.

Dad drew a deep breath and said, "I think we need to make a few phone calls."

Fear filled Mom's eyes. "What? What are you saying?"

"Now stay calm, Linda. Everything is going to be okay. We'll find him. It might just take a few calls to the neighbors."

We called all the neighbors, even a few of his friends from school, but by 6:00 the consensus was that nobody had seen him since earlier in the day. Panicked, Mom phoned the police. It took nearly forty minutes for them to arrive, which really pissed Dad off. When they finally got to the house, their presence wasn't very reassuring. They didn't look at all how I'd imagined. One of the officers looked like a pimply-faced kid barely older than I, and the other one looked like a broken-down, senile old man. The older officer must have sensed Dad's anger and quickly repeated the sentiments expressed by the dispatcher on the phone.

"Take it easy now. Most calls regarding missing children are false alarms. The child in question usually comes home within twenty-four hours or was never missing in the first place."

"What's that supposed to mean?" Dad asked.

The younger officer spoke up. "When little kids get overly tired or upset about something they sometimes wander off to be alone. Often, they hunker down in small or enclosed spaces such as closets, old cardboard boxes or underneath beds. I guess they find it comforting. It starts off as some sort of game or means of escape, but then they get tired and fall asleep and then we get calls from panicky folks because they can't find their kid. He's probably tucked away somewhere in the house. We'll look around and find him."

The tiny hairs standing up on the back of my neck told me that the officer was wrong.

2
The Bathroom
Fall 1987

As I waited for the water to warm, I studied my reflection and unlike Narcissus, the ill-fated character from Greek mythology, I didn't fall in love with my own image. I looked as insignificant as I felt. With my pasty skin and purplish moons shadowing the thin skin beneath my eyes, I resembled a sad, droopy-faced basset hound. The vibrating pipes hidden within the walls and ceiling grumbled and growled and reminded me of my isolation. And though the communal bathroom of a college dorm isn't typically perceived as a perilous place, I'd watched one too many horror movies. Paranoia set in. I turned from the sink to eye the floors of the stalls. I nudged open each door to make certain there wasn't a deranged, masked killer standing on one of the toilet seats wielding an enormous knife and waiting to snuff out my miserable existence. They were empty.

The bathroom door squeaked open and in walked my fellow insomniac. Though we never actually conversed, it was implied by our silence that we were cool with one another. Reaching into the pocket of her robe, she pulled out her bejeweled pillbox and dumped its contents into her cupped hand. Only after counting six times, never five or seven, she popped two of the confetti colored pills into her mouth before returning the rest to their safe vessel. Like every other night, I was tempted to ask if I could bum one, but once again, I decided against it. That wasn't part of our unspoken arrangement. I hadn't slept well in weeks, and I attributed my overwhelming anxiety to the debilitating insomnia that had hijacked my life.

After my satisfied companion exited the bathroom as inconspicuously as she entered, I made my way back to the sink and placed my hand under the running water. I embraced the comfort the warmth offered and concluded that my deserted surroundings weren't so bad. In less than five hours, I knew that the silent haven would be teeming with chattering girls readying themselves for their early morning classes. I took advantage of the solitude and tried to relax. The sound of the running water lulled me, and after a bit, I could feel my head inching slowly to my chest only to forcefully snap back to an upright position. It was as if, like a marionette, my head was attached to a wire that controlled my movement. The irksome buzz of a fluorescent light captured my attention and released me from my stupor. I wondered just how long I'd been standing in front of the sink like some drunkard perched on a barstool. It wasn't until I raised my hand to wipe the drool that had dripped from the corner of my mouth that I noticed the sticky medicine bottle attached to my other hand. Seeing it jarred my memory, and I remembered the reason behind my late-night visit to the bathroom in the first place. Desperate for anything that would knock me out and keep me asleep for at least a couple of hours, I resorted to cold medicine. Unable to remove the stupid cap, I tried running the bottle under the hot tap water for nearly a minute before taking a second crack at opening it. My hands were wet, which made it difficult to get a secure grip, so I used the bottom of my pajama top. Fortunately, the water had dissolved the hardened syrup from the encrusted neck and the cap twisted off with ease. I was quite certain that I had ingested more than the prescribed amount on the dosing cup, but I didn't care. I was desperate for sleep. Blurred vision followed by a strange spaced-out sensation washed over my entire body like a tidal wave, and I braced myself for what would most likely come next by placing both hands on the vanity in front of me and shutting my eyes. My breathing became labored and I prayed that the imaginary elephant that had plopped down on the center of my chest would just wander back to the fictitious circus inside my head. A desire to flee consumed me, but I knew there was nowhere to go. Back to my dorm room was out of the question and traipsing about campus or down Grand River Avenue in my pajamas in the middle of the night wasn't a viable option either. The Michigan State Campus Police would certainly have picked me up. Angry with myself for not seeing it coming, I unlocked my sealed eyes and gave myself a firm talking to.

What you're experiencing is disassociation and nothing to be afraid of. Disassociation is just a big word used to explain the detached feeling you're experiencing from yourself and your immediate surroundings. It's your mind's way of trying to cope with the tremendous amount of stress that's been thrown at you. You're not losing your mind.

The self-talk helped, and surprisingly, I managed a smile despite how lousy I was feeling. The voice I heard, spewing wisdom as it related to the psychological phenomenon I was experiencing, was not my own. It belonged to only one person. Though I hadn't seen or talked to the woman responsible for saving my life for some time, I thought of her often. The commanding, no nonsense voice that was egging me on was that of my former psychologist, Ava Blume.

Never one to mince words, her unwavering certainty and unapologetic conviction made it impossible for me to dismiss her views, no matter how "out there" they sometimes sounded. I came to construe her opinions as fact and not a matter of personal credence. There was something about her haunting eyes and heavy accent that spoke to me. Maybe it was her refusal to conceal the blurred identification number on her left forearm that endeared her to me. She made no attempt to conceal her past by pretending that it didn't happen. I suppose Ava had lost even more than my family had, but she'd somehow managed to flourish. When nobody else could say or do anything to put an end to my suffering, Ava had found a way to break through to me. She even understood the whole Will situation and didn't pooh-pooh it or make it seem like our breaking up had been just some silly, teenage *Romeo and Juliet* thing. Under her care, I managed to crawl out from under my blanket of sadness.

I closed my eyes and took deep calming breaths. I wasn't aware of any real medicinal qualities attributed to steam, but it felt nice on my skin, so I lowered my face even closer to the sink. Again, I heard Ava's persuasive voice as plain as day.

You're safe. Daisy, you're not losing your mind. You're not going to die.

There had been a time when I had wished I were dead. In that moment, I just wanted to find a way to silence my racing thoughts.

Water began pooling in the sink even though I hadn't inserted the rubber drain stopper. Hair was most likely the culprit, strands of swirling hair, compliments of vain girls with tousled manes who stood in front of the sinks brushing their hair and scrubbing away traces of sleep from their faces. I turned off the faucet and returned my focus to the Nyquil bottle. I replaced the cap. Guilt over helping myself to my roommate's cold medicine tapped me on the shoulder. Jane was a nice girl and I liked her. We had been well suited for one another because we kept to ourselves and didn't ask a lot of questions. I suspected that she too had experienced some tragedy or heartbreak so excruciating, that purging after every meal was the only way she felt solaced. I suspected that deciding what she ate, when she ate it, and when she rid herself of her undigested food might have been the only control she held in her own life. I could relate. Power over anything is therapeutic when you've lost everything. I didn't ask and she didn't tell...and vice versa. Our mutual silence was golden. We didn't speak of her eating disorder or of my brother or of my mom and her condition.

I wasn't certain if it was the medicine that made me feel all dozy, or if my body had finally thrown up the white flag, but suddenly I couldn't keep my eyes open. I made my way down the hallway and noticed light streaming out from under the closed door of my dorm room, and for a minute, I considered not going back in. I had assumed that Jane was out cold when I crept out, but I must've woken her.

"Hey," I announced, stepping into the room, "I'm so sorry for waking you." I forgot for a second that I was still holding her Nyquil bottle, but she didn't bat an eye as I clumsily attempted to hide it behind my back.

"Where were you?" she asked, stepping cautiously towards me with her hands awkwardly hanging by her side. She looked like one of those animal rescue workers approaching an injured animal and trying not to scare it off. I sensed that her strange behavior had nothing to do with me waking her. I'd pilfered her Nyquil and robbed her of sleep, yet she didn't appear angry. Empathy erupted from her expressive eyes and I could tell by her careful tone that she really wasn't interested in where I'd been. Her inquiry was nothing more than a segue for what she needed to say next, but she didn't wait for me to respond.

"Your dad called, Daisy. He needs you to call home right away."

I heard the urgency in her voice, but I didn't leap into action. Her eyes darted back and forth from the phone to me as if she were telepathically sending me a message to pick it up. Only when she began wringing her hands and blinking, as if she'd just walked from a dark theater out into the glaring sunlight of a parking lot, did I understand that if I didn't do something soon, she was going to start bawling. I took her hand and led her to the bottom bunk bed. We sat. In a motherly way, I patted her knee as if somehow the simple gesture would make everything okay. It soothed us both, but we remained silent. I was certain the call was about Mom. She was either dead or close to it and strangely, the morbid thought comforted me. For the first time in a long time, I felt that everything was as it was meant to be. Soon Mom was going to be reunited with her last born. I nodded and let go of Jane's hand. She walked over to the phone, picked it up and dialed the number as I rattled it off. Still holding the phone, she guided it to my ear. Dad answered right away, but did all the talking. I listened and nodded my head. When I finally opened my mouth to speak, I slurred. I couldn't tell if the words were really coming out in slow motion or if I was just imagining it. Dad must've sensed my incoherence and once again told me that I had to wait until morning to drive home. I confirmed that I understood, and then handed the phone back to Jane. My eyelids felt like sinkers had been attached to them. I shimmied up the ladder and passed out in my bunk. Somewhere between sleep and dreaming, my thoughts shifted from Mom to my brother Denny. He was in the room with me, but he wasn't a little boy anymore. He was a baby. The sight of him triggered something in my brain and I felt the muscles in the corners of my mouth turning up to form a smile. My heart ached thinking about how much I loved him then. We were inseparable. I even took baths with him when he was very little. Naturally, Mom never let the two of us out of her sight while we were in the tub. The water had barely covered my outstretched legs, but that didn't prevent her from being a mother hen. "Keep a firm grip on him," she'd warn. "He's as slick as a baby seal." Again, and again she lectured me on the importance of never leaving an infant unattended in the bathtub. "Always use caution, especially when you're a momma someday. It takes but a second for a little baby to slip under the water. And then," she snapped her fingers to emphasize how quickly it could happen, "gone in an instant."

As Denny grew from a baby to a toddler to an obnoxious little kid, I grew less enamored with him. I selfishly cared only about my own life. I turned away from my brother for what felt like less than a minute, and when I turned back around, he was gone.

3
Going Home

I struggled to awaken. My mind was trapped between two states of consciousness and I couldn't tell whether the sounds and smells wafting into my dorm room were real, or part of my fantastical dream. Temporary paralysis pinned me to my bed like a wrestler to a mat. If I stood, I feared that the weight of my upper body and arms would send me toppling over. My limbs felt heavy, like branches hanging from trees after a good rain. The sleep paralysis that I was experiencing was nothing new to me, but it was still infuriating. I knew the more I fought it, the worse it would get, so I tried to relax and focused on something else. My thoughts shifted from trees to water, and the sound of lapping waves. I saw a lake, and when I tasted the water on my tongue, I knew that I was dreaming.

Like most dreams, the scenes unfolded in no order but looked very real. The images were not grainy or muted. They were distinct, and caused my heart to twinge. I was back at the cottage on Lake Huron with my family. I saw Mom as she was then, so very happy. Her bald head tightly wrapped in a scarf like a Muslim woman in a hijab. She was all face and eyes and beautiful. Mom was dying. It turned out that the cyst wasn't as harmless as the doctors first suspected. They had been 99.9% sure she would respond well to treatment, but she hadn't.

"Glad I'm not a gambling gal," was her response after her oncologist informed her that his initial prognosis had been very wrong. Most people in her shoes would have come unglued, but not Mom. She kept it together for the sake of Dr. Barnes. Sparing his feelings trumped the fact that she had just been delivered a death sentence. It was just her way. Her breast cancer hadn't responded well to any of the treatments and was declaring war on her beautiful, left-sided brain. She didn't have a fighting chance, but she was hell-bent on making sure the rest of us were all okay before she died. She had been diagnosed the summer before my senior year, right around the time I was applying to colleges. She was resolute in her belief that everything was going to be okay. "I didn't finish college and there's no way in hell that I'm going to let you miss out just because I'm sick. It's breast cancer. Women beat breast cancer all the time. Look at Golda Meir. She had cancer for over ten years before she died." Golda, the former prime minister of Israel, was 80 when she died of blood cancer. Mom was in the prime of her life, but we all knew better than to ever argue with her. "I'll go through treatment and by the time you're ready to go off to college I'll be fine. We can't stop making plans just because I'm sick." She had been so confident. But when I left the following fall, she wasn't so self-assured and neither was I. "Now, you promise me Daisy, that you won't come home every weekend. Daddy will let you know when it gets bad, and when it does, he'll call for you. I don't want you missing a lot of school because of me. Promise me you'll try to have some fun this year, and that you'll make some real friends. Promise me that when it's over, you'll move on with your life, no matter how difficult it may be. Promise me that you'll try to be happy. The boys, including Daddy, will follow your lead."

We were all happy during those two weeks at the beach just before I started my freshman year at

Michigan State. It was probably the most normal any of us had felt in a very long time. The trip was exactly what the doctor ordered. In the evenings, we bickered over trivial things such as what to watch on the television set that only got three channels. We argued over which one of the boys forgot to put the toilet seat down, or who left the near empty bag of Funyuns open on the counter to get stale from the humid, lake air, but we also practiced being happy again on neutral ground. The best part of the entire trip was the small piano that Dad had arranged to get smuggled into the cottage before we got there.

Contrary to the rental agreement that came in the mail months before our scheduled stay, the keys to the cottage were not found in the lockbox to the right of the front door. Dad was furious.

"Maybe it's hanging on a hook under the front porch," I suggested. Keys to the other places we rented over the years were often stashed under the porch. Dad shot me a contemptuous look. "Check the flower pots then," I barked. I was only trying to be helpful, but it was hot and muggy and like all of us, he was grouchy and ready for our vacation to start. We were weighed down like pack mules. Our arms teemed with bags of groceries, beach chairs, inflatable water toys and luggage that held all the amenities that would help ensure our home away from home was as comfortable as our actual residence.

"Let's all say a prayer to Saint Anthony," Mom suggested.

"Old Tony better pull through," Dad groused. "If they're not here, we'll have to drive all the way over to the rental office to get another set."

In unison, everybody but Dad prayed fervently to the patron saint of lost things. "Saint Anthony, Saint Anthony, please come around. The keys to the cottage are lost and cannot be found." I don't know if it was all the praying or if we just got lucky, but out of the blue, Daniel spotted the key ring sitting in the middle of the picnic table.

With his one free hand, Dad shimmied open the stubborn front door. "Alright Linda. When we get inside, close your eyes," he said, "and don't open them until I say when." Mom was a sucker for surprises and was more than happy to comply. We trailed behind the two of them through the kitchen, passed the brightly lit dining room and into the nautical themed living room.

"Oh my!" she whispered from under her cupped hand. It was difficult to measure her reaction. There, amidst the white-washed wicker furniture and prints of lighthouses of the Great Lakes, sat a small piano. It wasn't much to look at, with its stained, wobbly keys, but it was a piano just the same.

"I figured that maybe since we're on vacation and at a totally new place, that just maybe you'd be in the mood to play a little bit."

"Where on Earth did you find it?" she asked.

"Do you like it? It's on loan from a Catholic school just outside Lexington. The principal's a buddy of mine from way back. We played on the same Little League team," Dad explained. "I got permission from the rental office and my buddy worked out the delivery with the owner and voila—you've got yourself a piano. Had to pay a little extra but what the hell. We're on vacation."

Mom gazed at the piano for some time before placing her right thumb on the middle C key and then the rest of her fingers on D, E, F and G just like she was a novice student practicing hand placement. Daniel, David and I still played the piano at home, but she hadn't touched it in years. After Denny died, we started taking lessons from a teacher at a music studio in town.

"Would you play something?" Dad asked, pulling out the bench for her to sit. From his briefcase he fished out a stack of songbooks and sheet music. The pages of the books were held together with yellow, brittle tape. While the rest of us unpacked and got settled in, Mom kept us entertained with one song after another. For the duration of our stay, if she wasn't outside basking in the sun or sitting on the screened-in porch working a puzzle, she was in front of the piano playing her heart out. Dad was in vacation mode too. He read one Stephen King novel after another under the striped awning on the side of the wraparound porch that faced the lake.

"This is the life. Everything I need is right here. I've got my books, a magnificent view of the water and best of all, my gorgeous wife by my side playing the piano." He didn't have Denny, but he didn't mention him. He didn't need to. Everybody felt his absence.

Arranging for the use of the piano had been a brilliant idea and I could tell that Dad was proud of his ingenuity. Ordinarily a very modest man, he paraded around those first couple days at the lake with his head held higher than usual. He, not God or the fickle hand of fate, was responsible for the smile cemented on the love of his life's face. My brothers Daniel and David hung out with the kids who had, like my family, been coming to the lake for years. Most of the places were private residences, but there were some, like ours, that could be rented for a week or two at a time. We hadn't been to Lexington since before Denny's death. I spent most of the time reading or taking long walks along the beach. Dad and I did most of the cooking and at night, after dinner, we played *Scrabble, Life* or *Monopoly*. Sometimes Dad built a bonfire and we'd sit outside around the smoky fire pit listening to music or the simple sound of the waves crashing on the beach. We were happy and nothing could spoil our "Shangri-La," as Mom so fondly referred to our time at the lake. She was right. Our time at the cottage was nothing short of magical.

I awakened again to discover that I was finally able to drag myself out of the bed. My skin felt clammy and gross. The hair on the nape of my neck and around my temples was damp with sweat. Even with the window slightly ajar, the room felt like a sauna. My eyes weren't ready for the harsh florescent dorm lights, but the room was still dark and it was difficult to see. My roommate was already gone. I held my breath as I gave the twisted nylon cord a gentle tug. Twice that week the battered aluminum blinds had come crashing down on me. The cool autumn air was a welcome reprieve. I cranked the window open as far as it would go and was greeted by the smell of burning wood emanating from the fireplace of a nearby residence. Instinctively I thought of home. I wanted nothing more than to stand in front of the open window and meditate, but there was too much that I had to do. For starters, I needed to pack. The clothes I shoved into my canvas tote consisted of mostly jeans and sweaters. I debated over whether or not to take the formal dress that hung in the closet next to my winter coat. Much to Mom's disappointment, the dress had never been worn. The tags were still attached. She and I had picked it out together, months earlier when Daniel and David were still away at Interlochen, a fine arts camp about 15 miles southwest of Traverse City, Michigan. They had been gone for several days and were scheduled to return when Mom suggested that the two of us have one last hurrah before they got back.

"Just the two of us," she insisted. "Lunch and then shopping. What do you think?" From her bedside table, she pulled out a small spiral notebook with a list of things that we needed to take care of before I left for school. "We need a comforter for a twin bed and sheets, at least two sets of towels, an iron and ooh, I almost forgot, a laundry basket." She rattled off a few other things, but I wasn't listening. "And Daisy, don't take this the wrong way, but you need to spruce up your wardrobe, especially if you're going to be in a sorority. We'll get a few new outfits as well. Jeans and sweatshirts won't cut it."

I wished more than anything that I could be happy. I knew how much me going away to school meant to her, so I pretended to be excited about our outing. "What about a backpack?" I asked.

Like wildfire, a smile traveled across her face as she scrawled the word *backpack* down in her notebook. "You could easily buy one at the campus bookstore, but you'll pay through the nose for it."

God, she was easy to please, I thought.

The plan had been to drive to JC Penny to look for all the dorm stuff and then to a quaint little café for lunch. After lunch, I agreed to shop for clothes. I felt guilty at the thought of shopping for new outfits. Contrary to what Mom believed, a new wardrobe wasn't going to get me jazzed about leaving for school, but I did like the idea of going to lunch. The restaurant was our special place. It was an old time sweet shop that offered handcrafted candies and desserts along with a simple lunch menu. Our order was always the same. Mom ordered a Reuben sandwich and for me, a cheeseburger. Within minutes of being seated, Dad appeared out of nowhere and slid into our booth next to Mom.

"What a surprise!" Mom shrieked, before leaning over and kissing him on the lips. "Look Daisy! Daddy's joined us for lunch." They weren't fooling anyone. It took only a few minutes for me to figure out that I had been had. The entire afternoon had been a carefully orchestrated emotional coup d'état. They knew I'd be forced to listen if we were out in a public place and that I wouldn't be able to stomp off to my room like I had done all the other times they broached the subject of me pledging a sorority. Over my cheeseburger and fries, I pretended to hear them out. They were so desperate for me to be involved in something that might possibly distract me from what we all knew would happen sooner rather than later that they didn't care that the Greek thing just wasn't for me. I'd never been a joiner and clearly didn't fit the sorority sister mold, but I told them that I'd consider it. I had to. After lunch, we went to a swanky department store where my parents bought me a beautiful emerald green dress to wear just in case I chose to pledge. Mom knew all about sororities because she had been in a sorority while at Michigan State. "You'll need something nice for your first formal," she explained, "and a few other nicer dresses for all the different events that you'll be attending, but you can shop once you're up at school. I'm so excited for you. You're going to love it."

As promised, I did go to a couple sorority open houses, but never went back. When the time came, I lied to my parents and told them that the sorority that I wanted to pledge didn't pick me. "Maybe next year," was the hope I left them with.

The dress was far too fancy to wear anywhere other than maybe to a wedding or a formal dance, but I brought it anyway. As I merged onto highway I-69, I tried the radio but it didn't come on. I scanned from one station to the next, but nothing, not even static, streamed from the speakers. I was left with only my manic thoughts to keep me company. Concern for mom was at the forefront, but I knew that it was only a matter of time before I'd begin thinking about Denny and of course, Will. It sucked that I couldn't think of Denny without thinking of Will and vice versa. They disappeared from my life at the exact same time. Their absence left a gaping hole in my heart. Ava once told me that if I never allowed myself to remember the bad, then I'd never be able to truly appreciate all that was good. For the next several hours, I remembered it all.

4
We're Moving
Fall 1982

Dad was offered a position at the bank in the fall of 1982, and he jumped at the chance to advance his career and to move out of the city. When my parents finally broke the news to my brothers and me that we were moving, I wasn't sure what made me angrier, the fact that they were uprooting our entire family without our consent, or the way they went about telling us.

I should've seen it coming. As a rule, my parents were happy, easy going people, but for several days prior to them coming clean with their dismal secret, they seemed a bit on edge. Everything about that week felt off kilter. For starters, Dad was uncharacteristically absent from the dinner table a few nights in a row. For many kids I knew, meals without the dads at the helm of the table were commonplace, but my parents believed that it was important to break bread as a family. Meals were eaten together whenever possible. What we ate was important to Mom, but what was most important to her was that we were together to recap the highlights of our days. Only a handful of times did I recall Mom covering Dad's plate with aluminum foil and leaving it in the oven for him to eat later. Most nights he was home on time, but periodically he'd get tied up with one thing or another and wouldn't get in until well past six o'clock. Denny was thrilled when we didn't have to eat so early, but the rest of us would be practically gnawing off our limbs by the time grace was said and the food doled out. Dad didn't like to eat the minute he walked through the door either, so that delayed dinner even longer. He was a creature of habit. First, he'd swap his work clothes for sweats. Then he'd turn on the nightly news and listen to it while sifting through the day's mail and throwing back a can of *Pabst Blue Ribbon* beer. Sometimes, when the beer can was nearly empty, he'd pass it around and let my brothers and I take a tiny swig. The beer was no longer cold and tasted gross, but the boys liked it. Sometimes he'd crack open one more but never a third. The only time he drank to excess was when he was hanging with his brothers. The men in the Doyle family liked their whiskey, so Dad threw back a few shots with them every so often, but at home—it was one or two beers with dinner. But that week, we ate twice without him and were even served frozen TV dinners. We didn't do either of those things very often. Mom took immense pride in cooking meals from scratch and was not a fan of processed food, so there were never very many boxes of pre-packaged meals sitting in the pantry or in the freezer at our house. The only time we got to feast on Banquet Pot Pies or frozen Salisbury steak dinners smothered in gravy so salty our tongues would swell within minutes of licking the aluminum trays clean, was when we stayed the night with one of our sets of grandparents.

Frozen dinners were all Grandma Nancy fixed for Grandpa Pat anymore. On the two nights that Dad was missing in action from the dinner table, Mom broke her cardinal culinary rule and served us frozen entrees. We didn't question, we just enjoyed. The other nights, he arrived home only slightly later than usual, but he was visibly exhausted and in no mood for putting up with the boys' shenanigans. The boys regularly talked with their mouths jam-packed with food and kicked each other under the table while they ate. Their poor etiquette was nothing new, so Dad becoming so angry with them was unprecedented. It wasn't that my parents didn't care how the boys behaved, they did. But I think after so many years of correcting their crappy behavior, they just threw in the towel. As soon as they cleaned their plates, Dad banished them to their rooms. As for Mom, she was normally an organized person. She had to be, with so many kids and all her piano lessons. A master at juggling many balls at one time, she had exceptional organizational skills. But that week she was a total scatterbrain. Three days in a row she had forgotten to pick up Dad's work clothes from the dry cleaners and he was forced to wear dress shirts that weren't exactly fresh and clean. He compensated by keeping his suit jacket on all day. Denny's school snack calendar also slipped her mind. It wasn't until she saw him standing next to his teacher at dismissal time that she remembered that it had been his day to bring in snack. Miss Michaels, his teacher, was a real sweetheart and assured Mom that the students didn't go hungry. Luckily for them, she always kept a box of snack crackers stashed away in her closet.

"If they were stale, none of the kids complained," she explained. She wasn't exactly certain how old they were and admitted they might have been left over from the previous school year. Mom laughed hysterically every time she repeated the part of the story when the teacher asked her, "You don't think they'll get sick from that do you?"

Mom's response, "Oh, God no. My kids eat stale French fries and whatever else they can fish out of the seat cushions of the station wagon and never get sick," she said jokingly.

Daisy Doyle

I'm sure Miss Michaels was mortified by her comment. By the time Mom shared the story with Dad, I had already heard it at least a half a dozen times. One of Mom's favorite pastimes, when she had a free moment, was talking on the phone to her family. She talked to her mom or one of her five sisters at least once a day, sometimes more, which was why I was a little surprised when I busted her several times that week in the laundry room speaking softly into the phone. I could tell she wasn't talking to family, but she denied it. It wasn't like I was spying on her or anything like that. Each time I was simply going into the kitchen to look for something to eat or to sharpen my pencil and happened to notice the phone cord stretched from the kitchen to the laundry room. When I asked who the heck she was talking to she brushed me off.

"Who you talking to on the phone and why are you whispering?" I asked.

She held up her finger to silence me and then covered the mouthpiece with her hand. "Shh! Please don't interrupt. I'm just talking to one of your aunties," she whispered

"Who? Let me say hi."

"You can talk to Aunt Julie later," she said with a straight face. I knew she was lying because she never snuck off into another room to talk to anyone in her family privately. Everybody in her family knew everybody else's business. Our extended families' triumphs and transgressions were fodder as we sat around the dinner table each night. Uncle Matt's drinking was always interfering with his ability to hold down a job and Aunt Rosemary and Uncle Gary's marriage was perpetually on the rocks because of Uncle Gary's infidelities. He didn't look the part of a Casanova,

35

but apparently, he had a way with the ladies. She even ratted out Grandma from time to time. It was Mom who spilled the beans that Grandma had started smoking again after 15 years. "Well, you're never going to believe it but guess who started smoking again?" she announced during breakfast. Dad was the only one who guessed because the rest of us really didn't care.

"Your sister, Kathy," he said.

"Nope. Mom. She blames it on Dad's dementia. Her nerves can't take all the constant questions and all the wandering around he does in the middle of the night. She's living on nicotine and caffeine. She smokes in the bathroom to try to hide it from Dad, but I don't know why she bothers. She could probably just tell him that he's the one smoking and he'd believe it."

The forgetfulness and the mysterious phone calls were all clues that something wasn't right, but when my parents announced they were taking us to the movies and then out to dinner on Saturday night, I knew something big was brewing. Our family did one or the other but never both. Not on the same night anyway. Dad only sprung for matinees and was a stickler about movie theater snacks. We couldn't get them. They were too expensive. Instead, Mom would smuggle in candy bars and cans of pop into the theater. Once the lights were out and the previews were dancing across the big screen, she'd pass out the contraband goodies that she had stockpiled in her over-sized purse. That night's movie experience was far from ordinary.

We went to the 6:30 show and not a matinee. There were so many good movies playing that it was hard for me to limit my choice to just one. I don't know why I bothered getting excited though. My parents never let me have the final say on anything. Of course, Denny wanted to see something stupid like, *E.T.* for the third time. Even Daniel and David didn't want to see *E.T.* again, but because my parents had never seen it, it didn't take much persuading by Dad to convince the boys to go along with Denny's choice.

"How is it possible that you two haven't seen it? I swear you're the only two people in the entire world who haven't seen that dumb movie!" I complained. I really didn't think the movie was dumb but seeing it once was enough for me. "How 'bout we see something cool or scary like *Amityville 2?*" I asked. My idea sunk like the Titanic.

"You haven't even seen the first one," Mom objected. "Besides, the boys can't see that."

I knew full well the movie would be too scary for the boys and that I'd probably regret watching it the next time I had to babysit, but I didn't care. I felt like being difficult. My parents always gave in to Denny's every whim but never mine. Just once, I wanted them to consider my feelings. "You don't need to see the first one to see the second one." I fired back. "Why can't you go with the boys and Dad go with me?"

"Be reasonable Daisy," Mom pleaded. "That's not an appropriate movie for you either. You'll never babysit again if you watch that movie. And besides, this is about us all being together. I don't want us to split up. That won't be any fun."

"It's never any fun going to the movies with the boys. Denny can't keep his mouth shut and has to go to the bathroom every ten minutes," I argued.

I knew that Dad wouldn't be able to resist putting in his two cents. "He's the baby. When you were his age, you got your way too honey. Besides, you get to go to the movies with your girlfriends all the time. Be a good sport, huh?" said Dad, patting the top of my head like I was an obedient dog being rewarded for learning a new trick. "Will you cheer up if I let you buy something from the concession stand?" he asked.

The snacks did little to help. Watching the movie with all of them was painful. The boys ruined any chance that I might have had for enjoying it a second time because they gave a blow-by-blow of every climactic scene before it happened. When the lights came on and we got up to leave, I noticed my parents dabbing their eyes with their crumpled napkins. Dad's voice sounded funny and Mom couldn't shut up about the little alien and talked about him like he was a real person. It was ridiculous.

"I'm so glad that little guy made it back home," she said over and over. "He's such a sweetie. I bet his family missed him."

"That was good. I haven't cried like that since watching *Old Yeller*," said Dad.

We drove straight from the movie theater to the restaurant for pizza. Any meal out was a treat for my family, reserved for special occasions or exclusively for my parents and their friends. The poor cinema and humdrum cheese pizza was only a preview for the fiasco that was to come.

I held my tongue as my picky family debated over what kind of pizza to order. I already knew how it would play out, so I didn't bother weighing in. Denny didn't like pepperoni because it was too spicy. He preferred sausage, which I thought was even hotter, but Denny couldn't be reasoned with once he got something in his head. Daniel liked pepperoni but was grossed out by the little fennel seeds in the sausage. David didn't like pepperoni or sausage or any vegetables for that matter other than green peppers, which was just plain old stupid. Dad didn't like green peppers, so we always ended up ordering a basic cheese pizza. Nobody said much throughout dinner. The boys talked more about the movie, but Mom and Dad were unusually quiet. Mom drank two glasses of wine and Dad had three beers. They never drank that much unless we were at a family party or wedding. When the waitress came to clear the dishes away, she asked Dad if we were ready for the bill, but he told her that we weren't quite ready.

"Why? Are you getting another drink?" I asked. I was cranky because I wanted to get home to watch TV. Next to Friday night, Saturday night was the best TV night.

"No, we're not getting another drink," Mom said. "Can we just take a few minutes to digest? It's been a hectic week."

"Can't she just bring us the bill? Digest in the car on the way home. What are you guys, sloths? Do you need a month to digest your dinner?" I asked.

"We'll get home soon enough, Daisy," said Dad. He then turned to the boys who were captivated by David and his *Rubik's Cube*. David was bound and determined to complete at least three sides. "Put down that darn cube and give us your attention. Boys," he said snapping his fingers, "for a second, please. Your mother and I have an announcement to make." When they didn't listen, Mom reached over and snatched the cube right out of David's hands and shoved it in her purse.

"Are we getting another dog?" Denny asked. "Is Gussy getting a baby brother or sister?"

Dad glowered. "No, we're not getting another dog. Not yet anyway."

"I thought you said that having one dog was enough," griped David.

"Never mind that," said Dad.

"It's even more exciting than a new dog," said Mom who didn't look very excited at all. In fact, she looked like she was going to throw up. "We're out tonight as a sort of celebration."

"Celebration for what?" asked Daniel.

"What we're celebrating is going to bring about some tremendous changes for the family," Mom explained, "but they'll be good changes. It's a win-win situation for all of us, but I'll let Daddy tell you what it is. It's his news."

"What's his news?" I demanded. All the secrecy was making me a little jumpy. "Tell us already!"

Dad cut right to the chase. "I've accepted a new job. It's a huge promotion. I'll be the chief financial officer of a bank up in Macomb County." Because none of us had a clue where Macomb County was, or what a chief financial officer did, we all just sat there waiting for him to tell us about the exciting part. "Now this new job does require our family to relocate. Mom and I have decided that I'll move up there first to get the lay of the land. You kids will finish out the school year while your mother packs and gets the house sold. In the meantime, I'll look for a new house. We're hoping to be all settled in by the end of June."

I was the first to speak. "That's your exciting news? How could you possibly think that we'd be happy about this? I don't want to move!"

"Me neither," said David. "What about you Daniel? Do you want to move?"

Daniel was unsure. "I don't know. Maybe. Where's Macomb County?"

"Atta boy, Daniel! Way to keep an open mind." Daniel's interest gave Dad the encouragement he needed to close the deal. "Well, Macomb County borders St. Clair County, Oakland County, Wayne County and a few others I believe, but that doesn't really tell you what you need to know. Macomb County is made up of several cities. We'll be living in either St. Clair or Richmond. We'll live out in the country. Your mother and I have always dreamed of owning a little property. With this new job, we can."

"That's good I guess," David reasoned.

"What? Are you kidding?" My disgust wasn't directed at Dad or my brothers, but at Mom. "Since when did you want to live in the country? You hate the country."

"No, I don't. When did I ever say that?" she asked. I knew that I was ruining their big moment, but I didn't feel bad about it. I was so mad at them. There was no way that they could think that we'd be happy about this. I wanted to cry. Mom reached for my hand, but I pulled it away and sat on it before she could grab it.

"This isn't a good thing. It's only good for you two. Don't we have any say in the matter?"

All at once, like a frantic coach on the sidelines with only a few precious seconds remaining on the clock, Dad borrowed a page from the Dr. Spock playbook and began rattling off a list of reasons why this move would benefit the entire family.

"For starters, we'll be getting away from all the riffraff. The old neighborhood isn't what it used to be. The smart people can see the writing on the wall. Everybody's moving out of Wayne County. I don't want to stay in the Detroit-Metro area anymore. I want land and fresh air. We'll finally have the physical space for everything we've always dreamed about. Wouldn't you boys like to have a baseball diamond in the backyard? You won't have to throw the ball in the street anymore. There'd even be room for a trampoline and possibly a pool. Land up there is cheap, so we can buy several acres. In the winter, there'll be miles and miles of open fields for snowmobiling and cross-country skiing. We could consider getting a couple of four-wheelers even. The list goes on and on."

I could tell by the look on the boys' faces that they were buying it hook line and sinker. "What are you talking about? We don't snowmobile. Mom would never allow any of us to set foot on a snowmobile or a four-wheeler. She thinks everything is too dangerous and when have any of us ever cross-country skied?"

"Well, it's never too late to start, right boys?" said Dad.

I shot Mom scathing looks from across the table, but she wouldn't meet my stare. The deed was done and she was desperate to make a clean get away before one of us truly comprehended the death sentence that was just delivered. "Where is the waitress with our bill?" she cried. "I think it's time we leave."

"I hate you guys!" I yelled. Everybody in the restaurant heard me and turned and looked at us. "I can't believe that you're doing this. You're making us leave behind everyone and everything that's important to us. Goodbye to our family, our school and all our friends."

"Honey, I'm sorry you feel this way," said Mom. "Right now, it feels like it's the end of the world, but you'll change your mind. Wait and see how good it will be."

For the next few weeks, I tried convincing them that the move would be a terrible mistake, but no amount of protesting and pouting, or acts of rebellion on my part could sway their decision. They were resolute. Dad and the boys were thrilled, but I wasn't and neither was Mom, though she wouldn't admit it.

"You seriously want to move?" I asked, trying to guilt her into crossing over onto my side. "You're a city girl. You're going to hate living out in the country. What about your piano lessons?"

Mom just shrugged her shoulders and gave her standard answer. "We're a family. We support each other. This is a huge opportunity for your father and for all of us. When you're married and have children someday, you'll understand. Life is about making compromises. We wouldn't be doing this if we didn't think that it was good for the entire family."

5
My Family

It was my belief that Mom agreed to the move out of guilt and not out of compromise. After all, Dad had made the ultimate sacrifice when he gave up playing ball to marry her. To hear Dad tell it, he wasn't good enough to go pro anyhow, but those who had seen him bat, knew that he was only being modest. He was a glass-is-half-full kind of guy, and he truly believed that his life had turned out according to God's master plan. Out of respect for Mom's feelings, he didn't talk much about his glory days, nor did he lament over paths not taken. They both gave up so much when she got pregnant with me.

My parents met at Michigan State University. Dad was a student athlete, a right fielder on the Spartan baseball team, and Mom studied music. He was a junior and she a sophomore. They had been dating only a few months when she got pregnant with me. She got pregnant the very first time they had sex but it wasn't until I was twelve years old, when I got my period for the first time that Mom shared with me her shameful secret. My period came while I was on a field trip with my sixth-grade class. I thought it was the worst day of my life at the time.

"Boys and girls, please," said Mrs. Webb. "I need everyone to stop visiting and to take one last bathroom break before getting on the bus. It's almost a two-hour drive back to the school and once we get going, there's no stopping."

There were three stalls in the girls' bathroom, and only the first one didn't have anything wrong with it. The second stall had a sign taped to the toilet stating that it was out of order, and the third stall had a working toilet, but the door wouldn't lock. To speed things along, I volunteered to use the stall with the busted lock while a girl from my class held the door closed. It wasn't until I was squatted over the toilet, my pants down around my ankles and ready to wipe, that I noticed the brownish, sticky stain in the center of my underwear. I had no idea what it was at first, but then I remembered how the school nurse explained during one of the sex education presentations that the blood that came with the first menstrual cycle might look brown and a little clayish instead of bright red. I wiped away the goopy sludge, placed a wad of toilet paper in my underwear, pulled up my pants and prayed to God that it wouldn't get any worse before we got back to school. It didn't, but by later that night, I was flowing steadily and couldn't put off telling Mom any longer. I considered just swiping a pad from her medicine cabinet but knew she'd be hurt if I didn't confide in her. With Mom and my extended family, my aunts and female cousins, getting a period for the first time was right up there with getting married or having a baby. They were so weird that way. By mid-day the next day, my entire family would know that I had started my period. Just as I expected, she made a big fuss.

"You're a woman now. My little girl is growing up." I wanted to gag, but I decided to let her have a few minutes of elation. She supplied me with a few pads and offered to show me how to use them, but I already knew how. Then she explained that my next period would most likely come anywhere from 28 to 30 days from then, but I already knew that too. I was bushed and just wanted to shower and go to bed, but Mom wouldn't get out of my room.

"Oh, and don't forget, this part is really important. You must remember to record on the calendar the first day of every period. Then you'll know roughly when to expect ovulation and the arrival of your next period. You remember learning that don't you?"

"Yes! Yes!" I said. I resented her rehashing information that was awkward to talk about the first time around "Why are you mentioning ovulation? It's just my period for Pete's sake. I'm not trying to have a baby."

Biting her lip, she said, "I know that, but now that you've gotten your period I need for you to understand that, theoretically, you could conceive a child if you had sex."

"Oh my gosh Mom! Duh! I know how babies are made. I'm not stupid. I'm not going to run out and have sex anytime soon. Why are you bringing all of this up? What's the point?"

Mom didn't beat around the bush. "You know that Daddy and I got married after I discovered that I was pregnant with you, don't you?"

Prior to that moment, I hadn't really given any thought to the fact that I was born in October, but my parents wedding anniversary was in February. I felt like an idiot.

"No, not really," I admitted. I was stunned. Shocked. Not because I was disappointed in them or because I felt betrayed over them not telling me sooner, but because I was 12 years old and I had never once done the math. It never occurred to me that unless I had been born a preemie, which I hadn't been, that I had come over a month earlier than I technically should have. Instead of being mad at myself for being so naive, I turned on Mom. "And how would I know that? I mean, I guess now that you say it, I realize that you must've been pregnant before you and Dad got married, but why are you acting like this was something we've talked about before?"

"You're right. We've never talked about it. I suppose your Dad and I never mentioned it before now because you were too little to really understand. There were times, especially when you were going through Human Growth and Development classes at school, and through catechism, that I thought about telling you. But it's a difficult conversation to have and—"

"For me or for you and Dad?"

"For us, I suppose," she admitted. "I'd never been with anyone before your Dad. I was saving myself for marriage, but we met and fell in love, and I just knew that he and I would be together forever. It happened the very first time we had sex. I was so stupid because it happened about two weeks after my period. We were in love and we were already talking about marriage after college anyway, so getting pregnant just moved things along a little faster. My point is that it worked out for the two of us, but most people aren't so lucky."

"Were you Dad's first?" I asked, cutting her off. I could tell by her reaction that she wasn't.

"Well, no, but boys are different. There were one or two girls before me, but it didn't mean anything and once he met me, he really regretted it."

"Hmm, interesting. All this time, when you've lectured the boys and me about saving ourselves for marriage, you were being a hypocrite."

Mom didn't fall back on the, *do what I say, not as I do,* cliché, but took her lumps. "I understand why you think Dad and I are hypocrites, because in a way, we are. But just because we slipped up doesn't mean that we want to give you kids the green light to behave in a way that defies the teachings of our faith. As I said before, it worked out for your father and me, but sexual relationships are very complicated, and can have serious repercussions. You're a smart young lady with a strong moral compass. I know that when the time comes, like it did for me, that you'll know who that right person is for you. But it is my hope that you will wait and be with your husband. Kids in middle school and high school are not emotionally equipped to be in sexual relationships. They often get hurt. Babies are a blessing, and I'm proud to be the mother of four beautiful children. I have a husband and we are emotionally and spiritually equipped to raise the four of you. I could go on and on, but what you need to know is that waiting until marriage, if you can, is the best option. Do you understand?"

"Yeah, I get it," I said just to get her off my back. "Can you get out of my room now?"

Mom's plan, all those years back, had been to return to school after I was born. Dad attempted to continue playing baseball, but it just got too hard. Eventually, he earned a finance degree, and then went on to get his masters, but Mom never went back and finished. David came 3 years after me. Daniel arrived just 11 months after David. David and Daniel were what Grandma called, "Irish twins." Daniel was supposed to be their last, but Mom was never good at remembering to record the first day of her period on the calendar, so lo and behold, she got pregnant for a fourth time with Denny. Once all of us kids were born, she started giving piano lessons from out of our house.

6
Meeting Will Banks
Winter 1983

Dad's new job took its toll on everyone. During the workweek, he rented a room at an inn not too far from where he worked, but on Friday nights he made the hour drive home to spend the weekends with us. Initially, my parents had agreed to let us finish out the school year but being apart from one another got to be too much for my parents. Mom missed Dad and Dad complained that he couldn't do the kind of job he needed to do only seeing us on the weekends. They made the decision to move just as soon as they found a house. It didn't take long. The 2,800-square foot brick ranch was purchased for an excellent price. It sat on two acres of land but needed some work. For the first time ever, we had to take a bus to school. We moved over Christmas break. My first day at my new school was a total nightmare.

I waited in line for what seemed like forever to purchase a stupid gym uniform. After manipulating the contents of the overcrowded storage closet, the secretary managed to locate what she was looking for and hoisted the dilapidated cardboard box up on the counter. It wasn't a wide box, but it was deep, and because she was so short, she had to place it on its side to see what was inside. "Okie dokie," she said, "let's see what we've got in here." She pushed up her sleeves and began sifting through the mishmash of items that had been tossed in the box along with the surplus of gym uniforms. She scrutinized each sticker located on the outside of the cellophane wrapped bundles before casting them off into the designated reject pile. When her search for a small or extra small came up short, she put each of the gym uniforms back in the box. "Now hold on a minute, I think there were a few that fell out of the box. Wait here a sec," she said before heading back into the closet. She came out a minute later with an armful of packages. Once again, she checked the size of each bundle before tossing them in the box with the rest of the gym uniforms. With only two left it didn't look very promising, but her demeanor remained upbeat. "Well, we tried," she said when her search came up short. "Let's see what one of these mediums looks like." She shrugged her shoulders, and with an apologetic smile, she tried handing me the bundle. Before I could protest, every phone in the office lit up.

"Mrs. Franklin," the principal barked from inside his office, "Who's manning the phones out there? Someone needs to tend to that incessant ringing."

"Excuse me dear. I must see to the phones. I'll be back with you in a jiffy." She took the uniform with her. The other secretary and the office aide, who were helping students only moments before were nowhere to be found, so it took several minutes for her to field all the calls. When the other two came back into the office, she resumed her position at the front counter.

"Alright then. Let's see what we've got." She tore into the package with both hands like she was Bruce Banner gashing at his shirt during his transformation into the Hulk. The neatly folded zip-up one-piece gym uniform plopped down onto the counter between us. She picked it up, shook it out and held it up so we could both get a better look at it. I could see that I was going to swim in it, but she acted as if that it was the perfect size. "100%

cotton. Oh, it'll shrink some. I think this will work just fine," she said, after reading the tag on the inside of the uniform. I didn't want to accept it, but I didn't have a choice. Even if I washed it in hot water a dozen times and dried it on high heat, it was still going to be way too big. "I guess I should probably put in an order for some other sizes. Seems like every other day someone's coming in here needing a new uniform. Kids these days can't keep track of anything. Always losing stuff," she complained.

"How long will that take?" I asked.

"Oh, not too long. They'll be here in a week or so. I'll be sure to mention on the morning announcements when they're available," she promised. I balled up the hideous uniform, stuffed it in my bag and stomped off. "Oh, by the way," she added cheerfully, "We're glad to have you at our school, dear." Halfway down the hallway on my way to locate my locker, a wicked cramp assaulted my lower abdomen. It felt like someone was carving up my uterus like a jack-o-lantern. The cramps and the sensation of slight dampness meant only one thing—my period. It came three days ahead of schedule, so naturally I wasn't prepared. I did an about face and marched back down to the health office, which was connected to the central office. Thankfully, no other students were in there to hear me explain to the nurse how I didn't have any tampons. She was cool about it.

"Don't you worry. I can help you out with that. No need to feel embarrassed." I wasn't embarrassed, I was pissed that my period came on my first day at my new school. I had the worst luck. From the bottom drawer of her desk she pulled out a pink wrapped square about the size of my fist and handed it to me. "Fresh out of tampons, but this will work in a pinch. You may use the restroom in here if you'd like."

The pad was ridiculously big. Nobody would be able to tell that I was wearing the diaper-like pad under my skirt, but my gym uniform was going to be a different story. I worried that the enormous pad would be like a blinking beacon. When I was younger and the idea of using a tampon was scarier than my actual period, I avoided wearing jeans or shorts or any other fitted clothing because I had been certain that everyone could tell that I was on my period. I knew better now, but I still felt awful, so when gym period rolled around, I bypassed the girl's locker room and went on a mission to find my gym teacher's office.

Thank God, I had the female gym teacher and not the male one. Her office wasn't attached to the actual gymnasium like his. Hers was in an odd space, one level up from the gymnasium on a floor of its own. It was a third gym. I suppose it was more of a weight room than an actual gym. There was a bench press and a rack holding dumbbells, and several pieces of gymnastics equipment. A long climbing rope hung from the ceiling. My gentle rapping on her fireproof door went unanswered, but I knew she was in there. I couldn't see cigarette smoke, but I could smell it. Like my old school, my new school had a teacher's smoking lounge, but because her office was so isolated from the other rooms in the building, I suspected that she smoked in her office in between classes or during her plan time. I knocked even harder and rattled the doorknob back and forth a bit to warn her that I was coming in. Sitting at her desk, behind the sports section of the *Detroit Free Press* and smoking a cigarette, was my new gym teacher. It was evident from her disdainful exhalation that she didn't appreciate the intrusion. I glanced down at my schedule to make certain I addressed her by the correct name. She had an undeniably German sounding name. It seemed that everybody in the area was of German descent.

"Excuse me, Miss Klein. I hate to bother you, but I'm Daisy Doyle and today's my first day of school." Crickets. She didn't respond.

Just when I thought that she might go on ignoring me forever, she lowered her paper, but didn't appear very interested in hearing me out. I forged ahead anyway. "I don't have the money for the gym uniform," I lied. "I mean, I can afford to buy one, but I left the check at home and you see, I'm in a skirt and clogs."

"And?" she questioned. "What is it that you need?"

"Well, if you could write me a pass to the library, I could just sit in there and read until gym class is over. I'll bring the check tomorrow and I promise that I'll be dressed and ready to go from here on out." I crossed my heart with my index finger and threw up my two fingers to indicate that my pledge was sincere. She glared at me like I was a space alien. She was clearly not the forgiving sort.

"I don't ever write passes for the library just because a student isn't prepared," she explained. "Besides, today's the first day of volleyball instruction." I wasn't sure what volleyball had to do with anything so I waited for her to explain. "You ever played volleyball before?" she asked.

"Yes," I squeaked, sounding like a little mouse. I wasn't usually the wishy-washy type, at least not in public, but I was desperate. The thought of putting on that uniform made me feel physically sick. Perhaps my hormones were out of whack because of my period or maybe I was suffering from first day jitters, but I felt like I was going to burst into tears at any second. The right side of my face began to twitch. As hard as I tried, I couldn't hold back the tears. I stood in front of my new teacher, crying with my shoulders slumped and pitched forward like a weeping willow. My tears did nothing to soften her temperament. As a matter of fact, they seemed to annoy her even more.

"For Pete's sake, dry up those eyes. What are you blubbering about?" she asked. I wiped my snotty nose with the back of my hand and straightened myself out. She shook her head with blatant disgust. "Oh, alright. Enough already. Because you're a newbie, I won't give you a detention." She crushed her cigarette out in the ashtray and sprayed her mouth with medicinal smelling breath spray. "But you're not going to the library. You'll sit on the bleachers and listen and learn."

"Uh huh," I mumbled.

"Now get out of here so I can get ready for your classmates," she barked.

I didn't push my luck by asking any other questions. Being banned to the bleachers was fine by me and far better than putting on the hideous gym uniform running around with gut-splitting cramps and an enormous pad wedged between my thighs.

Nobody seemed to notice me shivering on the empty bleachers as they filed into the gymnasium. The large, drafty windows located above the bleachers ushered in a steady stream of cool air. The room was an icebox. I buried my hands in the folds of my skirt and tried to get my mind off how cold it was by sneaking a look at my fellow students. The jocks were easy to recognize. They strutted in like flocks of prideful peacocks. I once read that the collective name for a group of peacocks is a party and the jocks in that class certainly behaved like they were at a party, a party thrown in their honor. Loud and boisterous, they commanded the attention of everyone already in the gym. They walked in flexing their muscles and taking imaginary jump shots from the free throw line. Two beefy looking boys, who from a distance could've been mistaken for grown men, began wrestling and nearly bowled over a small, timid looking girl who was bent over lacing up her shoes. Neither bothered to apologize. They both just laughed.

The less athletic, and hence, less popular kids were just as easy to spot. They slunk into the gym hugging the wall with their heads hung low. Unlike the cool, rich kids who had stylish hair and expensive gym shoes, these kids all seemed to possess flaws that would forever keep them on the outside looking in.

As the year progressed, I discovered that many of the popular kids lived in the houses that ran up and down the river. If they were afflicted with any sort of dreaded inadequacy, it was usually overlooked. I learned quickly that money could cover a multitude of flaws. At my old school, I was comfortable with my social standing. I fell somewhere in the middle of the pack. I wasn't wildly popular, but I had several good friends and was even liked by a few cute boys. Aside from having money, most of the boys at my new school weren't much different than the boys at my old school. For the most part, they weren't all that impressive.

The high-pitched shrill of the whistle interrupted my impromptu anthropological study and sent the stragglers sprinting to their assigned squads. Without the lit cigarette pinched between her index and middle fingers, Miss Klein looked the part of the stereotypical no-nonsense female gym teacher. Her sweatpants, which were a tad too tight, especially around her midriff, were also too short and exposed her thick ankles. And though she occasionally remembered to suck in her stomach, her slightly rounded pouch was a sure give away that she wasn't a serious athlete. Her visor, which I later learned that she wore every day, regardless of whether class was held outside or inside, did nothing to improve her look of authenticity. Her pristine, low-top Reebok running shoes didn't help her image either.

"Okay, listen up everyone," she said, raising her hand in the air to signal that it was time for everybody to shut up, "we've got a new student." She turned to where I was sitting and motioned for me to stand up. "This is Daisy." Clearly, she had forgotten my last name, and because she hadn't bothered to ask me the name of the school I was transferring from, there wasn't much else for her to say. Nobody smiled or waved or said hello. Miss Klein then walked over to the free throw line and stood with her hands on her hips. When nobody followed her lead, she sounded her whistle again and the students stood at attention. She led them through a rigorous warm-up regimen of basic calisthenics. It wasn't until the very end, when she and the students were bending at their waists and pressing their faces to their knees that I noticed a boy creeping across the gym floor.

"Mr. Banks," Miss Klein called out, startling him as well as everyone else. Her face, reddened from bending over, gave the impression that she was madder than she was. "Why do you have such difficulty making it to my class on time?" He didn't answer her rhetorical question. "It's the first day of the new semester, so why don't you make it a goal from here on out to be more punctual?"

He smiled sheepishly and did one of those *golly gee* shrugs that females, young and old, love. Then he flashed her a smile so unassuming that I could tell that she wasn't going to stay mad at him for very long. And she didn't.

"Alrighty then! Go on up to the upstairs gym and run some suicides since you missed the entire warm up. You know the drill. Throw in a few push-ups and jumping jacks for safe measure. Climb the rope." Before she could address the rest of the class, hands shot into the air in response to a question that had not yet been posed. "Who can accompany Will upstairs? We know that injuries are often a result of students neglecting to warm up properly." Attached to each hand was a female student. Miss Klein ignored them all.

"Daisy, why don't you go up there with him?"

I pointed with question to myself, "What about volleyball?"

"Go on and do as I ask. And if you're not dressed in uniform tomorrow, you'll be running with him. I won't care what kind of shoes you've got on."

Dejected, all the other girls lowered their hands and watched Will and I leave.

Will was handsome and confident, but not arrogant. His self-assurance wasn't at all off putting.

Neither of us spoke. Clearly, he wasn't as enamored with my appearance as I was with his. Using only my peripheral vision, I watched him race from one end of the gym to the other with long and steady strides. I didn't stare. The last thing I wanted was for Will to think that, I too, was a member of his female fan club. His blond hair was sweaty and his face slightly flushed.

He was Hollywood handsome, a notch above all the other boys. His arms and legs were long, lean and muscular. His eyes were expressive and the most unusual shade of blue. They were almost cerulean. His face was roundish with deep-set dimples. His smile was perfect. When he stopped running, he acknowledged me.

"You smoke?" he asked.

"Huh? What?" I understood the question, but I wasn't sure why he was asking me something so random. The last thing I wanted was for Will to think I was a prude, so I tried to think up an acceptable answer.

"Cigarettes? You know. Do you smoke? Because, I don't know 'bout you, but I could really use one right about now."

I lied and said something stupid like I used to smoke, but I really didn't care for them anymore. I don't think he believed me.

"C'mon and follow me," he said. I couldn't believe what he was proposing.

Against my better judgment, I followed him to Klein's office door, but then changed my mind.

"This is stupid," I told him, "I'm going back to class."

"Hey, hold up. Don't go," he said, and grabbed my hand. I felt giddy and I could feel my cheeks turning three shades of red.

"Oh, all right," I agreed.

"After you m'lady," he said, holding open the door to Miss Klein's office. His Cockney accent was horrendous and anyone else would have looked and sounded like an idiot, but it worked on me. The minute I set foot in her office, I regretted my decision.

"I'm not so sure about this," I told him again.

"Awe, c'mon, it's okay. Do you really think she's gonna leave all those kids unsupervised to see what we're doing? She's already forgotten all about us. I think she's on something," he said, making a gesture simulating a person taking a hit off a joint. "It's okay, really." He wasted no time and began ransacking her office.

The space was sparsely furnished with a single file cabinet, a small bookcase and several brightly colored mesh bags filled with basketball jerseys and an assortment of balls that needed inflating. Her purse hung over the back of her chair. "Let's see, does Klein keep her smokes in here?" he asked, reaching for her bag.

I spotted the box of Virginia Slims on a stack of manila folders on her desk. Everything about being in her office felt wrong, but Will rummaging through her personal belongings felt even worse. He was crossing a very serious line.

"Wait! They're right there." I said, pointing to the cigarettes.

Will commented that they were chick cigarettes, but he lit one anyway. Perfectly round O's filled the empty space between us. He held out the cigarette for me to take, but I pushed his hand away. I'd never smoked before. Clearly it wasn't his first time.

"We should get back. If someone catches us we'll be in big trouble," I whined.

He didn't protest, but he took a few more puffs before tossing the half-smoked cigarette onto the concrete floor and extinguishing it with the tip of his sneaker. The butt he tossed in the trashcan on our way out the door. Half way down the steps that would lead us back to the gymnasium, a breathy girl from class greeted us. Her uniform fit like a glove and hugged her curvy body in all the right places. The pull on the zipper of her uniform was missing, which may have been the reason why it kept inching its way down as she and Will spoke. I'm certain her gym uniform was an extra small, though she would have been better served by a medium.

"Hey Willy, whatcha doing?" she asked.

"Hey, Stacy," he flashed his best Cheshire Cat grin. "Just heading back to class. What are you doing?"

"Looking for you," she purred.

I didn't stick around to hear the rest of their conversation, but I did notice that neither of them made it back to class.

7
The Beginning of the End of Everything

The boys quickly made friends because there was no shortage of kids their age to play with who lived near us. They congregated at each other's houses for hours playing with their *Star Wars* figures, trading baseball cards or playing hockey. Several of our neighbors had ponds in their backyards. As for girls my age, there was only one who lived close by. She lived three houses down from us in a small brick ranch set back from the road. Her name was Debbie Schmidt, and her family was the opposite of ours. She was the youngest of four children and her three older brothers no longer lived at home. We got to know each other while riding the bus, but we didn't have any classes together, nor did we share the same lunch schedule, which meant I was pretty lonely at first. Occasionally we did homework together after school, and hung out here and there on the weekends, but she was always so busy. Unlike me, Debbie led an interesting life. She was the captain of our junior high cheerleading squad and she was a gymnast. Her parents drove her twice a week over to Sarnia, Canada to train with a coach who once held a spot on the Canadian Olympic gymnastics team. Once, just for something to do, I tagged along with her to one of her lessons. Afterward, I felt like the world's biggest loser. Debbie was not only an accomplished gymnast but had an amazing body. She was skinny, but super toned. I was slim too, but really had to watch what I ate. After watching Debbie's lesson, I resumed the secret diet I had come up with back in sixth grade. I went on it anytime I thought I was getting a little chunky.

Breakfast consisted of a poached egg. Mom insisted on making two, along with two slices of lightly buttered toast, but I slipped the extra egg and bread to Gus when she wasn't looking. For lunch, I had a sandwich and piece of fruit. I ate my sandwich without the bread and gave away all the other stuff she packed to whoever wanted it at my table. Dinner was tricky because she watched everything I put in my mouth, but I was pretty good at pretending to eat. I was good at pretending about a lot of things, but I was horrible at pretending that the move didn't suck.

Things were working out well for everyone, just like Mom had promised. Everyone was happy except me. Even Mom was digging the move.

Mom loved giving piano lessons but when we moved, she was so convinced that no one would want to drive out to the sticks to learn how to play the piano that she didn't bother placing an ad in the paper. She assumed that my brothers and I would be her only students, but word spread quickly of her talent among the moms at our church and the boys' school.

One Sunday morning, after the regular pianist became violently ill just before the 11:00 am Mass, Mom volunteered to take her place. Within a week she had secured two new students, and over the next month, five more. For the first time ever, she even had two adult students.

One was a retired Catholic schoolteacher who'd always wanted to learn to play the piano but never got around to taking lessons. "Between teaching and volunteering at my church," she had explained the first time I met her, "there was never enough time to pursue such a frivolous dream as learning to play the piano. I took lessons for about a year when I was six, but then my dad got hurt and had to quit working. There was hardly enough money to pay all the bills let alone pay for piano lessons. I was so sad to have to quit, but I suppose God had other plans for me." Though she was born in the United States, she had one of those Polish names that nobody could pronounce—Emilka Januszewski. My brothers and I called her Miss J for short.

Miss J was a walking, breathing saint. In addition to teaching first graders in a regular classroom for over forty years, she was an RCIA sponsor for adults converting to Catholicism, and taught Catechism. She dressed only in grey or navy blue A-line skirts topped with sensible, button-down blouses under boxy cardigan sweaters. She smelled of mothballs laced with a hint of vanilla. She was sweet though, so we all looked past her smell. Every time she came for a lesson, she brought sandwich bags filled with hard candies or Swedish Fish for each of the boys. Never did she have a bag for me. I guess she figured I was too old to get excited about a little bag of candy.

One day, while I was sitting at the table doing homework and waiting for the pot of potatoes to boil, she wandered into the kitchen looking for the telephone. "Dear, may I use your phone? I need to call my mother and let her know that I'll be late for dinner. She's been a little under the weather lately and I'm staying with her until she gets back on her feet." Mom was running behind schedule. After she made her call, Miss J watched me mash the potatoes. We talked about food and how she still cooked dinners twice a week for the priests living in the rectory. She gave me step-by-step directions on how to make potato pancakes. I'm not sure how or why, but our conversation eventually turned from traditional Polish recipes to God, and the IHM Nuns who educated her. She had a lot to say on both subjects.

Her life's ambition had been to become a nun, but her father's death when she was still in high school squelched that dream. Being the oldest child in her family, she got a second job and helped her mom raise her younger siblings. After college, she did the next best thing to becoming a nun. She got paid peanuts working at the Catholic school when she just as easily could've found a job at a public school and earned more money. She devoted all her free time and talents to the Church. From that day forward, after spilling her guts to me about wanting to please both God and her parents, she brought me daily devotional booklets for teens or other reading materials. I didn't have the heart to tell her that there was no way I'd ever become a nun. She was sweet and easy to talk to and wasn't at all like Mom's other adult student who barely said a word to anyone other than Denny.

Mom's other adult student was a middle-aged man who lived on a private dirt road not too far from our house. Mr. Boyd was his name and his lesson was every Wednesday afternoon from 4:30 pm to 5:30 pm. He was Mom's only hour-long lesson. To say that he was punctual was an understatement. He arrived 20 to 30 minutes early for every lesson. It didn't make sense that he showed up so early because Mom was booked solid on Wednesdays, but Mom, of course, didn't think anything of it. She went out of her way to defend him because she knew that we all thought that he was a little weird.

"He gets here early to avoid the rush hour traffic. He comes straight from work you know. Nobody ever plans to be late, but sometimes things come up like traffic jams and accidents. I appreciate that he thinks ahead and is considerate of my time."

Mostly he read the newspaper, but if Denny were around he'd talk to him. They talked about cars or medieval castles, which was something that Denny was really into at the time. Dad found it odd that a grown man would want to take lessons so late in life and joked that he didn't know how he felt about his wife alone with some strange guy while he was at work. "I can see a retired old lady wanting a hobby to help pass the time, but he's a relatively young man. He had better not be some kind of pervert who likes hitting on married women."

"His mother started teaching him to play when he was a small boy," Mom explained, "but for some reason she had to stop giving him lessons. He really is a sweet man."

"Well he sounds a little peculiar to me," said Dad.

Mom would just sigh or twist her face whenever Dad made sarcastic comments about Mr. Boyd. She assured him that he wouldn't speak such nonsense if he met him. Dad's comments became even more absurd once he did finally meet him. My family bumped into him one night at a hole-in-the-wall diner not too far from our house shortly after we moved and Mom started giving lessons again.

The diner was a local hotspot despite its lackluster façade and décor that consisted of dark wood paneling and mounted animal heads. All walks of life frequented the place, especially on weekend nights. It was known for its famous perch and pickerel dinners and casual atmosphere. Curious to see if the food was as good as the natives boasted and for something to do—my parents took us to eat there one Friday night.

The parking lot was packed, but our timing couldn't have been more perfect. Just as we were pulling in, a pick-up truck was backing out of a spot smack-dab in front of the entrance. We anticipated a long wait but didn't expect that it would be standing room only. After about ten minutes, Dad proposed that we get something to drink from the bar. "It's going to be a while," he said after surveying the crowd, "No point in being hungry and thirsty." He recruited me to go with him because he couldn't carry six drinks all by himself. Denny wanted to come too, but Mom told him no.

"There's not enough room at the bar to swing a cat. Stay here, Denny. You'll just get underfoot." Denny didn't like her answer and threw a temper tantrum. To shut him up, Dad let him tag along. It took a minute or two to catch the frazzled bartender's attention. When he finally did, she was very accommodating. In addition to our drinks, she supplied Dad with a small tray to carry our beverages and a take-out menu just in case we changed our minds about waiting for a table. Against Dad's better judgment, he agreed to let Denny carry his own drink back to our spot. Just as he was handing him his glass, a man stumbling away from the bar bumped his arm and the front of Denny's shirt got drenched with root beer. Denny just stood there, mouth gaping, his upper body slumped over like he'd just gotten punched in the gut. The drunkard's buddy, who was only slightly less inebriated, witnessed the entire debacle and rushed over to make amends.

"Sorry little man," he said to Denny whose teeth were chattering a mile a minute. "Let me make it up to you." He reached into his pocket and fished out a handful of quarters and held them out for Denny to take. To Dad he offered their seats at the bar. Dad assured him that neither the seats nor coins were necessary, but when the guy who was responsible for the accident in the first place pulled out his wallet and offered to buy us all a round of drinks, Dad changed his mind.

"Alright! Put your wallet away, please," he said. "Denny, you go ahead and take a couple of quarters for you and your brothers, but that's it." Accidents happen, seriously man. If you're leaving, I'll take you up on your offer for your seats at the bar."

Dad and Mom sat on the barstools, while I stood sandwiched between the two of them. With his quarters safely secured in his gummy hand, Denny along with Daniel and David, took off in the direction of the pinball and Pac-Man machines located in the back corner. Mom and Dad settled into adult conversation with one another while I nursed my Shirley Temple and people-watched. I quickly got bored and decided to go hangout with my brothers at the Pac-Man machine. As I was getting ready to leave, I noticed Mr. Boyd standing at the end of the bar underneath the flashing *Pick-up and Take-out Here* arrow. I could tell it was Mr. Boyd by the way he messed with his ill-fitting glasses. It wasn't very nice of me, but I thought he looked like an oversized rodent. His head appeared way too tiny for his fleshy body. He had a long nose and beady eyes. With his little ears, he reminded me of a mole that had just popped up from under the ground. Maybe the problem with his glasses was that his ears were too small.

"Hey, don't look now," I said, nudging Mom, "but your boyfriend's here. He's standing at the end of the bar."

Mom looked to where I was pointing. "Shush!" she cautioned. "He'll hear you."

There was no way he could've heard us over the loud music and the crowd, but as soon as she shushed me, he looked over in our direction. The three of us weren't engaged in idle chitchat or mindlessly eyeing our reflections in the gold vein mirror behind the bar, but instead we were all staring at him. Panicked, Mom shot him a sort of half smile before looking away. Dad smiled at him and raised his glass as if to say, *"Hey, we see you. Be social and come on over."* To everybody's surprise, he did. Dad didn't flinch or make a face when he shook Mr. Boyd's hand, but I knew exactly what he was thinking and it wasn't good. Dad took issue with men who didn't shake hands properly and Mr. Boyd's hand rested in Dad's hand like a dead fish.

"What's your poison?" Dad asked him.

"Oh, well, I..." Mr. Boyd stammered, as he checked his watch, "I suppose I may have time for a quick beer while I wait." Those in the take-out line weren't moving any faster than those waiting for a table. In the time it took for his order to be filled, he drank almost two beers and revealed more information about himself than he probably intended, thanks to Mom's prying. We learned that he was single but had been married for a brief time. He told my parents that he was divorced with no children and had lived his entire life, excluding his college years, in the same house that his dad's dad had built decades before. His parents died from carbon monoxide poisoning while he was in graduate school, and being their only child, he inherited the house. Only later when Mom mentioned that she was from a large family and couldn't imagine being an only child did he clarify that he had a younger brother who had died when he was only six years old from a ruptured appendix. For someone whose life seemed to have been a series of disappointments, he came across that night as a well-adjusted dude. He grumbled a bit about his daily commute to The Warren Tech Center—it took about an hour depending on the traffic but overall, he enjoyed being an engineer and liked living where he lived. "City life just isn't for me," he explained. Mom and Dad glared at me as he commented as if his statement somehow proved that they were right about living in the country and I was wrong.

"Geez," Dad said, after Mr. Boyd left the bar with his food, "That guy's life really sucks."

"See," said Mom, placing her head lovingly on Dad's shoulder. "He's a nice man. Living alone for so long has left him a little odd that's all. We should count our blessings."

Dad picked up Mom's hand and pressed it to his lips. "I count mine every day. We live a pretty charmed life." The two of them basked in their sappiness just long enough to make me want to hurl.

"You guys might," I interrupted, "but my life sucks. I'm hanging out with my parents on a Friday night because I've got nothing better to do."

"Don't be so dramatic. It'll get better," Mom said.

"Yeah, when? When I'm 102?"

"When you get a better attitude," Dad answered. "Life is what you make of it Daisy. When the world gives you lemons, you make lemonade. Haven't you ever heard that expression?"

"Lemons are sour," I said, ignoring his stupid attempt to make me feel better. "I just want to move back home," I insisted.

"Well, that's not happening," he said. I knew that I was really pushing the boundaries on the complaining, but I didn't care. "Give it a rest already. I'm not in the mood to listen to you gripe all night. Try to enjoy yourself, or at the very least, save it for later so we can enjoy ourselves."

His scowl told me that that he probably wanted to say more to me, like to put a sock in it, but he didn't because Mom was there. Mom despised bickering.

"Honey, I know this move has been hard on you, but give it some time. You'll make friends, and in no time, you'll love your new life. Think of all of this as an adventure," Mom said.

In so many ways, she had been right. I gave it time and things did get better, even good, but not for long. The move ended up being the worst thing for our family. The move was the beginning of the end of everything.

8
Lonely No More
Spring 1983

The first few weeks at my new school were a total nightmare. I was homesick and lonely and miserable. Because Debbie and I didn't share the same lunch period, being in the cafeteria was sheer torture. I was forced to sit at tables with kids I didn't know. It wasn't like they were mean to me, or anything like that. Nobody dumped milk on my head or refused to let me sit down in an empty spot like they did in all the teen movies about being the new kid on the block, but nobody really went out of their way to make me feel welcome either. Most days I scarfed down my lunch and then hid out in the bathroom.

The only bearable part of my days then was gym period. That's when I got to see Will. I passed him several times every day in the crowded hallways, but he never gave me a second look. It was only in gym class that I interacted with him, and even that was limited. I soon discovered that he wasn't just a pretty face. He was funny and easy-going. He didn't get laughs by putting other people down the way a lot of the other guys did. I never understood why boys one-upped each other the way they did, or why they thought a put-down was the secret to making or keeping friends. Will joked around, but his jokes were never mean-spirited. He was athletic, but not what I considered a jock. To me, jocks were blockheads consumed with sports and nothing else. Will was all about having fun and not taking anything too seriously.

One class period, I was lucky enough to be on his side playing volleyball. I don't know how it happened, but the team consisted of me, Will and four other girls. He referred to us as his harem, which was fitting because the other girls were more interested in flirting with Will than playing the game. This was especially true of Stacy, in her gym uniform that was two sizes too small, and her ditzy friend, Denise. It was so obvious they were both hot for Will. They were probably the most popular girls in eighth grade, at least with the guys. I hated playing with them. They screamed anytime the ball came within two feet of them and purposely fell onto the ground so that Will could help them up. They couldn't stand anywhere near him without finding a reason to put their hands on him. I could tell that their ditzy façade was getting on his nerves. I was the only girl on our team who tried, and knew what I was doing. Will kept saying, "Alright Daisy Doyle, it's you and me. You set the ball and I'll spike it over the net."

We lost both games in the end, but when the class period was over, Will high fived me and told me that I was a skillful player. Outside of gym class, I was invisible to him.

By the end of my second month in school, I managed to make two genuine friends, Kim and Shari. By genuine, I mean girls that I wanted to hang out with and not girls I simply tolerated because I had nobody else. Unfortunately, both lived in town, so getting together with either of them was never easy and took a ton of planning. Hanging out right after school wasn't a big deal, because Mom was a planner and would view the trip into town to pick me up as an opportunity to kill two birds with one stone. Sometimes she'd swing by the carwash or stop in at the library to return books before they were overdue. If the timing was right, she'd drop into the barbershop with the boys for a quick trim. Dad preferred their hair short, especially during baseball season, but buzz cuts required a lot of maintenance. My brothers liked their hair longer, but it drove Dad nuts when their hair hung in their eyes like scruffy sheepdogs. Mom, always the consummate peacekeeper, took them in at least once a month to trim their bangs and take the weight off the back of their hair. If she had no errands to run at all, she'd take the boys to the ice cream parlor. With their cones of Superman or Blue Moon ice cream, they'd sit down on the boardwalk and watch the freighters meander down the river.

Seeing my friends during the week was almost easier than on the weekends because my parents' schedules were so hectic. Weekends were always busy. When Saturdays rolled around, I practically had to get down on my knees and beg one of them to stop what they were doing and drive me into town. I wasn't opposed to having friends over at our house, but there wasn't nearly as much for us to do in the sticks as there was in the city. The movie theater, the arcade, and any place else remotely cool were all downtown. At my house, we were limited to listening to music, watching movies or giving each other manicures.

When the weather grew warmer, we had more options. Shari's dad had a work truck, and sometimes, if he wasn't bogged down with work, he'd load her and Kim's bikes in the back of his truck and drive them over to my house. Mostly, we just road around on the dirt roads to get away from my brothers and their obnoxious friends, but if we all had money, we'd ride our bikes down to one of the convenience stores that were within a mile or so of my house. The boys weren't allowed to ride their bikes that far.

With our bags of chips and bottles of pop, we'd sit out in front of the store laughing and gossiping about the same three subjects; cute boys at school (mainly Will), the girls that all the cute boys liked, and thus, we hated, and upcoming school events. Of course, I didn't have a bike of my own, so I had to beg David to borrow his stupid Free Spirit MX bike. I hated that bike, but I had no choice if I wanted to get out and have a life.

The summer before we moved, I received a beautiful pink Schwinn bike for an early birthday present. My three best girlfriends also had pink bikes and the four of us zoomed around the neighborhood like we owned it. Privately, we called ourselves *The Pink Ladies* like the girls from the movie, *Grease*. We were *Grease* junkies and huge John Travolta fans. Danny Zuko was every girl's fantasy. I rode that bike nonstop right up until the day it was stolen. I parked it out in front of the drugstore without locking it up. In less than five minutes, the time it took to buy a bottle of *Faygo,* somebody rode off with it. I couldn't believe it. I was devastated, but my parents showed very little sympathy. They were furious with me for being so careless.

"Well, now you don't have a bike and if you want another one, you're going to have to buy it yourself," Dad insisted. Like always, Mom backed him.

They held their ground for a long time, but eventually got sick of hearing David and I fighting over me taking his bike when he had wanted to ride it. They caved and bought me a new one, but it wasn't as nice as the one I had received for my birthday. My new bike was ultimately what led me to Will.

9
Tennis Anyone?

It turned out that Will lived about a quarter of a mile down the road from me. I'm not sure how he got to school, but according to my gossipy bus mates, Will had been suspended indefinitely from riding the bus. When pressed, nobody could recall the exact infraction that got him banned in the first place. Something about the conflicting stories struck me as a little fishy. On two separate occasions, I had spotted the late bus in front of Will's house. In the winter, Will played on the first-string basketball team, and in the spring, he ran track. The first time I noticed him getting off the late bus was during basketball season. I was in the car with Mrs. Wiseman on my way to babysit her children. Babysitting sucked, but I liked having my own money, and since I couldn't drive yet, I didn't have any other employment options.

Mrs. Wiseman and I drove by his house just as the late bus was pulling away. Will was at his mailbox sifting through a stack of mail. The other time, I was with Mom. She was driving me over to Kim's house for a sleepover. As usual, Mom had a million things going on, so we were late.

"The movie starts at 7:00. We're supposed to eat at the Coney Island before going to the show, but the wait for a table is going to be ridiculously long because it's a Friday night. We're not going to have time to do both now," I complained.

"You'll have time. Don't be such a pessimist. It's only 5:30," she assured me. No sooner did we get on the road than we were forced to stop because the bus in front of us had turned on its flashing red lights.

"Great, a stupid bus! Just go around it before it stops," I told her.

"That's against the law, Daisy. Boy, you've got a lot to learn before getting behind the wheel of a car." The bus stopped right in front of Will's house. From what I could tell, Will was the only person on the bus besides the driver. When the bus door opened, he stepped out then turned and waved and said something to the driver before crossing the road.

"Hey, isn't that Will Banks?" Mom asked in a way that suggested that she knew full well who he was and that for whatever reason she disapproved of him.

I leaned forward in my seat, pretending I needed to get a better look at him to be certain. "Yep, that's him. I had no idea that he lived out here," I lied.

She sighed. "It's a shame about his family. He looks like a sweet kid."

I blew off her comment about him *looking sweet* because there was no way she could know how sweet he was or wasn't by simply looking at him, but her deep sigh and cryptic statement about his family got my attention. I had to play it cool or she'd wonder what my interest was in Will.

From the time I was old enough to choose my own friends, she lectured me on the importance of associating with kids who came from good homes. In her Catholic mind, this meant kids whose parents were still together and went to church every week. "You lay down with dogs, you get up with fleas," was one of her favorite expressions. She had a memory like a hawk, so I had to be careful not to confide in her too much about the personal lives of my friends or their families. Once, back in fifth grade I made the mistake of casually mentioning how my friend's dad let us have ice cream for breakfast because my friend's mom ended up staying the night at her sister's house and wasn't home to make us breakfast in the morning.

"You mean to tell me that Jody's mother wasn't even there when you spent the night? She never mentioned that she wouldn't be home. Tell me that you didn't know before-hand that her mother wasn't going to be home," she demanded.

I hated when she wigged out over such stupid things. "I didn't know," I answered truthfully. "Why are you making such a big deal out of it? It's not like we were home alone. How was I supposed to know what her mother's plans were?"

"It's not proper for a man to chaperone two pre-teen girls overnight. Anything could have happened." I had no idea what she meant by not proper.

"Not proper? It's Jody's dad. What is that even supposed to mean?"

"Oh, I'm not going to get into all of that with you. From now on, no sleepovers unless the mom's home. You got it?" I didn't get it, but from that point on, I was careful not to offer up any more information than I had to about my friends or their parents. She would've never let me step into the homes of half of my friends if she knew how laid back some of their parents were.

"Why did you say that it was a shame about his family?" I asked, trying to sound as indifferent as possible.

"Oh, I don't know. I suppose I don't even know the kid," she admitted. "I shouldn't be so judgmental, but the fruit doesn't usually fall too far from the tree."

Mom had this thing about using expressions that nobody ever used anymore instead of just saying what she meant. She could carry on an entire conversation using one idiom after the other. It was remarkable, but so embarrassing at the same time. "What tree?" I persisted, "What's so bad about that person or the tree he fell from?"

Mom clammed up. By the worry lines on her forehead and scrunched up eyes I could tell that she was debating whether she should be totally honest with me or not. "Forget I said anything," she told me. I reminded her that she had started it by commenting about his family.

"Nope, you can't do that. You can't drop a bomb like that and then back-peddle. Just tell me what you meant." I wasn't letting her off the hook so easily.

She finally caved. "Well, it's not nice to gossip, you know that, right? And you know that adultery is a mortal sin, don't you?" Anytime she repeated a story involving someone committing an immoral act, she had to preface it by making some kind of statement that conveyed that she, in no way, shape or form was condoning the behavior. "Anyhow, Mrs. Schmidt shared with me some rather disturbing information regarding Will's home life." I expected the worst, like maybe he was abused, or Will's dad was in jail or something. "His parents are divorced and he lives only with his dad, Thomas Banks. Will's mom left his dad a while ago, and according to those who still have anything to do with Will's dad, she hasn't been around to see Will since. She moved to California."

The lights stopped flashing and the stop arm retracted. Mom resumed driving and I turned in my seat to steal one more glimpse of Will. With his disheveled hair and his red and white trimmed running shorts peeking out from under his oversized sweatshirt, I no longer saw the confident Will that all the girls fawned over. In that moment, he looked sweet, even a little sad. Maybe I was just imagining it. The thought of Will not having a mother's love broke my heart. "But that's not the worst of it," she added, just when I thought her story was over. "Will's parents split up because Will's dad cheated on his mom. He was having an affair with a woman named Donna Hanson. She and her husband didn't divorce, but they packed up and moved. I guess they didn't have a choice. Could you imagine living next door to the man your wife had an affair with? I couldn't." All I could imagine was how embarrassed Will must've been. "And if all of what I just said wasn't bad enough, some say that he's responsible for the break-up of the Thompsons," she said in a hushed voice. The Thompsons were the people whose house we bought. "Now that hasn't been confirmed, but you can bet where there's smoke, there's fire. There must be some validity to it."

For days I thought about Will and his parents. I couldn't help wondering how much of what my mom said was true, and how much was neighborhood gossip. In a strange way, knowing about his family made me like him even more. I knew what it was to come from a loving home. There was no doubt in my mind how much my parents loved each other and me. Knowing that his father was not the kind of man that Will could look up to was sad. My own dad was the best father a girl could ask for. He was crazy about Mom and would never have behaved so dishonorably. And no matter the circumstances, Mom would never leave us. Despite

Will's good looks and popularity, he was probably unhappy about his parents.

There was something about Will's smile and his eyes that melted my heart. Everybody, even the guys, wanted to be around him. When I saw him at school a couple of days later, I said hi to him even though he was standing with a bunch of boys in the hallway goofing around. One of his friends mumbled something about me being his new girlfriend and they all laughed, but I didn't care. He said hello back to me and smiled like we were old friends.

I wasn't a big believer in fate, but the stars must have been aligned that day. After days of practicing the basics—serving, forehand, backhand and overhead against the gym wall, Miss Klein finally let us play tennis outside on the courts. She assigned partners and Will was mine. At first neither of us said much as we played. Will had to really focus on returning the ball and keeping it in bounds. He wasn't very good at tennis, and he was blown away by how good I was.

"Whoa, dude. You really know what you're doing. Do you play, like, all the time? You're good."

I loved beating him. I was on cloud nine, but I played it cool. "I did. I mean, yes, I guess I still do, but my parents haven't found a club for me to continue taking lessons at. I'm not sure what they're waiting for. Before you know it, it'll be summer and that's really all I do in the summer. That and swim. My dad and brothers play baseball, but my mom and I play tennis."

I gave him a few pointers, which made playing more enjoyable. As Will's game improved, so did his confidence. When he grew a little too cocky for his own good, I put him in his place. "In your face!" I yelled, surprising him with a drop shot. The tennis ball landed just over the net, but he couldn't get to it fast enough. I beat him by a landslide, but I didn't gloat too much. I went around the net to shake his hand, but he purposely blew me off. He tossed his racket into the air and didn't catch it when it came back down. It bounced a few times and landed at my feet. I picked it up and handed it to him. "I see you catch as well as you play tennis."

"Whatever! Let's go again," he said, challenging me to another game.

"No time," I said, "Klein looks like she's getting ready to blow her whistle. I'll have to beat you again tomorrow." Will took up a dueling stance, placing one hand on his hip and his racket straight out in front of him, pretending it was a sword.

"Alright, put down your weapon," I teased. He lowered his arms and began bouncing the ball up and down on the face of his racket. He was pretty good and unlike most people, knew not to bounce the ball too high. "Hey, John McEnroe," I called. "I heard the girl's high school team is pretty good here. Any truth to that?"

His focus was on the ball and not on my question. "I guess," he answered. "I don't know. Maybe. I don't really follow girl's tennis."

I was distracting him, but I didn't care. Class was nearly over and I wanted to keep talking. "It sucks living out in the country because there's no place for me to play tennis. It must be the same for you with basketball. Besides, there aren't a lot of guys our age out where we live are there?"

"Oh yeah, that's right. You live down the road from me. I didn't know that until a few weeks ago when I saw you riding your bike past my house. Sweet bike by the way."

I wanted to die. He must have seen me on David's bike. "Yeah, I had to ride my brother's bike for a while because mine was stolen, but now I have my own. I was saving up for a new bike, but my parents ended up just buying me one. I didn't have a ton saved, but I guess now I can put that money toward buying a car. I turn 15 in October."

Miss Klein blew her whistle causing Will to jump and the tennis ball to skid off his racket. It bounced a few feet away from us on the court. "Crap!" he cried, "I almost beat my record. Oh well." He left the ball where it fell. "My birthday's in August, but I turn 16. Next year, I'll be able to drive myself to school. Pretty sweet, huh?"

"You're turning 16? How?" I asked.

"I was held back in first grade. It's not that I was dumb or anything, I was sick and missed a lot of school, but it's cool because now I'll be one of the first kids in our class to drive." It was the perfect opportunity to ask him why he didn't ride the bus, but there wasn't time. Miss Klein blew her whistle again and Will took off in the other direction.

"C'mon boys and girls! Get a move on it! If you want to enjoy the fresh air and sunshine you can't dillydally when it's time to go in!"

I collected my sweatshirt and started making my way to the doors. Miss Klein stopped me. "Not so fast, Daisy Doyle, I need to speak to you a moment." I couldn't imagine what she wanted to talk to me about.

"I'll see you around, Will," I called, but he didn't answer. I don't think he heard me. He was too busy messing around with some guys from the other class. We had made a real connection so I didn't sweat it.

Miss Klein only wanted to compliment me on my tennis skills. She was the JV girl's tennis coach and just wanted to encourage me to try out for freshman tennis the following school year.

"Hey, Daisy," Will called, just as I was pulling open the door "The next time you go for a spin on your bike, drop by my place. Maybe I'll go with you."

I couldn't believe it. Did he like me or was he just bored out of his mind like I was out in no man's land? Whatever the reason, I was going to hang out with Will. I wanted to say, "Okay, how about tonight?" but I just smiled and kept walking.

10
You'll Never Believe What Happened Today!

"You'll never believe what happened today," I whispered into the phone.

Kim's high-pitched squeal on the other end of the line nearly pierced my eardrum. I repeated word for word the conversation between Will and me while pacing back and forth across the kitchen with the phone cord coiled around my body like a python. With so many little ears around, I had to be careful about what I said. Denny was at home sick with the chicken pox and was sitting at the kitchen table in his underwear slurping down a bowl of chicken noodle soup. He looked a mess even though the worst was behind him. His lesions had started to crust over and he could swallow again without wincing. Pink dots of calamine lotion decorated his pasty white flesh. His chest and back resembled constellation maps. Mom's 4:00 pm appointment was pounding out *Twinkle, Twinkle Little Star* behind the French doors of the music room while his older brother, her 4:30 pm student, sat flipping through a *Ranger Rick* magazine on the sofa in the family room.

After many phone calls back and forth among Kim, Shari and me, the three of us finally reached a decision. I would wait a few days before dropping by Will's place. There was no point in coming across desperate, especially if he didn't really mean anything by it. Waiting until the weekend made the most sense. Because Will ran track after school and I was stuck with a million chores to do every night, there wasn't any time. Most of Mom's lessons weren't over until 5:30 pm, so I had the unfortunate responsibility of looking after Denny and helping with dinner. It was always, "Set the table, Daisy," or "Daisy, would mind loading the dishwasher?" Mom left something for me to do almost every day, while the boys could kick back and watch TV or play. My brothers were completely useless. Sometimes being the oldest rocked. For one thing, I didn't get dragged around to a bunch of places I didn't want to go because I was old enough to stay home alone. I had more freedom, but sometimes being the oldest was the worst. Sometimes I fantasized about being the youngest child like my neighbor, Debbie Schmidt. Maybe then my parents would've treated me like a princess instead of a free baby sitter or an indentured servant.

11
Operation Drop By Will's Part 1

The clock radio read 7:45 am, but it felt later. If I hadn't felt so relaxed, nestled down in my comfy cocoon of blankets, I might have gotten out of bed and checked my *Swatch* watch, which was sitting on top of my chest of drawers not four feet away. Sunlight filtered through my chambray curtains. They swayed in unison with the subtle breeze and cast squatty shadows on the floor and walls of my bedroom. I was certain that I must have once again messed up the time on my clock radio. I knew how to set it, but sometimes in the middle of the night while half asleep, I'd accidently press the wrong button and mess up the display time or reset my alarm clock altogether. Alarm clock mishaps frequently caused trouble for me in the morning during the school week. Being lulled to sleep by sappy music every night was the last step of my nightly regimen. I was pretty OCD back then and I wouldn't have dreamt of skipping any part of my routine. First, I'd brush my hair 100 times with a paddle brush. I read in one of my teen fashion magazines that brushing your hair stimulated the hair follicles, which led to faster hair growth. After brushing my hair, I'd pull it up in a tight bun and scrub my face with Noxzema and scalding hot water. Next, I'd brush and floss my teeth. Lastly, I'd change into my pajamas and crawl into my bed where I'd record in my diary my deepest and darkest secrets. Actually, I never recorded anything too deep because I didn't trust my brothers not to ransack my belongings in my absence.

The house rule on school nights was lights out by 9:30, but I was never tired enough to fall asleep that early. Instead of tossing and turning half the night, I'd lie in bed and listen to *WNIC*, a radio station that broadcasted out of Detroit. I'd listen to, *Pillow Talk*, a show hosted by a DJ by the name of Alan Almond. His deep, baritone voice was hypnotic. Between the continuous stream of love songs and the sentimental letters he read from love struck fans, I typically fell asleep thinking of how nice it would be to have a boyfriend. Rarely did I stay awake for his sign off or closing song, but I never missed a show unless I spent the night at someone else's house. Sometime before midnight every night, I'd fall asleep, but would then wake up hours later and fumble around in the dark for the off button. Thank God Mom always came into my room and woke me if she didn't hear me the next morning moving around.

When I finally crawled out from under my covers, my room felt like an icebox. I slipped a sweatshirt on over my nightgown and pulled on a pair of socks. I shut my window and ventured out into the hallway. The house was deserted and unusually quiet for a Saturday morning. I felt a little like a character from one of those sci-fi movies where the main character wakes up after a long sleep only to discover that some kind of catastrophic event has taken place, or the world's population has been taken over by aliens or apocalyptic zombies. I followed my nose to the kitchen. Dirty plates resembling a house of cards were stacked on the counter next to the sink. One lousy piece of bacon left on a greasy napkin was all that was left of breakfast. Because my parents had this thing about sleeping in—they viewed it as a sign of laziness—it never occurred to either of them to ever save any breakfast for me. When the boys gobbled up all the food, my parents turned a blind eye. Denny ate like a bird and never took more than his share. Instead he'd fill his plate, cover the food in ketchup or syrup or some other disgusting condiment, take one lousy bite, and announce that he was full.

"That's what you get, Lazy Daisy, when you sleep half the day away," was what my brothers liked to say when I accused them of being greedy little pigs. David wasn't too bad because he didn't eat like there was no tomorrow, but Daniel was a different story. He was a bacon hound who could easily eat a pound all by himself if Mom let him.

By the looks of things, I knew they couldn't have gone too far. Both Mom and Dad's car keys were hanging on the key rack next to the garage door. The sliding glass door was cracked open to rid the house of the lingering smell of bacon. I checked the backyard and sure enough, they were all there. Dad and the boys were in grubby jeans and flannel shirts and Mom was in an actual pair of bibbed overalls and gardening clogs. Her hair was in braids. She looked like a little Dutch girl. They were huddled like football players in the northeast corner of the yard that had been tilled for the vegetable garden. I tried sneaking back into the house, but Denny saw me and ratted me out.

"Lazy Daisy's finally up!" he cried. "Did you see that Daniel ate all of the bacon?" Then he turned around and shook his butt at me.

"Morning, sleepy head," said Mom, ignoring Denny. "You must've been pretty tired to sleep in so late. Grab a bowl of cereal and put some work clothes on and join us." It was a joke that she considered 7:45 sleeping in. I didn't dispute it, but instead went in to put on some clothes.

Mom and Dad were stoked to have a garden all their own and were happy to put urban gardening behind them. For years they had been members of a community garden that they themselves had started, but the experience wasn't all that it was cracked up to be. The plots were small and the other members were a pain in the neck to deal with. "If this is what farming on a kibbutz is like, no wonder so many Israelis throw in the towel and go it alone," Dad used to complain when the same people in the group did all the work. To my parents, the garden was about more than fresh produce. They were hokey and viewed the project as an opportunity for us to spend quality time together. It was a labor of love, and there was no way they were going to write me a pass. I too had to help.

Operation Drop By Will's *or ODBW,* was not scheduled to take place until later that afternoon, so in a way, I was grateful to have the distraction. I was nervous. The name of my top-secret mission was lame and not very covert sounding, but I had more important things to focus on. Shari, Kim and I wracked our brains for hours coming up with a plan that would allow me to hang out with Will without my parents knowing. I considered just telling them. But given the way Mom freaked out about Will's dad, I knew there'd be too many questions and too many restrictions. Knowing them, they would have insisted that David tag along as a chaperone. Our plan was simple. If I paid attention to the time, I'd be able to pull it off without a hitch.

12
Operation Drop By Will's Part 2: Daisy Diana Doyle

We slaved away in the garden until mid-day. When Mom announced that it was time to break for lunch, she heard no objections from David, Daniel or me. Dad and Denny were the only two not ready to call it quits. The half field that remained uncultivated was an albatross around Dad's neck and he wouldn't rest until the last row was planted. Mom went inside to tidy up the kitchen and to fix something to eat while Daniel and David grabbed their mitts and began tossing the baseball back and forth. What was left of Dad's patience was lost after taking a rake to the face. Denny had left it at the end of the potato row, so he shooed Denny out of the garden, which worked out for Daniel and David because they were looking for a third person to join them in a game of pickle. They begged me, but I wasn't in the mood.

The sun felt so nice. With my jeans rolled to my knees and the sleeves of my t-shirt pushed up onto my shoulders and secured with the straps of my bra, I planted myself in one of the Adirondack chairs on the back deck and sunned myself. I felt a little guilty about not helping Dad, but I think he wanted to go it alone for a while. Knowing Dad, he probably felt badly for telling Denny that he needed to go find something else to do. Sometimes I had a tough time feeling sorry for Dad and Denny. Denny because he was so hardheaded and couldn't figure out when he was getting on people's nerves, and Dad because he brought a lot of his frustration on himself. Both of my parents, but especially Dad, believed in the proverbial wisdom hogwash about giving a poor man a fish and feeding him for only a day and teaching him to fish and feeding him for a lifetime, which is why it always took our family forever to do even the simplest of tasks. Take planting the garden, for example. It would have gone a million times quicker if Dad had just made all the rows and let us kids sow the seeds, or place the plants in the parted soil, instead of insisting that each of us take a turn at making trenches with the furrower that was attached to the rototiller. David was probably the best at it followed by myself. Daniel did okay, but Denny could only do it if someone walked behind him and helped guide the machine down the rows. Working with Denny was a pain.

We ate our boiled hotdogs and *Better Made* potato chips under the warm mid-day sun. Mom and Dad discussed their plans for the rest of the afternoon. Daniel and Denny had 2:00 o'clock games, and David's game was at 3:00. It was agreed that Mom would take the boys to the ballpark and Dad would stay behind and work in the garden then come to the park in time to catch David's game. Dad was no fool—Mom was getting the short end of the stick. David's games were exciting to watch, whereas my younger brothers' games were snoozers. Denny's team stayed focused, but only for the first few innings. They were only interested in batting. Daniel's coach was a jerk and just yelled all the time, forcing Dad to bite his tongue.

Since plans were being tossed about, I decided it was an appropriate time to mention mine.

I spoke my lines convincingly, just the way I had rehearsed them. "Say, if you guys don't mind, I'm going to skip the boys' games today. Debbie and I talked about hanging out." I almost always went to the boys' games. Not because I liked watching them play per se, but because it was another chance to hang out with Kim or Shari who could usually find a ride to the ballpark. Mostly we just talked or got something to snack on from the concession stands, but sometimes we'd catch a game that someone we knew from school was playing. "We thought about going for a bike ride."

Smiling Mom said, "Well, that's fine by me. You haven't hung out with her in a while. You mean to tell me she doesn't have 4H or any gymnastic meets this weekend?"

"Yeah, but she's free this afternoon so—we're going to hang." I was a little nervous using Debbie as part of my alibi, but I knew it would make Mom happy. She and Debbie's mom were getting to be close, and Mom had expressed on more than one occasion her desire for me to hang out with Debbie more instead of just spending all my time with Kim and Shari. She probably liked the fact that she didn't have to drive me anywhere when I hung out with her. I liked Debbie, I really did, but we didn't have much in common, and truthfully, she was rarely ever home.

Mom left with the boys, Dad resumed planting and I went inside to get ready. It was warm enough for shorts, but my pasty white legs needed shaving. I was all about getting ready quickly, seeing Will, and returning home long before everybody else. I dressed simply in jeans and a striped tee. I dusted my cheeks with a peachy colored blush, swiped my new *Bonnie Bell Dr. Pepper Lip Smacker* across my lips and sprayed myself from head to toe with *Loves Baby Soft* perfume.

I did make a point of saying goodbye to Dad before I left, but he barely acknowledged me. He threw up his hand and sort of waved me off. My bike hung on a rack along with all the other bikes in the detached garage. Crammed with everything that couldn't fit in the attached garage or the basement, it was a pain in the neck to find anything. Dad's rusty Ford truck that he used solely for hauling wood, mulch and junk back and forth to the dump, was in the way. Getting my bike without it crashing down on his truck or on myself was a major feat. I pumped a little air into the back tire and peddled off down our gravel driveway with the same optimism as Julie Andrews in *The Sound of Music* when she was leaving the Abbey for the first time to meet the Von Trapp family. I too felt like singing, but as I got closer to his house my optimism began to dwindle. Maybe he wasn't home. Perhaps I'd catch him not showered or worse yet with his teeth not brushed or his hair uncombed. It was quite possible that he was helping his own dad with yard work and wasn't free to go off with me. My confidence suddenly became overshadowed by uncertainty. I was about to leave and go to Debbie's house when I heard his garage door opening. I slowed my peddling and anxiously waited to see what the open door would bring. Possibly Mr. Bank's car would come backing down the driveway, or Mr. Banks himself, pushing a lawn mower and whistling some corny tune that all dads whistled when they worked in the yard. But instead, Will came strolling out with a basketball spinning on the tip of his finger. He bounced the ball a few times and took a jump shot. The ball swooshed through the weathered net that hung above the garage door.

"Hey, you made it!" He said, as if he were expecting me the entire time.

The long pants were a bad idea. I was roasting. My underarms were moist with perspiration and my upper lip already salty with sweat. I couldn't remember if I had applied deodorant or not, so when he went up for a layup, I did a quick sniff test. My pits smelled decent. "Hey yourself," I said, trying to sound just as casual. I wanted him to believe that my decision to stop by his house was spur-of-the-moment, an afterthought, and not part of some elaborate scheme. He looked adorable despite his mismatched ensemble of basketball shorts topped with a red plaid shirt and grass-stained sneakers.

"I was just biking down to the store and thought maybe you'd want to go with." He contemplated my offer longer than I thought necessary, which I interpreted to mean that he wasn't interested. I withdrew the invite to save face. "It's okay if you're busy, it's not a big deal if you can't come. I was going anyway." When he didn't say anything, I turned my bike around and said, "See ya."

"Oh, hey-wait. I want to go," he called. "I was just thinking about how much time I have. I'll need to be back no later than 5:00 because my grandparents are coming for a visit."

"Awe, your grandparents? That's nice."

"Yeah, my dad drove down to St. Clair Shores to help them look for a new car and then he's driving them back up here for the night. He'll take them back home sometime tomorrow."

"If they have their own car, why does he need to drive them here?"

"The car is just for them to drive around town in. To go to the store and doctors and stuff like that. Grammy doesn't drive at all and Poppy shouldn't drive, but he won't turn over his license. He'd probably get lost or crash his car if he drove all the way up here alone," Will explained.

"Grammy and Poppy," I repeated. I couldn't resist.

My comment didn't embarrass him though. He just went on with his story. "Yeah, that's what they like to be called. My grandparents are both a little senile, but they're cool." I liked that Will wasn't too cool to show that he had a soft spot for his grandparents. It made me like him even more. "Let me go grab some money and we can go. Be right back."

When he came back out, he was wearing a *Led Zeppelin* concert shirt that read, *1968/1969 North American Tour*. He smelled nice, like aftershave and minty toothpaste. Patting his pocket, he said, "Wallet and house key. Alright, I'm ready when you are."

Traffic wasn't bad, but sections of the road had little or no shoulder, which made part of the trip a little harrowing. Contrary to everything I learned in bike safety class, we didn't ride with the flow of traffic.

"I don't want to end up road kill," said Will when I questioned him about it. "It's better to see the cars head on then to have your back to them," was his theory. I didn't agree with his logic, but I didn't correct him either. During parts of the trip we couldn't ride side by side, so we didn't speak until we reached the store. There was no bike rack, so we leaned our bikes up against the side of the building and went inside. Other than the cashier, whom I recognized but didn't know, Will and I were the only other people in the store. She said hello to us and called me by name. She was sweet, but I wasn't sure how she knew my name, or why she spoke to me as if we had met. I'd never spoken to her before in my life.

"Hey there, Daisy. How are you today? You kids here with your dad?" she asked, looking past me to see if he were straggling in behind us. I think she thought Will was one of my brothers. Like most old people, she rambled on about things that neither of us even asked about. Her chattiness made me a little nervous because maybe someone I really knew would stop by, or someone I didn't know at all would mosey in and she'd say something like, "Well, so and so, you know Daisy Doyle don't ya? Her daddy is a big wig down at the bank." I tried not to freak out, especially since Will didn't act the least bit concerned about anything. His dad probably didn't keep track of his friends or his whereabouts. My parents, on the other hand, would've flipped out if one of our gossipy neighbors mentioned to them that they saw us together.

"So...Linda, John, I bumped into Daisy at the convenience store. She was with the Banks boy. Is that her boyfriend?"

There would have been several reasons why they'd be angry. Mostly they'd be disappointed that I had lied to them about what I was doing. I didn't dawdle. It was a Saturday afternoon and the odds of running into someone else I knew were great. I fished an ice cream sandwich out from the *Good Humor* chest and placed the exact change into the cashier's wrinkly hand. I was ready to be back outside along the side of the store where I'd be less visible, but Will's transaction took forever. The penny-candy he wanted was stashed behind the counter, safely out of the reach of nose-picking children's grubby little hands. It took forever for her to scoop the candy out of the canisters and into one of the small paper bags. Once we both had what we wanted, we went back outside and sat at a picnic table situated underneath a massive tree next to a rusty steel fire ring. I had to inhale my ice cream sandwich to prevent it from melting down my arm. Will popped a jawbreaker in his mouth and handed me his brown paper bag, "The ice cream here is never frozen because their freezer sucks. Take something if you want." I pulled out a *Jolly Rancher* candy and tucked it into my pocket for later. For the first couple of minutes, we didn't say much. In all our scheming, my friends and I never considered what the two of us would talk about once we were alone.

Our entire plan, from the lie I told my parents to the fact that I didn't consider that I might run into someone that I knew was lame, but I was hell bent on making the trip worth it. "So, have you always gone to school here?" His mouth was all juicy with spit from his jawbreaker, so it made it difficult for him to speak. He turned his head and made a sort of slurping noise that reminded me of the noise the turkey baster makes on Thanksgiving.

"Nope. I was born in California, but my parents didn't want me growing up not really knowing my grandparents, so they decided to move back to Michigan when I was in third grade. We lived in Grosse Point for a while, but my dad didn't like living so close to my mom's parents, and neither of them liked how snobby the people in Grosse Pointe were, so we moved. But we mostly moved for my dad's job. I started school here in fifth grade."

"Did your parents meet in college? Mine did, at Michigan State."

"They didn't go to the same college, but they both moved out to San Francisco separately when they graduated. That's where they met, at Baker Beach. Supposedly my mom was walking her dog, and my dad was taking pictures of the Golden Gate Bridge. He was so taken with her beauty that he asked her if he could take her picture."

"That's so romantic. Do they still have the picture?"

"It's somewhere in our house," he answered. "Not sure though."

"That's a great story. San Francisco seems like a cool place, I bet you hate that they moved and you ended up here."

Will laughed. "Have you ever been to San Francisco? It's all right, I guess. I like the water and the climate. A lot of hippies still live there and they're not the kind you see on TV. They're not young with pretty flowers in their hair. They're old, crazy hippies who live on the streets. Harmless I suppose, but creepy. Mom ran away to San Francisco when she was in high school, which was years before all the hippies flocked to the Haight-Ashbury district in the summer of '67."

"Why did she run away? Did she run off with some guy or something?" I couldn't picture my own mother being so spontaneous.

"I don't know exactly why she went. Supposedly she was a beatnik or some crazy shit. At least that's what my grandparents have said. Mom never really talks about that time in her life."

"A beatnik? Like those people that wear all black and pretend to be trapped in an imaginary box?"

"No man, that's a mime," Will corrected me. "I don't know," he continued, "Poetry and artsy shit was her thing. My grandparents were scared and had to hire a private detective to go get her. When she came back, she was all messed up and went to an asylum or some kind of hospital to rest. She really changed out there, or so my grandparents always claim. Anyway, it took a while, but she got better, finished high school and eventually went to University of Michigan. But the minute she graduated, she went right back out there. My Dad moved out there for a job, but mostly because he wanted to live in the Bay Area. He's into photography and was a huge Alfred Hitchcock fan back in the day." The only Hitchcock movies I had even seen were, *Psycho* and *The Birds*, but I got his reference. After listening to Will talk about his parents, I felt embarrassed that my own family was so incredibly normal and boring. Other than Mom getting pregnant with me in college, our family was ordinary. I didn't ask him about his parent's divorce. If he wanted to talk about it, he would've brought it up. I told him all about Dad playing baseball for Michigan State and he was impressed. We talked about tennis and basketball and some of the teachers at school, basically everything I'd talk about with my girlfriends. I did ask him why he didn't ride the bus, but that didn't seem to bother him. He explained that his Dad took him to school because he worked at a plastics company in town.

Everything was going off without a hitch until he pulled out a pack of cigarettes. *"Not this again,"* I thought to myself. He handed me the pack. Plenty of people I knew smoked, but they were all adults. Both of my parents smoked occasionally, Mom more than Dad, but any time they did, they made comments like, "Don't smoke, kids. It's really a bad habit and that's why we only do it occasionally." I honestly never had the desire to even try smoking. Kids at school smoked, but they were burnouts and Will didn't strike me as the burnout type. He was a pretty decent athlete. I wondered if his dad knew. My guess was that he didn't. I removed a cigarette from the pack and lit it. It wasn't horrible, but I didn't enjoy it.

I took a couple more drags, but I wanted to put it out. "Why do you smoke?"

"Probably the same reason you smoke. I like it."

"But I don't smoke."

"Well, don't look now, Daisy Doyle, but you're smoking."

I looked at the cigarette burning between my fingers and tossed it to the ground. "I don't smoke. I just wanted to try it."

"That's not what you told me the first day we met. You said that you'd smoked before, but you just didn't like it."

I was surprised that Will had remembered what I had said. I could have made up some lie to tell him, but I didn't feel like I needed to. "I didn't know you then. It was the first time we met and my first day of school. I guess I didn't want you to think I was uptight, so I lied. Anyway, I didn't think you smoked-smoked. I mean, not on a regular basis."

Will took a hit off his cigarette and turned his head so the smoke from his smoke rings wouldn't blow in my face. "Nah," he said, ignoring my comment about his habit. "I can tell that you're pretty cool, Daisy Doyle. And besides, you shouldn't worry about what other people think." He was right, it was stupid to worry, but not worrying was easier said than done.

"What's up with you calling me, Daisy Doyle all the time? I don't call you, Will Banks."

"I don't know. I guess I like the way it sounds. What's your middle name?"

I didn't want to tell him. It was too humiliating, but he begged me so I did. "My middle name is Diana."

He closed his eyes and tapped his fingers on his pursed lips like he was contemplating my full name. "That's a great name," he concluded. "Sounds like you could be the main character in a fictional book series. You know, kind of like Nancy Drew or James Bond. Can't you see it? *Daisy Doyle's Got a New Bike* or *Daisy Diana Doyle Smokes Her First Cigarette*. It's catchy, that's all."

"I don't think it's catchy. What's your middle name Will Banks?" I asked.

"Don't have one."

"You do too. Everybody has a middle name," I insisted.

He shook his head. "Nope, not even an initial. Maybe when I'm an adult I'll throw in a letter for my middle name to make me sound more distinguished or change my first name to a letter and just make up a middle name. Something like John F. Kennedy or F. Scott Fitzgerald or Wile E. Coyote."

I laughed, "Yeah, those three dudes are pretty distinguished, especially Wile E. Coyote."

I didn't tell him that I hated the sound of my full name, Daisy Diana Doyle. The names Daisy, Diana and Doyle by themselves weren't too bad, but when they were put together they were kitschy sounding and not the least bit romantic. Mom got my first name from the character Daisy Fay Buchanan from the novel *The Great Gatsby,* and I loved how her full name sounded, but hated my own full name. It struck me as odd that Will mentioned Fitzgerald, because that was one of Mom's favorite authors.

After a few seconds of silence Will asked, "Hey, were you named after the chick from *The Great Gatsby*? That's my mom's favorite book and the only Daisy I know besides Daisy Duck."

"Daisy Duck? Who's that?"

"You know, Donald's girlfriend?" Will clarified.

"I know who Daisy Duck is. I was just yanking your chain, but you're right— That's exactly who I was named after, Donald Duck's girlfriend."

He shot me a side-ways glance. "Huh-uh, you're lying. You weren't named after some duck."

I smiled and shrugged. "Maybe, but that's pretty weird that that's your mom's favorite book because that's one of my mom's favorite books too. Have you ever read it?"

"Nah. Too busy reading *War and Peace*. I'll get to that one later." I knew he was just kidding with the Tolstoy reference, but I thought it was sweet that he knew what his mom's favorite book was. Most guys wouldn't.

I helped myself to another piece of his candy. The taste of the cigarette still lingered on my tongue and I didn't like it. Will glanced twice at his watch before announcing that he needed to hit the road. "Still need to mow the front yard and clean my bedroom before Dad shows up with the grandparents."

"Cool. Let's go," I said.

The entire ride home was spent thinking about whether or not Will liked me liked me, or if he just considered me a friend. It was hard to tell. Half the time he referred to me as *Dude* and treated me like I was one of the guys. But that day he opened up to me about his parents and family, and that sort of seemed like a boyfriend thing to do. He didn't try to kiss me or hold my hand, but he did spend a lot of time with me. I so badly wanted to be his girlfriend.

13
A Walk in the Woods

Somewhere between the onset of summer vacation and the announcement of the last dance of the school year, I started giving more thought to my relationship with Will. At school, not much had really changed between us. We acknowledged each other in the hallway, bantered back and forth during gym class, but we were still not a couple, nor did we interact in a way that anyone would make anyone believe that we were anything but friends. I wasn't sure how to classify our relationship, exactly. Outside of school, we hung out sometimes during the week and on the weekends, but we never spoke on the phone. It was weird. Our relationship had been disappointingly platonic, but one Saturday afternoon, when Will showed up at my front door, our relationship took a turn. Thankfully, I was the only one home when he stopped by.

"Will," I said, trying not to act too surprised, "what are you doing here?"

He smiled before giving me one of his standard smart-alecky responses. "What? Do I need to produce a search warrant before you'll let me in?"

I knew I should've told him upfront that he couldn't just pop over whenever he felt like it, but I didn't want to scare him off. "Hey, my parents aren't home and they'd kill me if they found out that I had a friend over without asking permission first, so what do you say we go for a walk?"

"I'm cool with that," he said, "Where do you want to go?"

We couldn't walk on the road. Too many people were out working in their yards and would see us, so I suggested the woods. "My brothers and their dorky little friends always go into the woods behind our house. I've heard that there are some cool trails. Have you ever been back there?"

"Eh, a few times, but not in a while. What the hell do they do out there?"

"I don't know. You're a guy, what would you do out there?" I asked.

Will wiggled his eyebrows up and down suggestively and laughed. "You don't want to know, but sure, why the hell not? Let's go exploring."

Like frontiersmen, Will and I forged our way through the woods for quite some time before I got tired from all the walking and suggested we take a little break. "I'm thirsty," I announced. "I wish we had something to drink." Will didn't have anything to drink, but quickly produced a pack of cigarettes and a roll of breath mints from the front pocket of his blousy basketball shorts.

"Can't help you with the water, but I brought other provisions."

I had grown accustomed to his smoking and convinced myself that it wasn't a big deal. Deep down, I knew it kind of was, but I didn't make a big deal about it. Whenever I gave Shari and Kim the play-by-play after one of our secret rendezvous, I left out the part where Will smoked. They wouldn't have approved, and honestly, if it were anyone other than Will, I probably wouldn't have either. Will never put pressure on me to smoke. As a matter of fact, the first time I asked for a drag off his cigarette after the time at the store, he said no. I didn't want a whole one all to myself, but I was curious to see if maybe I'd changed my mind about the taste.

"Nah, I don't think you're a smoker," he had said, "and besides, I don't like being a bad influence on my friends."

"A bad influence? I think it's a little late for that," I teased. His reference to our friendship made me cringe on the inside because I wanted us to be more than just friends.

He lit up a cigarette and asked, "So what kind of music do you like?"

"All kinds, really. I love Pat Benatar and The Pretenders."

Will made a face. "They both suck."

"Uh-uh. What are you talking about? They totally don't suck," I argued.

"Okay, let me rephrase that. Pat Benatar's voice is decent and so is Chrissie Hynde's, I suppose, but their songs are lame. Total chick lyrics. Please don't tell me that you only listen to girly music."

"No way," I said. "I listen to other stuff."

"Yeah, like what?"

I felt like no matter what I said, he'd take issue with it so I avoided answering him altogether. "So what bands do you like?" I asked. "Let me guess. Van Halen? Billy Squire? Loverboy?"

"Oh, hell no dude! I mean, Van Halen's alright, but I'm more into Zeppelin, Pink Floyd—The Who."

"Figures," I said. "What guy isn't? So, speaking of really cheesy music, are you going to the last dance of the year?"

"Ha-ha! I dunno. Maybe," he answered. "When is it?"

"Duh, this upcoming Friday. The Friday after next is the last day of school, Will."

He shrugged his shoulders. "I guess I will. What the heck, I've gone to all the other ones. Yeah, probably." Will's response left me scratching my head.

"Well, I haven't been to one yet. I wasn't here for the dance just before Christmas break and I had a wicked case of strep throat at the time of the *Spring Fling*. This one coming up is my last chance."

"If it makes you feel any better, you didn't miss much. They were lame. The music sucked and anytime they played a slow song, they turned up the lights instead of dimming them. The whole thing would have been a total bust if it weren't for Brian Miller who snuck in a fifth of peach Schnapps."

"Where did he get that?" I asked.

"We all snagged a couple of beers from out of our fridges at home, but Brian's older sister bought us the Schnapps."

"And you drank it while you were at the dance?"

"Hell yeah, we did." Will acted like it was no big deal, like he drank all the time. Unlike the smoking, I had sampled my fair share of alcohol, but never drank with my girlfriends. Mostly I just snuck sips of wine from Mom's glass or sampled my aunts and uncles' mixed drinks at the yearly Christmas party when they weren't looking.

"So, are you going or not?" I asked again.

"Yeah, I'm going. Maybe we could hang before the dance. I mean there'd be other people there too. Invite some of your friends. It'd be cool. I'll let you know what's what when I hear whose house it'll be at. Say, what's your number?"

I couldn't give him my number. If he called the house and either of my parents answered, I'd never hear the end of it. Back in seventh grade when they caught wind that some of my friends had boyfriends, they weren't happy about it at all. It was established there and then that I wasn't allowed to date until I was a sophomore in high school.

"Why a sophomore?" I had protested. "That's so arbitrary and archaic!"

Naturally Dad had a logical explanation. "For starters, most kids can't drive until they're in 10th grade anyway and there's no way you're dating an upper classman. And besides," he added, "I'm sure you wouldn't want me or Mom driving you and your dates around, and that's exactly what would happen if you started dating any sooner." My parents could be so hopelessly old fashioned at times.

"So, what's your number?" he asked again.

There was no point in beating around the bush. I just needed to be honest.

"Will, my parents don't exactly know about the two of us hanging out. They're strict when it comes to boys and talking to them and stuff like that. You can't call my house and you really can't just stop by because they wouldn't like it. My dad's stricter than my mom. He's always spouting off about boys having one-track minds and that how he knows that is because he was once a teenage boy. They just wouldn't like me hanging out with you." I prayed that he'd be satisfied with my explanation, but he wasn't.

"Hold up, I'm confused. So, you can't ever talk to any dudes or have any dudes as friends or hang out with them unsupervised? Or would they just not like you doing those things with me?"

His question was legit, but my answer was complicated. "I don't know. A little of both I guess.

"Geez! I'm surprised they'd even let you go to a dance with all those guys there. Maybe they should just lock you away in a convent or something." He wasn't kidding with his convent comment, but he didn't have it exactly right. They weren't totally unreasonable. Speaking with a boy on the phone wasn't totally out of the question if we were just friends, but as with any of my friends, they'd ask a million questions about his family to make sure they were good enough. And, if for even a second they suspected that we were more than just friends, they'd put the kibosh on the relationship altogether.

"I'm not sure the best way to say what I'm about to say without hurting your feelings, so I'm just going to say it. My mom heard some stuff about your dad and though she's not all judgmental and whatnot, she's pretty overprotective, and so is my dad." The look on his face was a combination of disgust and hurt. I should've just lied and told him that my parents were overbearing and left it at that, but I wanted to be honest. "Look, Will, I'm sorry. I'm an idiot. It's not you, it's them."

"Awe, Daisy, you don't have to lie. What did your mother say?"

I worried that maybe Will didn't know the entire story behind his own parent's breakup. Maybe his parents spared him all the unpleasant details and gave him the standard, *We just don't love each other anymore, but we'll always love you,* load of crap that parents in the movies tell their kids just before the carpet is ripped out from under them. Maybe he did know, but figured it was a whole lot easier for me to say it than him. In that moment, I realized just how deeply I cared for Will. It was more than a stupid crush, and unlike all the other girls in my grade, I didn't just like him because he was cute or popular. I liked him because he was sensitive and smart and funny. He didn't try to act all cool, he just was cool. And because I loved him, I lied to spare his feelings. Looking down at the forest floor I said, "Oh, not much. Just that your parents got divorced and your Mom lives in California."

Will was bolder than I and did not look at the ground when he asked, "So all that time when you were asking me about my parents, you already knew that my parents weren't together? What difference does any of this make? Would your parents really not like me because of my parents?"

"Oh, God no. They're just super religious that way." Clearly, Will wasn't Catholic. I wasn't sure if he was religious at all. He obviously didn't know that getting divorced was a big deal for Catholics. "It's not that they wouldn't like you. Oh, this is so frustrating. I'm not sure how to describe what I mean in a way that you'd understand,"

"Well try," he said defensively. "I'm not stupid!"

"You see," I said, choosing my words even more carefully. "My parents believe that marriage is a sacrament, and that when people divorce, they're breaking a sacred vow that they made before God."

"And so?" Will scoffed.

"Well, it's stupid, I know. I'm only 14 and not getting married any time soon, but neither of them ever does anything without overthinking it to death. If they thought that we liked each other, they'd worry that you wouldn't be a standup guy, like your dad."

My words, like a hard slap to the face, were going to leave a mark. There was no reeling them back in. I had cast my line and now the hook was set in Will's ego.

"What do you mean by that? Who says my dad's not a standup guy?"

I wanted to crawl under the closest rock. "Crap! That's not what I meant! Of course, he is. I'm not my parents, Will. I'm just trying to tell you how it is with them."

"Yeah, okay. I get it. We're cool. If your parents don't want to meet me, or you don't want me to meet them, that's fine, but I hope that you don't take what I'm about to say the wrong way. Your folks sound like uptight assholes."

His words stung, but I had it coming. "No offense taken," I lied. My parents really weren't assholes, but there was no point trying to defend them. Will's family and my family were just different. The conversation was over as far as Will was concerned. He wouldn't even look at me anymore. He pulled out his crumpled pack of cigarettes and lit up for a second time.

"Give me one of those." I said, not giving him the chance to say no.

He handed me the pack, "Okay, but don't inhale, they're not good for you."

We sat smoking, each of us lost in our own thoughts. I wanted to hear more about his parents, but the opportunity had passed, thanks to my big mouth. There were so many things I wanted to say to Will, but mostly I wanted to tell him that being with him made me happier than I'd ever been in my entire life, and that it was only when I wasn't with him that I missed everyone and everything from my old life. The rest of my family had slipped into their new lives effortlessly, but I wasn't there yet, at least not entirely. Will was the only thing that felt like a perfect fit. I wanted things to go back to the way they were before I put my foot in my mouth, but I was afraid that I had ruined everything.

Just as I began to think that it was a hopeless cause, Will's eyes lit up again. "Hey—I don't know about the dance, but we should definitely do some pre-dance partying."

"We can hang, but let's be clear. I'm not so sure about the partying part. Why do you need to drink in the first place?"

He didn't need to think about it. "I don't need to drink, but it's more fun when I do."

"C'mon, seriously. I don't want to get busted and kicked out of the dance because I'm wasted."

"Nobody's saying that you need to get sloshed. As far as that goes—drink or don't drink, Daisy Diana Doyle, the choice is yours."

"Okay, we'll see Will Banks."

14
What You Don't Know Won't Hurt You

I found myself in the midst of a moral conundrum. More than anything, I wanted to be with Will, but doing so required an astronomical amount of lying, or truth bending, as I liked to think of it back then, to everyone I cared about. The first semi-lie I told was to Kim and Shari. It wasn't a lie as much as it was omitting details that might have swayed their decision in the other direction. They were both into hanging with the guys before the dance. Neither one of them mentioned drinking and so neither did I. We'd cross the alcohol bridge when we got to it. The way I saw it, I was doing them a favor by inviting them. They'd have fun. I used the same, *if nobody asks, then don't tell*, logic with my parents. What they didn't know because they didn't ask couldn't hurt them. The only smidgeon of truth that I left out with them was the party before the dance and the guys. But in fairness to myself, neither of my parents asked me if my friends and I were going to a party at Brian Miller's house before the dance, or if we were going to the dance with a group of guys. When Mom asked if Shari's parents would be home, I told her the truth. "Her mom just started working afternoons, but her Dad will be home after he gets out of work."

"So, nobody's going to be home between the time you get home from school and the time you leave for the dance? I'm not sure if I like that."

"Her brother Walt's going to be there. He's a senior. Shari's mom said that you could call her if you had any questions."

Of course, Mom called. And after asking her a million and one questions, she agreed to let me go over there. "Well, I guess it's okay," Mom told Dad over dinner. "Shari's mom assured me that Walt is a very responsible young man and that he takes care of his baby sister all the time. She's going to leave money for the girls to order a pizza and Walt will pick it up for them. Her husband will be home later and waiting for them when they get home shortly after ten. Sounds like they'll be in good hands."

I knew my dishonesty was a slippery slope and that one lie typically leads to another, so I justified my behavior with a tiny rationalization. A half-truth, I told myself, is better that a full-blown lie. I'd get back to being forthright when Will and I were in a good place.

15
The Dance

Walt wasn't as responsible as Shari's mom claimed, but that wasn't anything I had any control over. When we came in from school, Walt barley acknowledged our existence. He was too busy playing video games. At 5:00, he put down his joystick and drove over to Little Caesars to pick up our cheese and pepperoni pizza, exactly as Shari's mom promised he would. But when we left the house at 5:30, an entire hour and fifteen minutes before Shari's mom anticipated us leaving, Walt didn't say a word. By then, a couple of his buddies were over and they were too busy polishing off what was left of the pizza and drinking beer to notice what we were doing or not doing. On the way to the party, I went over the names of everybody who was probably going to be there. The guest list read like a *Who's Who* of the most popular guys in the eighth grade. In addition to Will and Brian— the party was at Brian's house —Ricky Reynolds, Tyler Scott and Michael Maynard were also expected to be there. Kim was thrilled because a few days before the dance, the buzz around school was that Ricky liked her. Next to Will, Ricky was the most sought-after guy in the eighth grade.

Shari wasn't as excited because she feared that she'd be the odd one out.

"I hope this night isn't going be a total bust. Kim's going to have Ricky and you'll have Will and I'll be in the corner talking to Brian's dog."

"First of all, I don't have Will," I assured her, though secretly I was hoping that by the end of the night, I would. "We're just friends. And secondly, I'd never ditch you for a guy and neither would Kim. We're going over there, hanging out, and then we're going to the dance and having fun," I promised. My hopes weren't all that high. Ricky's interest in Kim only came about after Will arranged for all of us to go over to Brian's house. And as for Will and me, there had been no whispering around school about the two of us.

"Yeah," Kim added, "and I wouldn't be so sure about Ricky. He's cute and all, but I'm not really his type if you know what I mean." Every girl in our school got what she meant. Ricky was a lady's man who went to the movies with a different girl every weekend. Mostly he and his dates just held monster make out sessions in the back row of the theater. But from time to time, the stories that came in on Monday mornings were much more scandalous, especially when his date was with a girl from the local Catholic school. Contrary to what my parents believed, the girls from the Catholic school were far from chaste. Aside from the juvenile relationships in elementary school and the onset of junior high, none of us had had a serious boyfriend up to that point, nor had we even kissed anyone.

"Well, let's make a deal here and now," I proposed, as we approached Brian's house, "we won't ever ditch one another for a guy, and if we don't feel comfortable tonight, with anything, we'll leave." Kim and Shari agreed.

The sound of Roger Water's bass guitar and the smell of burning incense greeted us when Will opened the front door. Brian's house, which sat a block in from the river, was still swanky despite its location. The houses that ran on either side of the road that ran along the river were the grandest and most expensive homes in town.

"Hey what's up Daisy?" asked Will. "Hey Kim, hey Shari."

"Hey, yourself," I said, answering for the three of us.

Will kept looking over his shoulder for Brian or someone else to come along to make the interaction less awkward, but nobody did. Eventually Will yelled, "Brian, move your ass, dude. You've got guests." Kim, Shari and I must have had looks of awe plastered all over our faces at how impressive Brian's house was. Will said, "Pretty nice, eh?" He was referring to the entire house, but I misunderstood him and made a stupid comment about the foyer being bigger than my bedroom. "Yeah, I know what you mean. My house looks like a dump compared to this joint."

"Hey, hey," said Brian, slapping Will on his back when he joined us at last, "I see you've welcomed our guests. Come on in girls and make yourselves at home. Everybody's in the family room." The collection of beer cans and cups strewn across the coffee table was the first thing that caught my eye. If Kim or Shari had any reservations about staying, they hid it well.

"Alright," said Ricky to Brian, "After Pink Floyd, we decided that we're livening up this party with a little AC/DC. Pink Floyd is just too trippy."

Brian blew off Ricky's comment and turned his attention to us. "Can I interest you ladies in a beverage?"

All the guys started laughing. Beer shot from Tyler's mouth, spraying everything within a few feet of where he was sitting.

"Jesus Brian! You sound like some douche bartender from the country club," Tyler said.

"Shut your pie hole, Tyler, and be careful," Brian fired back. "You just doused my mom's couch in beer, you idiot."

Shari asked, "Do you have anything other than beer?"

"Yeah, I don't like beer either," said Kim.

"I guess I don't either. Sorry," I apologized.

"No worries. If you ladies will follow me, I'll show you what we've got," said Brian. The guys were right to laugh. Brian was trying to act like he was super mature and sophisticated, but normally he went out of his way to live up to his reputation as class clown. We crossed back through the grand foyer to a large sitting room. It too was gorgeous. An enormous liquor cabinet took up practically an entire wall. Brian threw open the doors and said, "Choose your poison." Bottles of liquor lined the shelves on either side of the doors. In the center there was a bar for mixing drinks, and below that, a wine rack. I noticed a bottle of Tanqueray gin along with a bottle of tonic water. Gin and tonic was always popular with Mom and her sisters, and if they weren't too strong, they were pretty tasty.

"If you've got some limes, I can whip us up some killer gin and tonics," I offered, trying to sound like I knew what I was talking about. I didn't really have the first clue how to mix a gin and tonic, or any drink for that matter, but I was sure I'd be able to fake it. I was getting pretty good at lying.

Kim scrunched up her noise and stuck out her tongue. "Yuck! No! What else can you make?" Brian suggested screwdrivers, but then confessed that he wasn't exactly sure what all went into making one.

"I know," he said, "What about a wine cooler? Have you ever had one of those? They taste just like Kool-Aid.

My mom and older sisters drink them all of the time and I think I saw some in the fridge." We all agreed that a wine cooler would be our best option.

Our next stop was the kitchen. Brian handed each of us a wine cooler, then loaded his arms with as many as he could carry and showed us back to the family room. I imagined that people got turned around in his house all the time because of its size.

With my tasty bottle of liquid courage, I wasn't shy and plopped down right next to Will. Kim sat next to Ricky who nudged Tyler out of the way. Maybe I was just imagining things, but I felt a little buzzed after taking only five or six sips. I decided to slow down so I didn't get too tipsy too fast. Kim and Shari drank theirs like water. After about ten minutes, Ricky said, "C'mon slow poke," picking up my wine cooler and shoving it into my hand, "Your friends are drinking you under the table."

"I'm okay," I said. I didn't care what Ricky or anyone else thought. My plan that night didn't include getting hammered, but the alcohol certainly helped lower everyone's inhibitions, including my own. Will behaved the same as he always did around me and was the only one of the guys who didn't act like he was trying to impress anyone. After a while, Brian suggested that we play a drinking game called Quarters.

"Alright," he said, "everybody gather around the coffee table, and I'll show you how it's done." Brian poured his beer in a plastic cup, pulled a quarter out of his pocket and bounced it off the table. The quarter landed in the cup. "Oh yeah! Lucky on the first try, everybody drink."

"Wait," I said, ignoring his order to drink. "So, what's the game?"

"Okay, the object of the game is to try to bounce a quarter off the table and into this cup. If the quarter goes in, the person who landed it can pick a person to slam what's in his or her cup or bottle or have the whole group drink all at once. I say let's play that way because I'm sure nobody will mind getting messed up."

"That sounds really stupid," I said. We girls gave his idea the thumbs down. The guys started tossing around other ideas.

"Alright then," said Ricky, "Who wants to shotgun a beer?"

"No way man," Brian objected. "You can't do that in the house. Go out in the backyard if you're gonna do that."

"Calm down, Mom," Tyler said, trying to razz Brian. "We won't spill. We'll be careful." Brian jumped up and tackled Tyler to the ground and the two of them began wrestling around on the floor. The guys started chanting Tyler's name. Between all the shouting and music, nobody heard the doorbell except for Will.

"Hey dude," he said to Brian, "Are you expecting someone else? I think I just heard your doorbell ring."

Brian went ballistic. "Awe man! It freaking better not be one of my nosy neighbors! Turn the music down a sec," he hollered to Michael who was sitting the closest to the stereo. I strained to hear the conversation between Brian and whoever was at the door, but I could only make out bits and pieces of their conversation. When I heard Brian laugh a few times, I knew it wasn't a disgruntled neighbor. A few seconds later, Brian came strolling into the room looking like the cat that got the cream. Stacy and Denise were behind him. "Look who I found just hanging out on the front porch. The two hottest girls in the school have graced my home with their presence."

"Hey guys!" Stacy said. They both waved. "Did we miss the party? Are we too late?" The guys shot each other curious looks as if they were trying to figure out who had invited them. Nobody spoke up, but nobody seemed to mind that they had crashed the party, either. The two girls were average looking at best, but they oozed a sense of sexuality and self-assurance that the rest of us girls lacked. Stacy's long, bleach blond hair had a just-rolled-out-of-bed look to it, while Denise's over-processed permed hair looked like it belonged on a washed-up rock star. There was nothing natural looking about either of them. Their make-up looked as if they applied it every morning with a spackling knife. Stacy's mouth was painted with a sparkly, cherry red lip-gloss 24/7, while Denise wore enough baby blue eye shadow to rival David Bowie during his androgynous phase. Everything Stacy wore fit like a glove, especially her tops, which she spilled out of every time she moved.

"Hey girls!" Stacy said with a sour smile. "What are you doing here?"

Denise, who stood by Stacy's side like a loyal dog said, "Yeah, what are you guys doing here?"

Thankfully Ricky answered for us. "They're just chilling with us before the dance."

"Hmph, that's cool, I guess," said Stacy, "So what's everybody drinking?"

"Beer," said Will, "and the girls are drinking wine coolers,"

"Ooh, yummy," Stacy gushed, "I've always wanted to try one of those."

"Shit, we're all gonna have to throw in a few bucks so I can find someone to buy for us to replace all the wine coolers you girls are sucking down. Don't any of you broads like beer?" Brian griped. When he grabbed two for Stacy and Denise, he offered Shari, Kim and me another one. I was still on my first one, but Shari and Kim were finished with their second. I had been stupid to worry so much over Kim and Shari taking issue with everybody drinking. I was beginning to fear that maybe they were drinking too much. Shari and Kim each took another one.

"Alright, if everyone's good on drinks, we need to settle on a game," said Brian.

"What game?" Denise asked. "I love playing games."

Shari said, "Brian wanted to play a drinking game, but we didn't think it was a good idea."

Surprisingly Denise agreed, "No, probably not. We can't get into the dance if we're all messed up. Stupid teachers would rat us out to our parents."

"I know," said Stacy, smiling. She didn't give it much thought before saying, "Let's play spin the bottle."

"Hell yeah! That sounds like a plan to me," said Tyler.

Will shot down the idea immediately. "That's pretty juvenile. What are we, in grade school?"

"Oh, okay, Mr. Maturity," Ricky said, trying to goad him.

"Well, I guess it's all up to the rest of the ladies because I'm not gonna play with just one girl and a bunch of dudes," Brian chimed in.

"Yeah, right! No way!" added Tyler.

Kim, Shari, Denise and I glanced at one another, each waiting for the other to speak up.

"I'm in," said Shari.

"Me too," said Kim.

"I guess I'll play since you're all playing," said Denise.

It was up to me. "Well," I said nervously. "I agree with Will, it does seem really immature, but I guess I won't be the only naysayer."

Brian jumped up and drained the last few swallows from someone's wine cooler bottle. "Let's sit on the kitchen floor. It's the only room in the house not carpeted."

Denise looped her arm through Ricky's and led the way into the kitchen.

We a sat in a large circle on the floor like we were holding a séance. Someone said, "We'd better get cracking. It's already 6:30."

Stacy volunteered to go first. "Before I spin, we need to set some ground rules. Girls don't kiss girls and guys don't kiss guys. Each person is allowed one pass."

"No," several of the guys objected. "No passes, unless it's the same sex."

With the rules in place, Stacy spun the bottle and it landed on Kim. "Oops, free spin," she yelled.

"Uh, no way man. Your turn's over," said Tyler who was to the left of her. "It's my turn." He set the bottle in motion and it landed on Stacy. "Pucker up, buttercup." He leaned in to kiss Stacy, but she turned her head at the last minute and he ended up kissing her ear. "C'mon, Stacy. On the lips or you're out. Kissing you is like kissing my grandma."

She didn't try to hide her displeasure, but she went along with it. "Hurry Up! Get it over with," she told him.

Tyler didn't hold back. "You asked for it." She didn't turn her head, but his lips barely touched hers before she pulled away from him in disgust.

"My spin," she said, rubbing her hands together and casting a lusty stare around the circle. "Who's the lucky guy?" she asked, her eyes set on Will. I watched with baited breath as the bottle spun in circles, secretly willing it not to land on Will. It didn't, but once again she got stuck with Tyler.

"Hot dog!" he shouted, practically knocking her over as he lunged towards her. Everybody heard the clink of his teeth against hers. Stacy reared back, shielding her mouth with her hand.

"Gosh, Tyler! Watch it. You practically knocked my teeth out," she complained.

Tyler spun again and it landed back on Stacy.

"Alright, no way!" she said, picking up the bottle and handing it to Will. "What the heck, Tyler. Do you have a secret magnet under the floor that makes it land just on me?"

Will tossed the bottle up in the air and caught it with his left hand before setting it on the floor and setting it in motion. Like a spinning top, it spun around and round.

"Please land on me, please land on me!" I chanted the private mantra to myself. Unknowingly, I must've closed my eyes, so I had no idea that it landed on me until Kim called my name.

"Daisy," she shouted, "Earth to Daisy, open your eyes!" I opened my eyes to find that everybody staring at me, including Will who was within inches of my face.

"I don't know, dude," said, Ricky nudging Will in his side, "I think somebody's a little excited that you've landed on her."

"Hi!" Will said sweetly as he fixed his eyes on mine.

The room grew silent or maybe I just imagined that it did. "Hi yourself," I whispered. I was nervous and began twisting a few loose strands of hair around my index finger before tucking it behind my ears.

"I like it better like this," he said, freeing the hair so it fell against my cheek, and then he leaned in and gently kissed me. His lips were moist and soft and tasted of cinnamon gum.

I don't know how long we were kissing before someone said, "Okay, lover boy, that's enough. Let some other sap get a turn."

Will went back to his spot and I spun. It landed on Shari. "Oh well. Someone can take my turn. I need to go to the bathroom," I lied. "Hey Brian, can I use your bathroom?"

"Yeah, but use the one upstairs, it's closer."

The second the door closed, I checked my appearance in the mirror to see if I looked any different. My cheeks were Pepto-Bismol pink, but aside from that, I looked the same. In the middle of reapplying my lip-gloss, someone rapped on the bathroom door.

"Occupied," I yelled.

"Daisy, it's me, Shari. Open the door." She pushed her way into the bathroom before I could get the door all the way opened and mouthed, "OH. MY. GOD!"

"I know!" I mouthed back.

Shari locked the door. "Are you freaking out or what?"

"Or what," I answered. "So, what's going on down there? Did anyone say anything after I left."

"No, but of course the bottle landed on Denise or Stacy every single time one of the guys spun it."

That wasn't what I wanted to hear. "Please tell me that Stacy didn't kiss Will?"

"She sure didn't. I just wished you were there to witness her disappointment. The look on her face was priceless."

"Good! So—Kim didn't kiss Ricky and you didn't kiss anybody?"

"Nope and nope," said Shari disappointedly

"Figures."

Kim checked her hair in the mirror and then glanced at her watch. "Shoot! We'd better get going. If we're late, they're not going to let us in." The school had a standing rule that nobody got in after 7:30 and once in, nobody could leave unless a parent came in and signed out their child. We all filed out of Brian's house in no particular order, but when we got on the sidewalk, everybody walked in pairs or groups of three. Naturally Kim, Shari and I walked together. Like magnets, Stacy and Denise clung to Will's side, which is where I wanted to be, but I refused to ditch my friends. We had made a pact. But even if they had given me the green light to go to him, I wouldn't have. I didn't want to look desperate like Stacy and Denise.

When we reached the school, Shari, Kim and I headed straight to the front doors, but everybody else goofed around outside near some large bushes.

"If you've got 'em, smoke 'em," I heard one of the guys yell. An orchestra of flicking lighters followed.

"Can we go in?" Kim begged. "I don't feel so hot. I need to go to the bathroom."

Miss Klein and the other gym teacher, Mr. Simmons, greeted us. "You're cutting it a little close ladies, aren't you?" Miss Klein commented.

Kim and Shari hit the bathroom right away, but I decided to wait for Will. "Go ahead without me. I'll be there in a second." For over 10 minutes I paced in front of the door, but Will and the rest of them never showed. 7:30 on the dot, Miss Klein and Mr. Simmons shut the double doors to the gym and set their chairs in front of them to prevent anyone from leaving. I wanted to cry. Will was off somewhere with Denise and Stacy doing God only knew what. I pushed past swarms of dancing kids and ran up the stairs to the girl's locker room. Normally it was packed, but except for the few quick-change artists who were swapping outfits and reapplying makeup like harried actors changing costumes between scenes, it was deserted. Shari and Kim were in the bathroom crammed into a stall. Kim was on her knees with her head hanging over the toilet. Her body heaved again and again as it rid itself of wine coolers while Shari stood behind her and held her hair out of the way.

"Kim's really sick, Daisy," said Shari, "And we can't leave."

Kim looked up from the toilet when she heard her name. Chunks of undigested pizza peppered one side of her face. She looked awful.

"I'm sorry, guys," she said. "I hope you don't hate me."

"Don't say that," I told her. "You okay?"

She shook her head. "I just want to go home." I grabbed a handful of paper towels from a dispenser on the wall and ran them under cool water. As I wiped her face, I explained our predicament.

"You know there's only one way to leave the dance and we can't very well call any of our parents to come sign us out. We'd get busted. We're just going to have to find a place to hide out until the dance is over." A pathetic whimper was the only objection she offered. "Shhh, I know. I'm sorry, Kimmy, but it's the best we can do." We helped her up from the bathroom floor and guided her over to a large shower stall. It wasn't the ideal place to spend an evening, but it was dark and quiet and thankfully, dry. I removed the sweater draped around my shoulders, balled it up and placed it on my lap so Kim had a soft place to rest her head. Without the wine coolers sloshing around in her stomach, she felt better, but was sleepy. A few minutes passed and then she was out cold. Shari and I kept watch in the abandoned stalls until a few minutes before 10:00 pm and then joined the rest of the kids in the gym. When the lights came on, I scoured the crowd for Will, hoping that just maybe he had somehow made it in, but he was nowhere to be seen.

The fervor that drove our walk over to Brian's house at the onset of the evening had faded. I imagined us as weary soldiers trudging home after years of combat. The front door was unlocked for us, but Shari's house looked battened down for the night. A dim light coming from the family room was the only sign that someone was home. "I'm surprised my dad's not up," Shari commented. "We'll need to be quiet, but I think we should raid the fridge before heading up to bed." We left our shoes near the front door but didn't make it to the kitchen before a voice from the family room stopped us.

"Girls, come in here a sec." Kicked back in his recliner with a book resting on his roundish stomach, was Shari's dad. He removed his reading glasses and gave us the once-over, "Whoa some dance-huh? You all look exhausted. Did you have fun?"

"It was alright, but we're tired. I thought we'd find something to eat and then crash," Shari answered. Her dad volunteered to whip us up a batch of his famous banana chocolate chip pancakes. We took him up on his offer. None of us were still buzzed, just starving. After eating, we spread our sleeping bags across Shari's bedroom floor and collapsed in a heap. Nestled between my two closest friends, I felt comforted and cared for, but after they fell asleep, a feeling of isolation and loneliness crept in. Before I knew it, what felt like a trickle soon turned into a swell of tears, washing away any semblance of emotional well-being I had left. I wanted to be home. More than anything, I wanted to be near Mom, and though I'd never be able to tell her exactly what went on that night, I knew that she was part of me and could feel my suffering even when I was silent. Will and I had shared a kiss and I should've felt elated, but I didn't. The softness in his eyes when it was over said more than his words could probably ever say, but I needed verbal affirmation. I needed to hear that it meant as much to him as it did to me. To me, it was everything.

16
He Loves Me, He Loves Me Not

I spent both Saturday and Sunday refereeing my conflicting emotions, which fluctuated between loving Will and hating him. The thought of facing him at school made me physically sick. Two new zits popped out on my face. If it weren't for the fact that it was the last week of the semester, I would've planned to stay home on Monday.

Twice on Sunday, I left my house to confront him, but didn't end up making it past the end of our driveway. I chickened out. He needed to be the one to make the next move. I decided to ignore him by making myself scarce and if I ran into him at school, I'd give him the cold shoulder. His locker wasn't far from mine, so I devised a plan that I hoped would prevent us from running into one another. I'd purposely hide out in the girl's bathroom until after the second bell rang to avoid running into him first thing in the morning. After first period, I'd make a beeline down the hallway to my civics class without going back to my locker.

My plan would've worked if I hadn't left my branches of government poster in my locker. That's when I ran into him. It was obvious that he was waiting for me.

"Excuse me," I said, pushing past him. "I need to get something out of my locker."

He stepped out of the way. "So, how was the rest of your weekend? I guess the dance was a total bust, huh?" I pretended not to hear him, but Will was persistent. "It's been a little weird not seeing you these last couple of days."

"Weird?" I asked, placing my hand on the poster that was in front of me the entire time. "How so?"

"Well, obviously I didn't make it to the dance and then I didn't see you Saturday or Sunday. I thought about calling you, but then remembered how you're..." he made air quotes with his fingers, "not allowed to talk to someone like me on the phone." His cynical comment rubbed me the wrong way.

"I didn't say I wasn't allowed to talk to you. I just said that my parents would drill me with a thousand questions if you called the house and that I just wasn't up for them pestering me all the time. Don't put words in my mouth," I said, slamming my locker shut. "I've got to go."

"Daisy, hold up. What's wrong? You seem like you're mad or something."

"Nothing's wrong. I just need to get to class."

"Well, can I talk to you for like two seconds?" he asked. I stopped walking and turned to face him. "I'm sorry about Friday night. After you and Shari and Kim split, we finished our smokes and were about to head in, but then Ricky got sick, I mean really sick. He hurled all over the place. Since I was staying the night at his house, I was stuck taking care of him. I walked him over to the elementary playground and sat with him on the blacktop for an hour or so until his buzz wore off."

I wanted to believe him, but I was blinded by my jealousy. "So, you all didn't just go back to Brian's or hang out somewhere else"

"Nah, his parents were home by then, so they all went to Stacy's, I think."

"Hmm, too bad that you couldn't go. I bet you hated not being with Stacy." I looked at my watch and said, "I really have to go. I don't want to be late for a second period in a row."

"Not really," Will said.

"Not really what?" I asked.

"I really didn't care about being with Stacy or any of them. I just wanted to be with you," he said, no longer looking at me, but at the ground. "I missed seeing you this past weekend and I'm sorry I missed the dance."

My heart melted. "You missed me? Really?"

Will flashed one of his irresistible smiles. "Yeah, I kinda did. Is that okay?"

Before I could answer, the bell rang. "Crap! I'm late again!" I cried.

"Oh well," he said. "So am I. I guess we'll serve detention together." He never exactly asked me out, nor did we tell anyone that we were girlfriend and boyfriend, but from that day forward, Will and I were a couple.

17
Summer Loving
Summer 1983

School concluded on the third Wednesday of June. The next almost three months that followed passed so quickly that it felt like we had no summer break at all. Between being shipped off to music camp for two weeks, babysitting, and tennis every Tuesday and Thursday nights, I didn't have a lot of free time to spend with Will. He wasn't quite as busy as I was, but he still had a summer job that always seemed to conflict with my schedule. He worked for a neighbor who owned a small trucking company. He washed rigs or did whatever odd jobs the man needed him to do around the shop. The work sucked, but the pay was good.

On the days when we found time to sneak away, our trysts were always rushed, but wonderful. It was hard for me to relax because I was so afraid of getting busted. Sometimes we managed to finagle hanging out in town with our group of friends, but then I was constantly looking over my shoulder for people who might recognize us. By mid-July, I was at my wits end. I couldn't take not seeing or talking to Will every day. The only time I could talk to him freely on the phone was when my parents weren't around, which wasn't very often, so I decided to come clean with them about Will and me in a very roundabout way.

I arranged for Will to call my house at a time when I knew both of my parents were guaranteed to be home. At precisely 8:45 pm, on a boring Friday night, our phone rang. Normally I bowled people over trying to get to the phone, but not that night. Mom, Dad and I were watching TV in the family room and the boys were still outside jumping on the trampoline with some of their friends.

After the second ring, Dad looked at me and asked, "You going to get the phone, Daisy?"

I wanted one of them to answer it so that they knew for sure that it was a guy on the other end of the line that I was talking to. "Are you for real? I can't get up. I've got this furry beast on my lap," I protested. Minutes before, Gus had moseyed into the room and plunked down on me like he was a lap dog. Good old Gus had unknowingly provided me the perfect excuse for staying glued to my seat. "Gussy just got comfortable."

Dad and Mom were snuggled up together on the loveseat and there was no way Dad was getting up to get it. "Oh, heaven forbid if we inconvenience the dog. I know how he busts his hump all week long and likes to relax and take it easy on the weekends," Dad said sarcastically. "Don't be so lazy, Daisy. Go get the phone. It's always for you anyway."

Before Dad could stop her, Mom got up and said, "I'll get it, honey. My wine glass is almost empty."

I could feel Dad giving me the evil eye, but I didn't acknowledge him. To Mom I said, "Hey can you be a doll and bring me back some chips or something to snack on? And while you're at it," I added, "I'll take a glass of wine too."

"Fat chance," Mom said. "John, you want a beer or something?"

"Nah, I'm good," he told her.

A few seconds later, Mom was in back in the family room, sans the snacks.

"Daisy, the phone is for you. It's Will Banks."

I got up, careful not to disturb Gus, and walked to the kitchen. Mom was whispering something to Dad, but I couldn't completely make out what she was saying. My conversation with Will was brief and a few minutes later, I was back in the family room with a bag of Doritos and a can of Tab.

"Anybody want some?" I offered.

Dad grabbed a handful of chips and asked, "Who was that you were talking to?"

"Oh, didn't you hear Mom? It was Will Banks."

"Yeah, I heard her, but why's he calling? I didn't know you knew him."

"Sure, I know him. He goes to my school. He's in my grade and lives just a couple of doors down on the other side of the road from us."

"I'm well aware of where he lives," said Dad.

"Then why are you acting so surprised that I know him?"

"Mind your tone, missy," said Mom, "Dad's simply pointing out the fact that we weren't aware that the two of you were friends. You're just friends, right?"

"What else would we be?" I asked defensively.

"Well what did he want?" Dad asked.

"Geez! What's up with the billion questions?"

"What did he want, Honey?" Mom asked evenly.

"Tomorrow afternoon a bunch of us want to meet up at the city pool. We can't do it during the week because we all have summer jobs and he just called to see if I needed a ride, that's all."

"Well, who's all going?" Mom asked. "I can drive you and Will. Maybe your brothers and I will go to the pool while Daddy's doing yard work."

"Are you kidding me? Forget it. I'm not going if you guys are going. No way."

"Calm down! It was just a thought," Mom assured me.

"So, you're friends with Will, huh?" Dad asked again. "Just mind your P's and Q's around him. His dad's a little shady."

"What's that supposed to mean? Do you know his dad?"

"Know him?" Dad asked. "Not really. I know of him. He's been into the bank a few times. Seems like an okay guy, but I've heard some stuff about him. Don't think he takes the reins when it comes to parenting. Will isn't someone I think you should be getting too buddy, buddy with, that's all."

Dad's reaction was exactly what I anticipated. "Since when do you listen to hearsay, Dad? You and Mom are always lecturing us kids to think for ourselves and not to be followers. You're being a hypocrite. You're letting what other people say shape your opinion of someone you don't even know. Let's say for the sake of argument that you're right, and Will's dad is some kind of lowlife. Does that mean that Will couldn't be a good kid?"

"Here's the thing," Dad responded in a holier-than-thou-tone, the kind that implied that he was the authority on everything, "You're right and I'm sorry for being judgmental. I'm sure Will's a fine young man or you wouldn't be friends with him. Sometimes a child becomes what he or she sees. I'm just saying that I'm not sure that he's had the best role models. Without a proper upbringing, children make poor choices. I know you're old enough to choose your own friends, but I don't want you getting too comfortable with Will. You can pal around with him in a group situation, but I don't want it to be just the two of you. So, if you want to go to the pool, Mom will drive. It'll be a chance for her to meet him, but she won't stay. She'll check everything out to see that it's on the up and up, and then leave."

I wasn't crazy about the terms, but I knew they wouldn't budge.

"And," he added, "I guess you can be friends with him, but remember, no dating until you're 16. Not him or anybody else. Not yet."

"Not that again. I get it! I get it! No dating, sheesh."

"Daisy, Dad and I have all the faith in the world in you. If you say Will's a good guy, then I believe you, but just remember, we know a few things because we're older. This is the age when both guys and girls are looking for more than just friendship with the opposite sex. Though Will's dad may be a decent enough guy, his lifestyle and beliefs don't jibe with ours. He's had numerous affairs and most likely doesn't parent the same way we do. You may not like hearing it, but you're our precious gift from God, and it's our job to make decisions concerning your welfare until you're old enough to effectively make your own. Do you understand?"

"Yes, I understand. Can I go to my room now?" I asked. There was no point in correcting her claim that Will's dad had numerous affairs. When she first mentioned him, it was one affair and an unsubstantiated report of a second one. Now it was numerous affairs. Their minds were clearly made up about him.

"Don't you want to watch TV?" she called, "*Dallas* is on."

"Nah, I need to call a few friends. I'll see you in the morning."

Mom was disappointed. Dad didn't really like watching *Dallas*, but he did so to appease Mom. He was sweet that way.

The person I really needed to call was Will. For over an hour we spoke about going to the pool and about how much summer sucked because of work and never getting to see each other. He didn't sweat the fact that Mom was taking us. My next call was to Shari and Kim to confirm that they were still going. Shari had started dating a guy from our school who wasn't exactly friends with Will or any of Will's buddies, but they played basketball together. Her finding a boyfriend took the pressure off me a little bit. At the beginning of the summer, they both hinted at the fact that it seemed like every time we hung out, Will was around. Poor Kim was still holding out for Ricky, even though he'd never settle down with just one girl. The four of us—Will, Kim, Ricky and I went to a movie one Saturday night, but it was awkward between the two of them. Ricky knew better than to try anything too risqué because Will had given him fair warning that Kim wouldn't be cool with him getting all touchy. At the end of the night, they kissed, but it was nothing major, at least that's what Ricky said. According to Will, Ricky thought Kim was hot, but didn't want a steady girlfriend. He was just looking for someone to have fun with, aka, someone to fool around with. I worried that maybe Will was tired of just kissing too. We kissed and held hands all the time, but it never went beyond that. He didn't even try. Every night, I ended my prayers with the same request. *Please, God. Don't let Will grow tired of me and morph into Ricky overnight and dump me for someone like Stacy.* My prayers were shameful. There were so many other worthy causes to pray for, like an end to the famine plaguing Africa or world peace, but I was on cloud nine dating Will and didn't want anything to come between the two of us.

Will was sitting on his porch with his towel around his neck waiting for us when we pulled up. Mom's window was down, so she waved and called to him even before putting the car in park.

"Hey there, Will! Is your dad home? I'd love to meet him."

"Oh, hi Mrs. Doyle. No, he isn't home. I'll just hop in the car."

"Alright! That's fine," Mom said, "some other time then."

Will slid into the back seat, keeping a fair amount of space between the two of us. Mom was good at making small talk and getting answers to questions without seeming overly pushy. She was a sly fox.

"So, Will, how long has your family lived in the area?"

"Oh, it's going on about four years now I think," he said.

"And you like it here?" Mom asked.

"Yea, it's cool. I guess I wished we lived in town because it's kind of a pain to have to get rides everywhere, but I'm getting my license in August, so that'll be sweet."

"Really? Your driver's license already?"

Will explained how he had repeated first grade.

"Well, you be careful out on these country roads, especially in the winter. I'm sure your parents will be worried sick every time you get behind the wheel."

"Mom! He doesn't need a lecture from you," I said. "You're so embarrassing."

"Will doesn't mind. He's got a mom. She probably tells him the same thing all the time. Moms always worry more than dads. We're just more overprotective I suppose."

I knew exactly what she was getting at by bringing up his mom.

"Well, my mom's in California, so she's not around to nag me so much. My dad's blasé about everything. He's been letting me drive for the last few years."

"What? By yourself?" she asked.

"Not by myself," he quickly clarified. "Only with him and mostly on the dirt roads."

"Whew," said Mom. "So, your mom's in California, huh?" she asked, playing dumb. "Is she there temporarily for work? Or visiting family?"

"Nah, she lives there. She moved back to San Francisco after my parents' divorce. I'm going to visit her in August though. She really wants me to live with her, but I don't want to. All of my friends are here."

"I'm sorry to hear that. Divorce is always the hardest on the children, but just remember, your parents will always love you. Nobody falls out of love with their children, that's for sure," said Mom. When her question and answer session was over, we drove the rest of the way listening to the radio. Periodically she smiled at us in her review mirror.

"That wasn't so bad," Will said, as Mom's car pulled away. "Your mom seems pretty cool."

Little did he know how uncool she really was.

18
The Real Summer of Love

Like all great love stories, the time came for Will and me to temporarily say goodbye. Will left for San Francisco to visit his mom, and I headed off to Lexington with my family. The week at the lake went by in the blink of an eye because there was so much to do. But once I got home, I was bored out of my skull. Both Kim and Shari were on vacation. I missed Will horribly and the remaining week and a half without him felt like an eternity. Getting his postcards everyday was the only thing that kept me from completely losing my mind.

Before we left for vacation, Will and I agreed to write to each other every day. My postcards went directly to his Mom's apartment, but mine were mailed to my actual house—mail wasn't delivered to the rental properties, so when I got back into town there were several waiting for me. Will mostly sent me letters, but the few postcards he did send he placed in envelops, per my instructions, before mailing them. I didn't want Mom or anybody else to be able to read them if they happened to get to the mailbox before me. My postcards to him were sappy and oozed with sentimentality, while his to me were generic, but still thoughtful and sweet. *"Today we visited Alcatraz..."* or *"Saw a gazillion sea lions at Fisherman's Wharf..."* The last correspondence I received was a postcard with a panoramic view of Baker Beach. It read:

> *Dear Daisy,*
> *Spent the day at Baker Beach and thought*
> *of you and your whacky obsession with the*
> *movie, Grease. The lyrics to that stupid song*

kept running through my head, 'He got friendly holding my hand. Well, she got friendly down in the sand.' Thanks to you, I can't get those dumb lyrics out of my head.
    Love and miss you,
    Danny Zuko.
    P.S. Can't stop thinking about you either.

I read that postcard at least a hundred times before stuffing it under my mattress. His letters and postcards sustained me until we were reunited.

The day Will was scheduled to come home passed like a slow-moving train. It was hot and humid and though angry clouds hovered in the sky from sun up to sun down, it never rained. Minutes felt like hours and hours felt like days. I did whatever it took to make the time pass faster. I took a three-hour nap, helped Mom make blueberry and strawberry jelly, and finished reading a tawdry Harlequin Romance novel instead of one of the books from my required summer reading list for Freshman English Lit.

I had started reading the romance novel while on vacation, but never finished it. I had swiped it off the bookshelf at the cottage. I didn't steal it or anything like that. The owners had a policy allowing renters to take a book as long as they left a book. Most of the books were lousy, but there were a few decent ones. Dad volunteered to leave one of his books behind so that I could finish my book at home.

Will's plane landed at Detroit Metro at the scheduled time, but because he went out for pizza afterward with his dad and grandparents, he didn't get home until after 9:00. Lucky for us, my parents went to a movie that night, which meant that I got stuck babysitting my brothers. Ordinarily I hated being left alone with them, but it worked to our advantage because my parents weren't home to harangue me about being on the phone all night. I could talk to Will without any interruptions and without lying about who I was talking to. Before we hung up, we arranged to meet the next day.

19
Take Your Hands Off My Sister

"All right," Dad asked with a beer in one hand and a ham sandwich in the other, "who's watching the *Tigers* game with me?" His TV tray was already set up next to his recliner waiting for him.

"I am! I am! I am!" Denny chanted as mushy pieces of white bread flecked with bologna chunks flew from his mouth. He was always enthusiastic at the beginning of every game, but rarely made it to the end. Nine innings was too much for him.

"Gross! Watch what you're doing!" Daniel shouted, "You just sprayed the entire kitchen table with your disgusting sandwich." Daniel carefully examined his food to make sure it hadn't been contaminated before joining Dad in the family room.

"Can I bring my lunch in with me too?" Denny asked.

"Knock yourself out!" Dad answered.

David, who was already done with lunch, was stretched out on the couch with Gus. Dad hollered at him to scoot over and make room for Denny.

"C'mon, can't Denny just sit on the floor? Gussy shouldn't have to move just because of him," David complained.

"I'm sick and tired of everybody constantly worrying about the damn dog's comfort level. If you boys don't stop bickering I'm going to toss all of you, along with the dog, outside and none of you will watch the game.

Mom wasn't home and Dad wasn't in the mood to play referee all day. She'd driven up to Lexington with Mrs. Schmidt to an antique store to pick up an old steamer trunk she had found during our stay at the lake.

145

No matter how many times Dad packed and unpacked the station wagon, he couldn't make it fit. The owner of the shop agreed to hold it for her until Labor Day.

"Count me out," I said, placing my dirty dishes in the sink. "I'm going for a walk."

David's ears perked up. "What's up with you suddenly turning into a nature freak? You're always hiking or biking or going on marathon runs."

I was certain that David was only busting my chops and really didn't suspect a thing, so I didn't bother coming up with an excuse. "Don't worry about it, dumb-ass and watch your stupid game."

"Awe! Daisy!" Denny said hopping up and down on the couch and pointing his grubby little finger in my direction "Dad, did you hear her? She just called David a dumb-ass."

"C'mon you guys, knock it off," Dad said, without taking his eyes off the television or exiling them to the yard. "Daisy, watch your mouth. And Denny, sit down before you fall down." Since Dad was preoccupied with the game, I left while the leaving was easy.

When I arrived, Will was sprawled out on the grass noshing on a piece of fruit from one of the trees in Mr. Schneider's orchard. He gazed up at me—his eyes squinty from the sun and told me to plop a squat. "Take a bite of this," he said, pressing the pear to my lips. I hadn't intended on taking such a big bite, but because it was so ripe, it fell apart as soon as I sunk my teeth into it. Juice squirted from my mouth and trickled down my chin.

I felt like such a slob. "Geez, that's some pear. I'm a mess. How come you're not all sticky?" I asked, swiping my chin with my hand.

"Here, let me help," he offered, kissing my chin and cheeks before moving to my mouth. His kiss, slow and deliberate at first, intensified as he placed his one hand on the back of my head and the other on the small of my back and gently leaned into me until I was flat on my back. At first, he hovered over me, but then he was completely on top of me—our bodies stacked atop one another like folded shirts. His hands quickly found the waistband of my shorts. Without asking, he began tugging at my tank top, so his hands could slip underneath it. Like his mouth, his hands were warm and urgent. I could feel his excitement—his racing heart and his quickening breath. "God, I love you," he whispered. "You're so hot." My body burned with embarrassment and desire.

"I love you too," were the only words I could get out before his tongue was back in my mouth. After a few minutes, I asked him to stop, even though I really didn't want him to. "Will, don't. Not here," I said. He stopped, but he gave me a wounded look. "It's not that I don't like it, but someone might see us. Let's go for a walk in the woods," I proposed. Will helped me up after picking a few stray sprigs and pieces of grass from my hair.

"Don't want you to look like you were just rolling around in the hay with someone," he teased. I tucked in my tank top and he adjusted himself before we sprinted off for the woods. Once shielded by the leafy trees, he went right back to groping me. He was an octopus. With his hands on either side of my hips, he guided me three steps backwards until I was leaning up against the trunk of a tree. Bumpy bark pressed into my flesh, but I was too distracted by what Will was doing to care. His face was nuzzled deep into one side of my neck while his hands ran up and down the length of my torso. His hair still smelled like the ocean, his skin like sunscreen. Just as Will was going for my tank top again, I heard a tiny voice yell, "Hey, take your hands off my sister!"

I opened my eyes to find Denny standing a few feet away. Denny squelched our make-out session. "Denny! What are you doing out here?" I boomed. "Did you follow me?"

"I sure did," he said proudly. Then to Will he asked, "Who are you?"

Will gave it to him straight. "I'm Will, Daisy's friend. Who are you?"

"Hmm... her friend?" Denny asked. He wasn't buying it. Gullible little Denny understood that Will and I were more than friends. "Well, I'm Denny, Daisy's little brother and it doesn't look to me like the two of you are just friends. You were practically sucking each other's faces off."

Will smiled. "Daisy's little brother, huh? What's up little dude? I guess you are smarter than the average bear," he said, referencing Denny's Yogi Bear t-shirt. Underneath the decal of the wisecracking bear was his famous catchphrase, *I'm smarter than the av-er-age bear!*

"Hey yourself," he answered. To me he said, "Do Mom and Dad know that you're out here kissing Will?"

Because Denny *was* smarter than the average bear, I knew that I had to keep one step ahead of him. I could see the imaginary gears in his puny brain turning as he contemplated his next move. He was acting a little too big for his britches, so I decided to turn the tables on him. "No, but they don't know that you're out here either. As a matter of fact, you're not allowed out here. Where did you tell Dad you were going?"

He looked down at his flip-flops and wriggled his dirty toes, "I said I was going to Jeffery's house."

"Oh, so you lied huh? They wouldn't like the fact that you were being dishonest." Guilt washed over Denny's face. Tricking Denny was a piece of cake.

"I only sorta lied," he admitted. "I was going over to Jeffery's to play on his new Slip N Slide, but then I saw you and him and I wanted to see what the two of you were doing."

"When did you first see us?" I asked, praying to God that he didn't see us making out in the grass.

"When you were walking in the direction of the woods," he answered. I could tell that he was telling the truth. He was too nervous to lie.

Will wrapped his arm around Denny's shoulder and said, "We're just two friends going for a little walk. You want to go with us?"

I didn't think it was a good idea, but Denny was all over the invitation. "Heck yeah, I'll go!"

"Here's the thing," I told him, "We'd both be in big trouble if Mom and Dad knew we were out here, so mums the word, okay?"

Denny mulled over my proposition and then said, "I'm pretty sure that you'd be in more trouble than me, but don't worry, I won't say anything. Will's your boyfriend, isn't he? He's the person you're always talking with on the phone. All the whispering and giggling and gross stuff is to Will, right?"

"That's right. He's my boyfriend, but you can't tell Mom or Dad that either. I can trust you, can't I? You and I are tight. Like this," I said, crossing my middle finger over my index finger, "Right?"

Denny began chanting, "Daisy and Will sitting in a tree. K-i-s-s-i-n-g. First comes love, then comes marriage and then comes the baby in the baby carriage." I wanted to tell him to shut his face, but I held my tongue.

Will was great with him. When Denny finally stopped singing his idiotic nursery rhyme he said, "You lead the way, Denny. Daisy tells me that you're a regular ole Grizzly Adams. Where do you want to go? You're the leader, dude."

Denny stayed at least ten steps ahead of us the entire time. When he stopped to scoop up a large toad that he nearly squashed as he leapt and slashed his way through the woods, Will and I sat down on a tree trunk and talked. After a while, Will reached into his pocket and pulled out his closed fist. For a second, I was afraid that he was reaching for his lighter, but that wasn't the case. "Close your eyes. I have something for you," he ordered. I closed my eyes. "Now don't get too excited because it's not a big deal. Give me your hand." He took my hand and slid something over my ring finger. "Okay, open your eyes."

"Oh Will, it's beautiful," I said, because it was. The heart shaped rhinestone ring was too big for my ring finger, so I slid it off and put it on my middle finger.

"There, that's better. Now I won't lose it, but I'm not sure I can accept such an extravagant token of your affection."

"Oh, well—" Will sputtered, "It really didn't cost anything. I got it at the San Francisco Giants game from one of those massive bubblegum machines."

"I'm kidding, Will. I know."

He blushed. "You do? Good. Sorry if it's too big."

"I love it," I gushed. How could I not? It's from you." After stealing a few more kisses, Will told me to shut my eyes again.

"A second gift?" I asked. "I feel bad. I don't have anything for you."

"Just hold out your hand and be quiet," he told me, but before he could gift me a second time, Denny came bustling over with the toad he had found.

"She's a beauty, ain't she, Will?" Denny beamed as he thrust the wriggly toad in Will's face.

"Err, hold on buddy," Will started to say, but Denny noticed Will had something in his hand.

"Hey, hold up. What kind of rock is that you're holding?"

Will opened his hand. "It's for your sister."

"Ooh, cool! Where did you get it?" Denny asked. "Can I hold it?"

Denny handed me the toad and Will handed Denny the rock, "You'll never believe it. I found it on a beach in San Francisco." While Denny was drooling over the rock, Will took my hand and gazed into my eyes. "You see, I was thinking about your beautiful sister here and how much I missed her back in Michigan and happened to look down at the sand and voila, there it was. Talk about serendipity, man."

Denny made a face in response to Will's comment about my beauty, but then said. "Hey—you interested in making a trade? This rock is super cool. It looks just like the state of Michigan on the map!"

"A trade? What kind of trade? I might be up for a little wheeling and dealing."

Denny's eyes grew as big as saucers. "Whatta ya say my toad for your rock?"

Will looked to me for approval. I couldn't say no. "I don't know, Will. I think that's a pretty fair trade," I said. "I'll bet there are all kinds of rocks that look like

Michigan lying around Baker Beach, but probably not too many toads."

"I'll tell you what," Will said after pretending to consider his offer, "Daisy's probably right. I can find a million rocks that look like Michigan in San Francisco, but I also have plenty of toads at home. You keep the rock, but what do you say we release the toad. She's probably got a family and her babies will be sad if she doesn't come back home to them."

Denny liked that idea of keeping the rock, but he was reluctant to let his toad friend go. Eventually, Will persuaded him to do the right thing. Will was sweet with Denny, which made me fall in love with him even more. The ring, the rock, and the fact that Will didn't dis Denny only reinforced my belief that Will was truly perfect in every way. Denny liked Will, which was a real positive for me. True to his word, he didn't breathe a word about Will to anyone, and kept the rock hidden from my parents. From that point on, every so often, Will and I allowed Denny to tag along with us when we rendezvoused in the woods. A happy kid was a quiet kid, I reasoned.

20
Cards on the Table

Each day with Will was better than the previous one, at least for the first month or so of my freshman year. We were a full-fledged couple and I was the envy of every girl in ninth grade. Will could've had any girl he wanted in our class, but he chose me. The only glitch in our relationship bliss was that Will drove to school every day without me by his side. I was condemned to riding the bus and no matter how many times I asked my parents to let me catch a ride with Will, they said no. They still didn't know the truth about the two of us, so I always had to pretend that getting a ride with him was a necessity because I was running late or had to finish an assignment before school started and I couldn't get it done on the bus, or there was something going on at school that required me to stay after. Their answer was always no, but the reasons varied depending on who I asked.

"That's what we pay taxes for, Daisy. For things like transportation to and from school," Dad maintained. "And even when you're able to drive, you'll still be taking the bus. There's just no reason why you need to catch a ride with someone when you've got the bus. If for some reason you can't take the bus, your mom will give you a ride to school."

Mom's reason was just as lame. "It's a safety issue," she insisted, "Not a girl/boy issue. Young drivers are easily distracted and boys have lead feet. It's just not safe."

I had no choice but to ride the bus, but in the big scheme of things, not driving to school with him didn't matter all that much because I found other ways to be alone with him. At least once a week, I'd lie and say I was going over to Shari or Kim's after school and eventually I would, but for the first hour or so, I'd cruise around town with Will in his 1976 Ford Thunderbird. Sometimes we'd drive out to a dirt road or to the cemetery next to the ball field and just talk or listen to music or make-out. We'd kiss so much that later my lips felt bruised. Eventually Will grew tired of just talking and kissing, and though he didn't come out and say it, I could tell that it made him angry that I didn't let him go further. Once I let him go up my shirt, but not under my bra. That made him happy for a while, but then the next time he did it, he slid his entire hand under my bra and I totally freaked out. I screamed because I wasn't expecting it.

"Jesus, Daisy! You just blew out my eardrum!" he said, jumping up and moving back over to the driver's side of the seat. I scooted over next to him, placing my head on his shoulder and tried sweet-talking him, but it didn't work.

"You just surprised me that's all," I lied. "Don't be mad." He was ticked, but he wouldn't admit it.

"Maybe I should just drop you off at your friend's house," he suggested.

"So now you're mad at me?"

"I don't know. I guess not. I mean, is it okay if I do that or not?" he asked.

It wasn't okay, but not because I didn't like it. It wasn't okay because I knew where it would lead. I never banked on waiting until I was married to have sex, but I figured that I would at least be out of high school. During catechism, when our teachers talked about chastity and how much more special the act of sex would be in matrimony, it sounded like a good idea. But messing around with Will stirred feelings in me that I didn't know I had, and I was no longer sure if I could wait another ten years or so to have sex with him or anyone else.

I certainly wasn't naïve enough to believe that Will and I would be together for that long anyway, but occasionally, I caught myself fantasizing about us staying together throughout high school and college and then getting married. It was a stupid pipedream.

Other times I felt like I had no idea what I really wanted at all. My goals and my parents' goals for me sometimes got blurred. Deciding how far to go with Will was really a predicament. I didn't want to be one of those gross girls that all the guys talked about. I didn't want to be the girl that nobody dated, but everybody messed around with. I knew that Will genuinely cared about me, so I decided to make an exception. I told him that it was okay for him to put his hands under my shirt if there was no touching under the bra. From then on, every time we were together, I spent half the time worrying about what he would want to do next and for good reason. It didn't take long for him to want more.

A few days after school started, Mom agreed to be the assistant den leader for Denny's Cub Scout troop. David and Daniel's Boy Scout troop met on the same day, which meant that every Tuesday, I had almost two hours to myself after school. I spent practically every minute of it over at Will's. The bus dropped me off every afternoon between 3:35 and 3:40. I was at Will's by 3:50. The uninterrupted time alone with him was amazing. We made food, watched TV, listened to music and of course messed around. The second time at his house, we ventured into his bedroom under the guise that he wanted to show me his record collection.

"My gosh, how many albums do you have? You might have even more than my parents, and they have a ton." Four wooden crates, the kind that held peaches and other fruits, lined his bedroom wall and were stuffed full of albums.

"Some of them I inherited from my parents, but the newer stuff I bought. I don't listen to half of them, but figured I'd hang onto them and sell them some day. They'll be worth a fortune in another twenty years or so. Pick something out and I'll cue it up."

I flipped through the albums, trying to pick out something that I thought he'd like too. Hey, what about this?" I asked, only half seriously. I really didn't think he'd go for Cat Stevens. "Look how cute he was back in the day with all that curly black hair. My mom loves him." Commenting about my mom was something I could do around Will without him thinking I was a total geek. Most kids I knew acted like their parents didn't exist, but I talked about my parents and family to Will all the time.

"Well if your ma likes him, that's good enough for me. I guess old Cat ain't too bad."

While Will was messing around with his turntable, I snooped around his room. It was a typical teenage guy's room. It could have been one of my brothers' rooms, only Will's didn't smell. The walls were covered in rock and roll posters, and his dusty shelves were cluttered with trophies, Detroit sports memorabilia, and odds and ends left over from childhood that he never bothered to pack away. There was a picture of an older couple, presumably his grandparents, pinned to the corkboard hanging on the wall. On the nightstand, there was a black and white framed photo of a woman whose resemblance to Will was uncanny. A beach and the Golden Gate Bridge served as the background. I was certain that it was the picture that Will's dad took of his mom on the day they first met.

Will noticed me eyeing the picture. "That's my mom, if you haven't already guessed."

"It's the picture your dad took, right? Did you just find it?" The thick layer of dust on the glass suggested that it had been in the same spot for some time.

"Huh? What do you mean?" he asked.

"When you told me the story about how your parents met, you know, how your dad took a picture of your mom on the beach, I asked you if your parents still had the photograph and you said it was somewhere in your house, but you acted like you didn't know for sure where it was." It took a second for him to catch my drift, but then he acted a little put off by my prying.

"What the heck, you writing a book or something? What's with the third degree?" he snapped.

"No, I'm not writing a book. I'm just curious about why you lied about the photo. You can trust me. You know that, right?"

Will went silent. I couldn't tell if he was thinking or sulking. Eventually he answered. "So, that is the picture that my dad took way, way back. The one I told you about. My mom had it in my parents' bedroom for as long as I could remember, but when she left, she put it in my room. I guess she didn't want me to forget about her. Most dudes don't keep pictures of their moms in their bedrooms unless they're Norman Bates and pyscho, but it's all I got. I guess I felt a little weird admitting that to you when we first talked about her. Truth is, my mom's pretty messed up."

"Messed up? How so?"

"She's not crazy or anything like that. Mostly she just gets depressed. Like one day she's working and doing everyday normal stuff, but then on a dime, her mood turns. It's like the lights go out, and when they come back on, she's a totally different person. She can't get out of bed, she cries all the time and doesn't care about anything. I think that's the real reason why my folks split up."

"The real reason?" I asked. We hadn't discussed any reasons up to that point.

Will covered his face with his hands, and for a second, I was afraid that he was crying and was too embarrassed to let me see, but he wasn't. Like a character in a comic strip, he pulled both sides of his hair and yelled, "Argh! I hate this!"

"C'mon Will, what is it?"

"Don't tell me you don't know. Everybody around here knows."

"Nope, not me, not everything."

"My dad screwed around on my mom. He had an affair with one of her best friends. She was our neighbor. Everybody knew about it. The lady's husband and my dad got into this huge-ass fistfight and the cops were called. When the dust settled, my mom said that she didn't care about the affair because she didn't love him anymore. She even said that she was glad that it happened, because it made her realize that a lot of her unhappiness was because of not loving him anymore. And as for my dad, he's so pathetic. He still loves my mom. He wants her to come home and everything."

My heart broke for Will, but I couldn't think of a single thing to say that I imagined would make him feel better. To avoid saying the wrong thing, I did the only thing that felt right. I kissed him. My kiss was meant to be reassuring, but our wires must have somehow got crossed because Will was really turned on by it. Maybe it was being in his bedroom or the fact that he had shared something so deeply personal with me, but he was even more uninhibited than usual. He threw me on the bed and immediately started pulling at my shirt. I didn't protest. Then he grabbed my hand and placed it near his inner thigh. I could feel his penis through his sweatpants. I'd felt it before, pressed up against my pelvis, but it felt weird to have my hand on it. I knew what he wanted me to do, but I didn't want to. I jerked my hand away, but like a game of tug-of-war, he pulled my hand back in the direction he wanted it and began twisting and turning his hips like he was Elvis Presley. I felt degraded even though I knew that he had no idea the effect his behavior was having on me. After several minutes of continued kissing and the cat and mouse game with my hand, he sat up and yelled, "What? What's wrong now, nobody's here! It's just the two of us and you're acting like a total tease. What's your problem?"

His words sounded so ugly. They were words belonging to a sleaze ball, like Ricky and not my sweet, sensitive Will. I wasn't trying to be a tease. "Will, don't say that. Let's talk about it," I begged.

"That's all you ever want to do is talk. Talking's cool, but c'mon, I don't want to talk and kiss. I want more. Don't you?"

There it was. His cards were on the table, and I had no choice but to fold or play the hand I was dealt. Either way, it felt like a lose-lose situation. "Will, please," I started to say, but was interrupted by a knock on his bedroom door.

"Will? You got someone in there with you? Can I come in a sec?"

Will mouthed, "It's my dad." He stood and motioned for me to do the same, but it didn't seem realistic that the both of us would be just standing in his bedroom doing nothing, so I sat down at his desk and opened his Algebra book as he smoothed out the comforter on his bed before granting his dad permission to enter.

"Hey buddy, what's going on?" Mr. Banks asked. "Who's your friend?"

"Hi," I said, "I'm Daisy. I'm helping him study for tomorrow's math test."

It was obvious by his dad's curious stare that Will had never mentioned me to him, because if he had, his dad would've said something like, "Ah, so you're Daisy. I've heard all about you." Nor did his face light up like it was nice to finally put a name to a face, but he was very welcoming.

He said, "Will doesn't bring too many friends around as of late. He's always holed up at other people's houses. It's nice to meet you. I presume you live around here?"

I nodded. "Just down the road. My parents bought the Thompson's house last winter."

"Hmm, so your dad's the banker, huh? That's a nice house. I was in it once or twice before. I don't know if Will told you, but in addition to being an engineer, I dabble in a little photography on the side. I took some family pictures for the Thompsons after their second son was born. Even sold them a few pieces of my own work. Nice people, but they didn't live there too long."

"Oh? How come?" I asked, hoping to detect by his answer whether or not Mom's claim that he had a second affair was true or not.

Like a forgetful old man, Will's dad scratched his head trying to recall the exact reason why they moved. "I believe the wife was originally from North Carolina or Tennessee. Her husband was able to transfer with whatever company he was working for at the time, and so they moved there to be closer to her family."

Mom was wrong about Will's dad.

"What are you doing home so early in the first place?" asked Will, changing the subject.

His dad reached into his pocket and pulled out three tickets. "I snagged us some tickets to a Tigers game. My buddy gave me three, so Daisy, if you'd like to join us, we'd love to have you. Only thing is, we need to get going soon or we'll be late. I hate getting to games late."

I wanted to go, but there was no point in asking. My parents would never go for it. They didn't know Will's dad and even if they had, they'd never let me go down to Detroit with people that weren't family or good family friends. I had to pass on the offer. Will's dad eventually excused himself but told Will to shake a leg. "We're leaving in ten minutes. I'm going to call Grandpa and see if he wants to go to the game with us."

As soon as Will's dad left the room I asked, "Do you think he suspects anything?"

"C'mon, he's not stupid. We're teenagers, and you were acting so jumpy. He knows that we're more than just study buddies." I knew Will was right. "Don't worry about it," said Will. "I'm psyched to go to the game, but bummed he barged in. It was just getting good. Now, where were we?" he asked. Before I could protest, his mouth was on mine.

"Are you crazy?" I said, pushing him away. "Your dad could come back in at any second."

"Nah, he won't," he assured me. I didn't object when he slipped his hand under my shirt, but when he grabbed my hand and guided it south, I pushed him away. "Okay, I lied. I don't like you going up my shirt and I really don't like how you're trying to get me to grope you. It's gross."

"I'm gross? Really? Grow up and stop acting like a little girl. There're plenty of people our age that do a lot more than this. I love you and I want to be with you and you think I'm gross. Thanks a lot!"

"I didn't say you were gross. It's just that things are moving too fast."

Will didn't give me a chance to say anything else. He flung open the bedroom door and called to his dad, "Yo, old man. I'm ready to go." I wanted to be invisible, but there was no bypassing his dad on the way out the front door.

"Well," Will's dad said, standing as I entered the room, "it was nice meeting you. I'm sure I'll be seeing you around." I don't recall telling Mr. Banks goodbye.

Will wasn't at school the next day. He probably overslept because he got home late from the game, but as usual, I let my imagination run wild. I convinced myself that his absence was linked to what happened between the two of us the night before.

After school, I barely acknowledged poor Gus who was waiting to greet me at the front door. I kicked off my shoes and raced to the phone.

"Whoa! Where's the fire?" Mom asked, as I breezed past her and Miss J who were sitting in the living room flipping through an *Avon* catalogue. Miss J had recently become an *Avon* representative, which was pretty ironic considering she didn't wear a stitch of make-up, ever. "Can't you say hi to Miss J?"

"Oh, hey Miss J. I didn't see you there. Sorry, but I forgot to copy down the stupid directions for an English assignment that's due tomorrow and I need to call someone from my class. My teacher is a total joke. Supposedly her class is college prep, but the only challenging thing about it is keeping up with all the tedious homework." Miss J shook her head and commented about the need for teachers to create more stimulating assignments instead of doling out mindless busy work. "Tell me about it," I agreed just to shut her up.

Will's phone rang and rang. I left a message, which was pointless because what I really wanted to say to him I couldn't leave on a machine. I called several more times, but I didn't leave any more messages. Before calling it a night, I tried one more time and his dad answered. He explained that Will was in the shower, but he promised to have him call me back after I told him that it was urgent. Will never returned my call that night. I didn't speak to him until school the next day.

I was late getting to school because my bus had to make an unplanned pit stop at one of the houses along the route to allow a kid to use the bathroom. "It's an emergency," the kid tearfully explained to the bus driver. I guess she didn't want to risk one of her passengers messing his pants, so she stopped. I didn't even wait for the driver to park the bus before standing and making my way to the front. I needed to be the first one off. After running up two flights of steps, I was huffing and puffing, but managed to make it before the tardy bell rang. Will was leaning against his locker with a glum look on his face, waiting for me. A few feet away stood the assistant principal, barking at kids to get to glass. He was the sweeper—the person responsible for clearing out the hallway of stragglers. None of the kids could stand him because he was a big jerk.

"I need to talk to you," Will said, not bothering to say hello. His serious tone and inability to look me in the eye reaffirmed my suspicion that something was seriously wrong.

"Okay, what's up?" I asked.

Will was blunt. "Not here," he said. "Meet me outside on the north side of the building when you're finished eating lunch."

"Why outside? Why can't we talk during lunch?" I asked.

"Move it along," the assistant principal ordered, shaking his detention pad at the two of us in a threatening manner. I had no clue which side of the building was the north side, but I had until noon to figure it out.

The cafeteria was already half empty by the time I got there. Only a handful of kids were seated at each of the tables, so it took no time for me to see that Will wasn't there. We always ate together, whether it was in the cafeteria or somewhere outside. According to our school handbook, we were a closed campus, except for ninth graders who were permitted to leave school grounds for lunch. Most kids didn't bother because our lunch period wasn't any longer than the seventh and eighth graders'.

I ate my lunch as I circled around the building in search of the north side. I figured I'd eventually run into him and I did. He was sitting on the steps with Ricky, Brian and a few other guys, but as soon as they saw me, everybody but Will bailed. Usually I waited for Will to make the first move, but I wanted to see how he'd respond if I kissed him first. Something about the kiss didn't feel quite right. He was the first to break from our embrace, which was almost never the case. Will didn't give me the chance to ask about the game with his dad or why he wasn't at school the day before.

"Look—" he started to say, but I cut him off.

"Stop! Whenever people start a sentence with the word *look,* it means something bad is going to follow. Promise me you're not going to tell me something bad."

Will made no promises. "I didn't want to do this over the phone, so that's why I didn't call you back. I really don't want to do it at all, but I think we should call it quits."

"Call it quits? You mean breakup? Why?"

"I love you, Daisy, I really do, but this whole dating thing just isn't really working for me anymore."

My brain knew what was coming, but my heart was ill-prepared. "Listen, I'm sorry about the other night for freaking out on you, but I've had some time to think about it and I decided that I'm okay with taking our relationship to the next level. I mean, not sex, but other stuff. Whatever you want. Please don't do this." I reached out to him, but he stepped back from me like I was a carrier of a deadly disease.

"No!" he insisted. "I don't want you to do that. It's not only because of that, I mean it is a little bit, but it's other stuff."

I didn't believe him and told him as much. "You're lying. It has everything to do with that."

"Okay, it's a lot about that," he admitted, "but I love you so much. I mean, if you let me do the stuff that I want to do, you'd hate yourself. Man, the look on your face the other day was just too much. You looked at me like I was scum and I suppose that maybe I am. It's weird, but I almost liked it better when we were just friends and I didn't feel like I was always letting you down. I've never been able to talk to anyone the way I talk to you. But now when we're together, all I think about is being with you. You make me feel like there's something wrong with wanting you."

"That's not true!" I cried. "I want you too and I acted the way I did because I was scared. Before you, I'd never even kissed anybody. You've done more stuff than me and I just didn't want you to think I sucked at it."

Will laughed. "What are you talking about? I've never done anything like that before. You're the first. Not the first girl I kissed, but everything else."

I was shocked. I wasn't sure if I believed him. "Really? What about Ricky? What about all the stories I've heard about your friends?"

"C'mon, I'm not Ricky, and I'm not sure what stories you're talking about. You know this place. Everybody likes to talk shit, but it doesn't mean anything."

He was right. Maybe I was the one who had it all wrong. "So, what do you think about what I said? What if I agreed to more because I want to do more?"

"Are you sure about that?" he asked. "I don't want to force you to do anything that you're not comfortable doing."

"Let me worry about it," I said.

In the end, we agreed to keep seeing each other and decided to see how things played out. Those were his words, not mine. All I heard was that we weren't over. I had successfully negotiated the terms of our relationship—at least temporarily.

The rest of September through late October was unseasonably dry and warm. It was an Indian summer and the perfect time to be in love, but eventually, our relationship, like the leaves, began to change. Half of the orange, red and yellow leaves fell to the ground, but the other half clung rebelliously to the branches. Summer seemed to stretch on forever, which didn't make our teachers very happy. They reminded us daily that summer vacation was over and it was time to buckle down and commence learning. I loved the weather because it wasn't quite summer, but not full-fledged fall. Mostly I loved it because I could still ride my bike and sneak away with Will without anyone getting too suspicious. Halloween night in particular couldn't have been more perfect.

Nobody complained that it fell on a Monday night because for the first time in a long time, kids could wear their flimsy dime store costumes as they were intended to be worn and didn't have to dress in layers to stay warm. There were no bulky sweatshirts or sweatpants pulling at the seams of the girls' dainty nylon costumes and the boys' sinewy little muscles were visible under their Super Hero costumes. Nobody rushed home early to get out of the cold or rain. I volunteered to stay behind and pass out candy. I was too old to go out trick-or-treating and besides that, all the good parties had been the weekend before Halloween. I only went to one, Shari's. Hers had been an actual costume party, and though her parents were around to chaperone the entire night, it was still fun. She handed out invites at school along with explicit directions to wear a real costume and not just a mask.

I dressed up as Princess Leia. Mom was the mastermind behind the costume. The best part of my costume was that we didn't have to spend a single dime making it and everybody agreed that my costume was by far the best. To achieve the cinnamon bun hairdo, we used round steel wool scrubbing pads. Mom parted my hair down the middle to make pigtails. Each pigtail was then pushed through the small hole in the center of each pad. Then we wrapped my own hair and some hair from an old wig that my grandma used to wear back in the 70's around the pads and secured each bun with bobby pins. For my white robe, Mom starched the only white sheet in the linen closet that wasn't stained and draped it around my body like a toga. David's brown dress belt was used to cinch the waist and I carried Daniel's *Han Solo Blaster gun*. My costume looked legit. Will went to the party with me, but only after I begged him. None of his friends went. Shari's party wasn't cool enough. He went as Han Solo, but if it weren't for the second *Star Wars* gun that I swiped from Denny, nobody would've been able to figure out who he was supposed to be. I suggested that he go as Luke Skywalker, since they were both blonds and boyishly handsome, but coming up with a costume was tricky since Luke dressed mostly in all white like Leia. Since Han's costume was generic— black pants, a white shirt and a black vest, it was a whole lot easier for him to go as Han Solo.

The next night, Ricky had a party, but I didn't go. I went to my Aunt Susan's annual Halloween party, but only because I was forced to. My Aunt Susan was a Halloween nut and every year she threw a party for all the nieces and nephews and their parents. Normally, I couldn't wait for her party, but not that year. Will was going to Ricky's party without me. Because Kim and

Shari couldn't go either, I spent the entire night worrying about what other girls were there. As it turned out, I had good reason to worry, but I didn't find out why until later.

21
A Season of Change

It wasn't until two days after Halloween that Mother Nature conceded and the weather turned brisk. The cooler weather didn't deter Denny from playing outside every chance he got. Whether he was obliterating abandoned pumpkins and squash left to decompose in the untilled soil of our vegetable garden with his baseball bat or playing football with our brothers and their friends, outside was where he could be found. With his Carhartt jacket and faux raccoon cap, he tromped around in the backyard or on the edge of the woods for hours on end. The jacket was a hand-me-down from our cousin Kevin, whom Denny idolized. His reasons for looking up to him were straightforward and typical of a seven-year-old boy.

Kevin was older, which automatically made him cooler, and unlike Denny, he could participate in activities that our parents deemed too dangerous for someone Denny's age. Kevin's family had a cottage on a lake in Irish Hills and there, on the gravel road that followed the lake, he fearlessly rode his moped and four-wheeler until both were out of gas. He even had his very own gun and it wasn't just a BB gun, but an actual hunting rifle. Denny would have been content with just a BB gun, but my parents still said no. Kevin was the only child of Aunt Jinny and Uncle Tom, so naturally he was a little spoiled. Mom held her tongue around Dad because Uncle Tom was his older brother, but she vocalized her misgivings to all of us kids.

"That kid's lucky that he hasn't lost an eye or broken his neck," she'd lecture. Her speeches were lost on

Denny though. Kevin was a real outdoorsman, and Denny wanted nothing more than to be just like him.

As for me, I hated the colder weather, especially that fall. The change in temperature seemed to usher in a change in Will's affection for me. I couldn't put my finger on it, but something was different between us because something was different with Will. He brushed off my concerns claiming that basketball was the culprit. The two-hour long practices were gobbling up all his free time after school or so he claimed. When Will announced that his dad was going to his older cousin's wedding down in the city the weekend after Halloween, and that he'd have the entire place to himself, I felt hopeful that Will and I could rekindle our relationship, but Will had other plans.

"Well, I didn't think that you'd be able to pull anything off with your parents always breathing down your neck, so I invited the guys to come over and hang with me. They're probably going to spend the night."

I was hurt and disappointed that he made other plans, but knew he was right to assume that we wouldn't be able to hang out. "Oh, well, yeah if you've already made plans, don't change them on my account."

"No, I can tell them not to come. It's not a big deal," he said unconvincingly.

"Don't do that. I'll be fine. I guess I just miss you because I hardly get to see you anymore, but just think, in less than a year, we can date freely and won't have to worry about sneaking around."

I had no way of knowing that Will and Denny would be long gone by then.

Part Two

22
Ava Blume
Spring 1984

My understanding of psychiatry, psychologists or anything relating to the treatment of people suffering from emotional or mental ailments was limited to what I had seen in the movies or from my brief stay at the hospital, which didn't really count because I barely remember my time there. I suppose that's why my first visit with Dr. Blume was not at all what I had expected. For starters, the office itself wasn't how I imagined it would be. I envisioned a contemporary lobby with funky inkblot paintings hanging on white walls and modern, geometric furniture strategically placed throughout the room to ensure that patients didn't have to interact with one another, but that wasn't the case.

Instead, it looked like a typical American family's living room. A comfy looking L-shaped sectional sat in the center of the room with a worn Oriental rug underneath it. A loveseat and two armchairs occupied the remaining two sides of the square seating arrangement. In the center of the cozy space was a coffee table with newspapers and magazines strewn across it. Along the perimeter of the room were more chairs and a sideboard that held a coffee pot and a hot water dispenser for making tea.

The old building smell that greeted us in the foyer was replaced by the smell of greasy, spicy smelling food the moment we approached the glass partition that separated the front desk from the rest of the lobby. Nobody was there to greet us. After about a minute, a young, blondish woman came barreling back toward the desk with what looked like a warmed-up plate of Chinese food and a can of Vernors in her hands.

"Oh, uh good afternoon," Dad said awkwardly. "Sorry to interrupt. Looks like we caught you in the middle of your lunch break?"

"No not at all," she said, shuffling around a few loose papers from atop her cluttered desk to free up a spot for her plate. Once situated, she looked up and gave us a proper greeting. "Now that's better. Good afternoon. Please forgive me, I don't normally take my lunch at my desk or this late, but Martha, the other gal, has been out sick the last few days and this is the first chance I've had to eat all afternoon. Who are we seeing today?" she asked.

"My daughter, Daisy" he said, glancing back over his shoulder as if he needed to check for himself that I was indeed present for the appointment. I didn't bother looking up or acknowledging the receptionist when I heard my name, which I knew was a pretty shitty thing to do, but I didn't care. I stepped off to the side and let Dad do all the talking. "Oh, did you mean which doctor? Geez, I can't seem to recall the doctor's name, but I've got a card here somewhere," he said, patting his pockets in search of the business card that Mom had given him before we left the house. Before he could find it, the receptionist located my name on the appointment calendar in front of her.

"Ah yes, here she is. Daisy Doyle with Dr. Blume. Now if you don't mind, I have a little paperwork for you to fill out, sir." She attached several forms to a clipboard and handed it to Dad. "And for you," she said, leaning slightly forward over the counter and craning her neck so that she could address me, "I've got something for you as well, but don't worry, you can sit down to work on it if you'd like. Leave it on the counter when you're finished."

I suspected that she suggested that I sit down because I looked like the walking dead, or maybe because she noticed me ogling the couch. I was tired all the time and even the short walk from the car to the building left me longing for a place to sit and rest. I could barely make it up and down the steps of school without feeling like I was going to have a heart attack.

Dad removed his coat and hung it on one of the empty hooks on the coat rack. "Whew, it's like a blast furnace in here. Give me your coat and I'll hang yours up too." The room was hot, but I declined his offer. "Suit yourself," he said, not bothering to debate it. I'd agreed to the visit, but I didn't want to give the impression that I was getting comfortable with the idea of seeing someone on a regular basis. I melted into the corner of the sectional with my clipboard. Naturally, I shut my eyes. "C'mon, Daisy," Dad called from across the room where he stood with a mug of coffee in his hand. "You need to complete the form for the doctor. You promised your mother and I that you'd cooperate."

A strong cup of coffee or tea was probably the very thing I needed to get through my appointment, but I was too lazy to fix a cup for myself and wasn't about to ask dad to fix one for me, considering how bitchy I'd been on the drive to the office.

"Geesh, I am," I answered, "give me a sec, will you?"

In the end, there were very few questions on the form that I bothered to answer. Most of them were stupid, redundant, and a total waste of the paper they were printed on.

1. Are you currently experiencing overwhelming sadness, grief or depression?

Uh, that's why I'm here. What do you think?

2. Are you experiencing any chronic pain? *"Depression hurts," says so right on the poster hanging on the wall.*

3. How would you describe your current sleeping habits? – *Sleep all the time, like Rip Van Winkle. Could barely find the energy to make this stupid appointment.* Number four just about killed me.

4. Can you identify the source of your sadness or anxiety? – *Again, duh. Dead brother and my life sucks. Surely my parents and/or the shrink at the hospital have already disclosed the reasons behind my paralyzing depression.*

Just as I stood to return the clipboard to the receptionist, the door to the lobby opened and a distinguished looking woman stepped out whom I assumed was my doctor. Dad rested his clipboard on the seat cushion next to where he was sitting and walked over and introduced himself.

"Hello Dr. Blume. I'm John Doyle and this is my daughter, Daisy," he said, motioning me to join him. Her accent was strong, but her English was flawless. For someone so scrawny, she had a pretty impressive handshake. My hand felt like a deflated balloon when she finally released it. Dr. Blume was an attractive, older woman in an understated, European sort of way. Her silvery gray hair was thick and shiny. It brushed the top of her shoulders and complimented her long, angular face. The crow's feet that formed around the outer corners of her eyes were not very pronounced and overall, her face didn't look too craggy for someone so old. I guessed her age to be somewhere between late fifties and early sixties. Her best features were her wide-set eyes and her hawkish nose, which provided much needed character to her stoic face. Through her cardigan I noticed her arms, which unlike my grandma's arms, weren't loose and wobbly. Her arms appeared thin and taut.

After answering a few of Dad's basic questions concerning insurance and billing, questions that were probably more suitable for the receptionist, she turned to me and said, "So what do you think, Daisy? Should we head to my office and get to know one another?" She filled the empty mug she held in her hand with hot water, grabbed a few tea bags and offered to take my clipboard. "I can take that if you're all finished with it." And without bothering to check if I had actually completed the questionnaire or not, she slipped it into the manila folder that she kept secured under her arm. "If you'd like," she said pointing to a tray displaying an assortment of tea bags, "fix yourself a cup of tea or grab some coffee."

I'm not sure why, but I didn't fix myself anything to drink. "Uh, I think I'm good. Can we just go ahead and get started?" I asked.

"Of course. Right this way then," she said, leading me down a short hallway.

We passed three other offices. Dr. Blume's office was located at the end of the hallway. Much like her appearance, it was unassuming but attractive. The built-in bookcases situated on either side of the non-working fireplace were filled with impressive looking burgundy and forest green embossed medical volumes and encyclopedias. Framed photographs, presumably of her family, also lined the shelves. Some were displayed on her orderly desk.

"Please have a seat," she said, pointing to a comfy looking couch and two high-back leather chairs. I had my sights on the couch, but before making my final decision I asked what I considered a totally logical question. "Should I sit or lie down?" I wanted to prove to her that I wasn't a rookie when it came to therapy and that I couldn't be easily manipulated.

My question didn't faze her. "I'll leave that up to you," she said. "By all means, do whichever makes you most comfortable, but you should know, I'm not a psychoanalyst." The psychoanalyst reference went right over my head, so I settled for the chair and she sat on the couch. "So, how are you feeling today?" she asked. I expected her to hit me with a bunch of trick shrink questions designed to help her quickly diagnose me, but she didn't. Her question was pretty straightforward, so why I couldn't just answer her with an equally generic response frustrated me. The brain fog that piggybacked my depression was a drag. I ignored her question and began playing with the snaps and zippers on the front of my coat.

"Would you like me to hang up your coat? Maybe you'd be more comfortable if you weren't so warm," she suggested. "Someone's coming in later today to check the thermostat. I'm always cold, so I don't mind, but my receptionist and several patients have complained over the last few days."

To avoid looking completely obstinate, I met her halfway and removed my coat, but didn't give it to her to hang up. Determined to get me to open up, Ava took another crack at breaking the ice. "Do you understand the difference between the two?"

"The two what?" I asked.

"The difference between a psychiatrist and a psychotherapist, or therapist, as we are most commonly called. There are quite a few different titles in the mental health profession, which can make it a little confusing for patients to understand who they need to see. There are psychiatrists, psychologists, psychoanalysts and psychotherapists.

"Wow! That's a lot of psychos," I commented.

"Indeed, it is," Ava agreed. I appreciated Ava's persistence. The shrink in the hospital often just stared at me for long stretches of time, waiting for me to have an epiphany or something. Either that, or he pestered me into answering his dumb questions. I really despised that man.

"You all basically do the same thing though, right? I mean I've already seen one shrink. He prescribed meds to me, which I hate, by the way. I mean, I do feel a little better, but barely. So, no offense, but I'm not sure why I need to talk to you too. He didn't really help much."

She studied my chart for a second and then commented. "So, the antidepressant is helping only somewhat?"

"It's helping okay, I guess. I'm not better, but at least I can get out of bed. I'm still tired all the time and I don't have much of an appetite yet."

"Different medications have different side effects. I can call your psychiatrist and we can consider putting you on something different. Sometimes it takes a while to figure out what works best for the individual patient. One size doesn't fit all in this case."

"Yeah, okay. I guess we could do that," I agreed.

Ava wrote something down in her notes. "Well, getting back to the differences— you're correct in your assumption that psychiatrists or shrinks, as you refer to them, do some of the same things as a psychologist or psychotherapist, but the roles we play in the treatment of patients varies. Would you like me to try to explain the difference between them?"

"Sure," I said, not caring one way or the other, but we had almost an hour to kill, so I figured that her doing all the talking was better than me spilling my guts. Convinced that her explanation was going to be a real snoozer, I regretted not taking the couch.

"I'm not a medical doctor like your psychiatrist at the hospital, which basically means I'm unable to prescribe medicine. I hold a PhD, which is why the word doctor precedes my name. I'm not big on titles, so you may call me Ava if you'd like."

I nodded. "Okay, I'll call you Ava." In my head I already was.

"Well, now that we've got that settled, I'll continue. Psychiatrists deal mostly with patients suffering from clinical issues, like schizophrenia for example, or other conditions brought on by chemical imbalances, and their primary job is to help patients manage their medication. My job is to help my patients identify the source of their emotional stress or depression, and to give them the tools they need to help manage the stressors in their day-to-day lives. In simple terms, the medication prescribed by the psychiatrist helps the brain be more receptive to therapy. For most of my patients, medication and therapy combined works the best, especially in the beginning. Medicine alone cannot fix the sadness, or the feelings or thoughts that are preventing the patient from living a healthy and productive life."

After several more minutes of discussing other misconceptions about psychiatrists and psychologists, she stopped talking altogether. We sat in silence for several minutes. I had no idea why, and I figured she must have lost her train of thought. She was pretty old, after all. I mistakenly interpreted her pause to mean that she was done speaking. I'd learn later that silence was part of the therapy.

"So, what is the job of a psychoanalyst?" I asked. "You didn't explain what they do." I was impressed that she had found a way to capture my attention. Most adults, like my teachers at school, just sounded like the adults in all the *Charlie Brown* cartoons, *Wah-Wah-Wah*, when they spoke.

Ava continued. "Many psychiatrists and psychologists are psychoanalysts, but I am not. Psychoanalysts often work with people who are trying to come to terms with a traumatic event buried deep in their psyches. Sometimes memories are so horrific that they are repressed or trapped in the subconscious. An unresolved traumatic experience from childhood is often the culprit. The person doesn't realize that the unsettled issue is negatively impacting his or her life. Bouts of depression and/or self-destructive behaviors may plague a person until the issues are worked through.

Psychoanalysts see their patients much more frequently than a psychiatrist or psychologist, sometimes up to three or four times a week. Patients treated by psychoanalysts sometimes lay on a couch but not always. Patients say whatever comes to their minds with prompting by a doctor with a single word or image, which is how the subconscious reveals itself. Subconscious hurts often stay hidden unless they're drawn out," she explained.

"So, in other words, you could have been any psycho you wanted, but you chose to be a psychologist."

"That is correct. I would've had to have gone to medical school to become a psychiatrist and taken different courses if I wanted to practice psychoanalysis, but rest assured, I love what I do."

"Hmm. Interesting. So basically, what you're saying is that you're the best person for me to see because I'm not crazy. You're saying that you think the root of my problem isn't buried deep in my subconscious, so there's no need to pull it out of me through hypnosis or electric shock therapy or anything too drastic. You just need to figure out a way to help me forget about all the crappy stuff that's happened to me over the last few months."

Ava quickly corrected me. "You're not a suitable candidate to receive ECT. Where did you get such a notion?"

"ECT? What the heck's that?" I asked.

"Electroconvulsive Therapy or electric shock therapy as you referred to it. You're absolutely right though. You don't need that." I was mostly kidding with my crack about electric shock therapy, but I was relieved to hear that she didn't think I needed it. "Is that what you want me to do, make you forget? Erase your memories?" she asked.

Here we go! Time for all the introspection! I thought to myself. My real answer was, *Yes, make me forget. Help me find a way to erase the past,* but I wasn't so far gone that I believed that she could do either of those things. Instead of telling her what I really thought, I said, "I just want to stop hurting. I want to be in control of my feelings. I want to go to bed and wake up tomorrow or a year from now and for all of this to be behind me. I want to feel normal again. I'd like to be able to pretend that this past year was all just a bad dream. "Can you help me do that?" I asked. Hot, angry tears sprung from my eyes. I hadn't planned on crying, but I was too exhausted and too weak to hold them in. I reached for a tissue, but the box was empty. Ava walked to her closet and fished out another box of tissue and set it in my lap. I expected her to rub my back or to say something uplifting, but she didn't.

"Don't dab at your eyes with the same tissue that you just used to blow your nose," was the only solid advice she gave. When I was reasonably composed, she resumed our session. "Daisy, I need you to do something for me. When you get home and over the course of the next week, I want you to compile a list of topics that you'd like to discuss with me. I don't want you to over-analyze your list or write down things you think we should talk about based on what you've heard or seen on television. I want your list to reflect genuine issues or feelings that you're struggling with. Do you understand what I'm asking you to do?"

I understood what she was asking me to do and it pissed me off. My parents had practically strong-armed me into meeting with this woman, and she expected me to do all the heavy lifting by deciding what was important for us to talk about. She was the doctor. I wanted to express my anger, but because my response was punctuated with hiccups, I ended up sounding like I was intoxicated instead. "I thought it was your job to figure out what we're supposed to talk about and not mine. You're the one with the Ph.D."

"Your assumption is fair, but not accurate."

"And why is that?" I asked.

"I'm not a mind reader. If I presume to know how you're feeling based only on what little information is made available to me, and I treat only what is at the surface, only what is buoyant, while ignoring what lies beneath, then you will eventually sink. It would be comparable to a doctor applying bandages to a serious wound when stitches are required. That wound would remain vulnerable for a long time because it wasn't treated properly in the first place, and extreme caution would need to be taken to avoid reopening the wound. I can't wave a magic wand and make your pain disappear. I need you to be an active participant. Healing is a process. Do you understand that?"

Her bandage analogy made sense, but I had so many wounds to heal that determining which one to treat first felt too overwhelming. My spirit was broken. Biting sorrow had edged its way into the space of my heart that once was reserved for happiness. Like a bad dream, sadness crept into my room every night and woke me from my sleep. It shadowed me throughout the day and was there to tuck me into bed again when the day was over. For someone who spent every moment I wasn't at school curled up in the bed, it was mind-boggling to me how tired I always felt. Sleep or thoughts of sleep was all consuming. Ava's little speech reminded me of something Dad would say to my brothers before every game. He gave the same pep talk every time. He'd say, "Remember, you don't have to go out swinging like you're Babe Ruth and the bases are loaded. A ground ball to the outfield can send a player 'cross home plate just as easily as a homerun. It just takes a little longer." After some inner debate, I decided to try taking my turn at bat.

"I suppose I can work on that list," I announced after weighing my dismal options. My parents weren't about to let up on me. They'd for sure force me to see her every week. The way I saw it, I could let her do all the talking, or I could confide in someone who might listen, and not just pretend to listen. "I really don't need a week. I can think of something right off the bat."

She nodded her head and asked, "So what would you like to talk about?"

"Alright, here's one for you. It's maddening how nobody will listen to me about taking the rest of the school year off, not even my academic advisor. I don't see why I can't just go to summer school to make up what I've missed. Last year there was a girl at my school who had cancer. She was gone more than she was there. I thought for sure she'd flunk the 8th grade, but when I walked into my first hour 9th grade English class, there she was, sitting in the front row. By summer I'm sure I'll be feeling better and besides that, being at school stresses me out. Everybody tiptoes around me like I'm some kind of head case, which I suppose I am. My teachers are all afraid of me and somehow, even though I've only turned in a handful of assignment from when I was in the loony bin, I'm not failing a single class. My point is that I'm certain they'll promote me no matter what, but even my parents won't budge. Why is everybody making me jump through so many hoops? I swear, God must hate me, He really must."

"I would prefer if you refrained from saying things like, 'loony bin' and 'head case.' And for the record, the world's not against you, Daisy. It sounds to me that your teachers are merely trying to be supportive. It's possible that they're cautious around you because they're afraid they might say or do the wrong thing. As far as taking more time off from school, I don't think that's a very wise idea. As difficult as it may be, it's important that you get back into your routine. Avoiding uncomfortable situations will only slow the healing process and..."

"Give me a break already. My brother just died, like, not that long ago and I think I'm entitled to shut down for a while, don't you? My mom has, but I don't see her sitting here."

The comment about Mom wasn't entirely true. Like everybody else, she was still reeling, but she only completely checked out for a few days. Only after the funeral was behind us did she allow herself to come completely unhinged. Grandma even had to come stay with us because she was so bad. She didn't come to take care of my brothers and me, but to take care of Mom. I was so afraid that Mom would be the next to die. Our once attentive mother could barely drag herself out of bed and slipped further and further away from us with each passing day. I suppose the pain she felt eventually grew too big for her to contain, and like an arthropod that's outgrown its exoskeleton, she had to shed her former self to break on through to the other side. Eventually, she got out of bed. But she wasn't the same.

"Oh, and for the record," I added, "it's not like she had a complete mental break down or anything like that. I mean she wasn't exactly like the woman in that old movie, *The Snake Pit*. Did you ever see that movie? My parents love old movies and I guess now so do I." Ava raised an eyebrow but let me continue. "You'd probably say that she's functional now, but barely." I didn't mention that she hadn't so much as looked at her piano, let alone play it, since Denny's death. Most people wouldn't find that too unusual, but those of us who know her know it's a big deal. To her, playing the piano was vital, like the fourth basic need behind food, clothing and shelter. She'd played the piano almost every day since the age of four, but not once since

Denny's death. For all practical purposes, Mom had stopped breathing.

Ava finished recording something in her notes before addressing my comment. "I'm not treating your mother, but it sounds like your mother is a topic you'd like to discuss. Would you like to tell me about your mother?"

"I dunno." I said, noticing the two-sided clock displayed on the coffee table. It was beautiful and looked like something Mom would like. "Your clock is cool. Are there two sides so we can both see the time without coming across as rude by constantly checking our watches? Where did you get it?" I asked.

"I don't know is not an answer, Daisy. Either you do or you don't," she said, again ignoring my questions.

"I guess we can talk about her. What do you want to know?" As soon as the words passed through my lips, I realized my error. She wasn't going to tell me what to tell her about my mom. We continued sitting there for several minutes, neither of us willing to be the first to speak up. It wasn't until a few sessions later that I asked her what the deal was with the long silences during therapy and why she seemed to blow off so many of my questions. In true Ava fashion, my question was answered with a no-nonsense response.

"Silence is a fundamental part of the process. I'm listening to you, and I need you to listen to me. I remain silent at times so you can digest the meaning behind my words and your own. We all need think time. Words serve as clues to what we are really feeling and thinking. You are a smart girl and I'm not going to waste your time or mine by answering nonsense questions that are meant to change the subject or to avoid honesty. You are smart, but I'm too old of a cat to be fooled by a kitten like you." Ava's attempt at a joke made me smile for the first time in a long time.

To talk about Mom, I had to start by talking about Dad. "It was business as usual for my dad after Denny. A week after the funeral, he went back to work, back to the bank to crunch numbers or whatever it is he does there. I suppose you think him jumping back into his routine was a good thing, huh?"

I thought it was weird, but I didn't tell her that. His son was dead and there were still so many unanswered questions swirling around his death, but Dad reported back to his office like a dutiful worker bee. With his dated ties and conservative, charcoal suits, the average person would never have suspected that his life had just been derailed, but he wasn't fooling me. He was just going through the motions by pretending to care about insignificant things like interest rates and Big Ten football rankings. I suppose all that pretending prevented him from losing his mind altogether.

"What should he have done instead? You said your mother shut down. Is that what you think your father should've done?" Ava asked.

"No," I said defensively. "I get that he has to work, but his behavior is almost worse than Mom's."

"Worse? How so?" Ava asked.

"He's like a zombie. It's like he's walking around in his own body, doing all the same things that he did before, but he's got somebody else's brain inside his head. Take football for example, when it was on. He'd stretch out in his recliner in front of the TV and watch one football game after another just like before, only not really because he didn't actually watch them. He just stared past the TV. The games were on, but the volume was completely turned down. When my brother asked what was up with that, he gave him some stupid excuse like he was sick of the biased commentators always singing the praises of Bo Schembechler." I wasn't sure Ava knew who Bo Schembechler was, because she didn't strike me as the football type so I said, "You do know Bo is the coach for U of M, right?"

"I know who he is," she replied.

"It's no secret that Dad hates him, but he never, ever watched any game with the volume turned all the way down."

"So why does he do that?"

"He watches mindless television and goes to work every day to prove a point, to be an example for the rest of us. It's his way of saying that if we try, we'll eventually move on and forget about Denny."

She didn't address my Denny comment, but focused on the first half of my statement. "You seem upset that he's trying to move on."

"You're missing the point. I don't think he's really moved on. He's just pretending. I don't think any of us will be able to move on. Mom cries a lot, I mean all the time. Sometimes she comes into my room or one of my brothers' rooms and lies down next to us. She cries and then gets up and packs lunches or cries and then forces herself up and drives to a Boy Scout meeting. Dad never cries. Never. Never mentions Denny either."

"People deal with death differently. Maybe your dad puts on a brave face because your mom can't right now."

Her comment incensed me. How could she lecture me about people dealing with death differently? "Are you kidding? So, it's okay for Mom and Dad to deal with Denny's death however they want, but it's not okay for me to deal with it in my own way? That's such a double standard. It's bullshit."

"Daisy, do you remember why you were hospitalized?" Ava asked.

I waited too long to answer. My time was up. My session was over.

23
Everything We Can't Say

I embraced the quiet. No radio, no talking and no cross-examination. If Mom had taken me to my first appointment, it would've been a different story. Dad said nothing, which initially I appreciated because I was tired. But after a while, his stoicism unnerved me. His silence had everything to do with his own feelings and nothing to do with respecting my privacy. I could tell that his mind was somewhere else. He gripped the steering wheel as if it took all the strength he had to keep the car from careening off the road. The muscles in his face and neck strained as he clenched his teeth. My jaw hurt just watching him. I wanted to reach out, console him with a small gesture like touching his forearm to show that I understood his pain, but I couldn't. My time with Ava had taken too much out of me. Going into my session, my expectations had been low, which was understandable based on my experience with the psychiatrist at the hospital. I discussed Denny's death with him, but only in a generic sort of way. We talked mostly about survivor's guilt and finding closure, but we never talk-talked about Denny, or Will, or specifically, my role in their disappearances. I just couldn't connect with him. Also, I couldn't get past his appearance. His face resembled an old-fashioned catcher's mitt—puffy and puckered around his darting eyes. His small, sunken mouth was turned down in a permanent scowl, and his voice was full of skepticism. And on the rare occasion that he gave me a chance to speak, I felt like he was rating my responses. My responses were never a perfect ten. At best, they were always a five or six.

Back at the house, I didn't stop to talk to Mom who was clanging around in the kitchen trying to get dinner on the table. "Hey, how did it go with Dr. Blume?" she asked. The hopeful expression on her face dissolved the minute I opened my venomous mouth.

"Fine," I said, bitterly.

"Just fine? Why just fine?" she asked. Her voice was laced with disappointment.

Mentally fatigued, I had no patience for her questions or disappointment. I just wanted to be left alone. "It was fine. I mean, what did you expect? Did you think I'd be cured after one visit?"

"Hey!" Dad said, his head whipping around like a vigilant owl, "don't talk to your mother that way!"

"Whatever," I said waving them both off. "I'm going to lie down for a while so don't bother calling me for dinner, I'm not hungry."

"Well don't sleep long. We're eating within the hour," she added, discounting my comment about not being hungry. Before reaching my room, I heard Mom ask, "Did something happen to upset her?"

My inability to confide in her bruised her ego. Hurting her feelings was yet another offense I could add to the lengthy list of crimes committed against the people I claimed to love. I should have mentioned to Ava that guilt and sadness were two emotions that we could just skip over discussing. I was capable of feeling both unequivocally. I despised my depression and how it jumbled my thoughts and feelings, but I hated even more how it impacted my relationship with my family. I didn't have a beef with Mom, but I had no desire to interact with her or anyone else. Shutting people out was easier than letting them in. Most nights, after the kitchen was cleaned and homework was completed, my parents and brothers congregated in the family room to watch TV or read. The four of them paired up like animals marching onto Noah's Ark. David, too old to snuggle, would instead sit really close to Mom on the couch, allowing some part of his body to touch hers. She was his touchstone, and by the contented look on her face, I could tell that she reveled in the fact that she was able to console and comfort her eldest son.

Daniel and Dad had their routine as well. Together they would squeeze into the oversized armchair and watch silly sitcoms until Daniel and sometimes even Dad, fell asleep. With the tops of their heads touching, they resembled a set of Siamese twins joined at the temples. I was always invited to join them for the family love fest, but I could never participate. There wasn't enough love to go around, or so I thought. Aside from that, the sight of Gus stretched out on his dog bed without Denny curled up beside him hurt my heart too much. My presence was toxic and I didn't want to inflict any more hurt on them, especially Daniel, who already seemed to hate me.

Daniel was a bed wetter until third grade. Toward the end of that humiliating stage in his life, he could manage the nightly cleanup without disrupting the rest of the household. He'd strip the bed, change the sheets and his pajamas and then crawl back into bed without anyone being the wiser. (Mom of course would find out the next day when she emptied the hamper in his bedroom.) But when he was much younger, no longer a toddler but too old to still be flooding the sheets every night, he'd peel off his urine-drenched underwear, slip on a fresh pair and then crawl into bed with me, David or Denny. As a courtesy, he never invaded the same bed two nights in a row. David and Denny were deep sleepers, so they usually didn't discover him passed out in their beds until morning, but I inevitably woke up each time he showed up. It was never the weight of his body or the sound of his shallow breathing that woke me, but always the salty, slightly maple syrup urine smell that still clung to his skin that woke me from my blissful slumber. My parents took him to all kinds of specialists and tried every home remedy in the book to get him to stop wetting the bed, but nothing worked. They restricted his liquids before bed, woke him up in the middle of the night to pee, but had zero luck. Then one day, out of the blue, he just stopped wetting the bed. After Denny's death, he woke every morning again to soaked sheets. He never peed when he fell asleep next to Dad in the chair though, and since Dad could sleep anywhere, many nights the two of them stayed there until morning.

One day before school, I overheard Mom talking to Daniel in his bedroom. Just as she had years before, she was reassuring him that he'd stop wetting the bed. "It's a temporary setback," she promised. "The doctor said that the stress from Denny's death might be triggering it." When she left his room, arms full of squishy bedding, I knocked on his open door and asked if I could come in.

"Hey, Daniel. Do you have a minute?" I asked.

He was sitting on his pee stained mattress in his underwear. "I guess," he said. He grabbed a towel sitting on the bottom of the bed and covered himself. "What do you want?"

"I just wanted to tell you that I'm sorry that this is happening to you again."

"What do you mean? What are you talking about?" he asked defensively.

"You don't have to be embarrassed. It's me. Everybody understands. You're just really freaked out now, but Mom's right, you'll stop." I took a few steps toward the bed. I wasn't going to hug him or anything like that because we didn't have that kind of relationship, but I wanted to tell him that I loved him. He looked at me as if I was some kind of piranha, even held his hands out in from of him like he needed to prevent me from coming any closer.

"What do you care? You don't give a crap about me or anyone else in this family. All you care about is your stupid boyfriend and how he left. He probably killed Denny," he said.

Daniel's comment stopped me like a fist to the face, but I deserved it. I knew my brothers were grieving, but I hadn't really stopped to think how his death had impacted them. Grief didn't seem to consume them as it had me. They still saw their friends and played their sports and went to school just as they had before Denny's death. I went to school, but for me everything felt surreal, like a dream that I couldn't wake up from.

I'd been vocal about not wanting to see Ava, but secretly I prayed that she'd be able to cure me. Like Mom, I suppose I had been too optimistic. I was an idiot to think that after one visit I'd miraculously feel better. My session did little to help. As a matter of fact, it had the opposite effect. It opened Pandora's box, and all the unpleasant feelings and memories associated with Denny's death descended upon me with a vengeance. I pulled down my shades and stretched out across my bed with my pillow over my head. And though I tried not to,

I recounted the events that unfolded the night Denny went missing.

24
Remembering the Night

The search for Denny began shortly after the two officers arrived. The entire family followed them from room to room as they opened closet doors, looked under beds and into any receptacles that were big enough for Denny to squeeze into. The basement took the longest because of all the boxes my parents hadn't unpacked yet. When they couldn't find him anywhere in the house, they looked in both garages. Surprisingly, the officers didn't appear outwardly concerned when their search came up short. They questioned my parents for what seemed like forever and kept asking them the same questions over and over, re-wording them slightly differently each time.

Did Denny have any reason to run away? Why would Denny have reason to run away? Was there a friend he played with that nobody knew about? Did he have any friends that he might not have mentioned? Was it common for him to take off without telling anybody where he was going? Did he always say where he was going or did he sometimes just take off? What exactly was he wearing? Describe the clothes he was wearing.

Their responses were pretty cut and dry and always the same.

No, he'd never run away. Maybe he had a friend that we didn't know about, but it was highly improbable. Yes, he was always running off without telling anybody where he was going. He was wearing his tie-dye vacation bible school t-shirt, jeans and his Carhartt jacket.

Reinforcing the gravity of the situation, a horrific storm began to unfold outside in the middle of their questioning. The wind blew hard, causing the entire house to shake. The rat-a-tat-tat of the clattering windows grated on everybody's nerves. I couldn't shake the image of loathsome children, with their greasy faces and flattened hands pressed up against the glass of the gorilla exhibit at the zoo, pounding away and antagonizing the bored primates.

We were all in shock. Rain and hail the size of golf balls plunged from the combative sky. The storm and sudden drop in temperature caused the remainder of leaves in the woods behind our house to fall like raindrops from a cloudburst on a hot, humid day. The next day, the ground and everything lying on it was covered in leaves.

Both the local and Detroit papers ran stories about his disappearance and then later, stories about his death. He had died of natural causes, but the events preceding his death are what left the police scratching their heads.

Word of Denny's disappearance had spread quickly in the community. People we never even met before showed up to help search for him. The police recommended that Mom and Dad not go with the search party, but Dad wasn't too keen on that idea. Mom sided with the police. "What if he comes home and there's nobody here. We need to be here just in case he finds his way home," she argued, repeating the words, *find his way home*, over and over as if Denny were just lost or had left of his own free will on some sort of far flung adventure. In front of the window in the living room was where she sat, 24/7 waiting for his return. The pink trimline phone, on loan from my parent's bedroom, rested in her lap along with a notepad and pen. She had been so certain that someone would call with information concerning Denny's whereabouts. Every call was answered on the first ring, but not a single person who called had any useful information.

It had been true what my parents told the police about Denny. He was always wandering off to a nearby friend's house, failing to let anyone know where he was going, but not in a million years would Denny leave and stay gone for so long. He usually showed up just about the time Mom began questioning why he wasn't home yet. He'd eventually slink in through the back door and make a beeline to his room. I guess he figured that's where he'd end up anyhow. He behaved just as Gus did after one of his all-day excursions in the woods behind our house, or down at our neighbor's place where they owned the sheep. Gus loved chasing after those fat sheep. After being run off by the owner, he'd come home and stand at the patio door whimpering and peering through the glass with the most pathetic look on his face. It was like he knew he had done wrong and needed to ask for forgiveness. Dad had no problem ignoring his apologetic stares, but the howling and carrying on was always too much for Mom, who would then convince Dad to let him in. "See how sorry he looks? He doesn't know any better," she'd say. Dad would give in and let him in the house. With his tail between his legs and his head practically sitting on the floor in front of him, Gus would slink off to his crate. Like our Gussy, Denny only came out of his room when Dad summoned him.

Once the organized searching got started, it took two days to find my brother.

Denny's body was found in the cavity of a hollow tree. Our neighbor, Mr. Schneider, and not one of the police officers, spotted Denny's tie-dye camp T-shirt sticking out from under a blanket of rust colored leaves that carpeted the forest floor. The foliage made it nearly impossible to detect the fallen tree that housed his body. After the last of the volunteers were rounded up from the woods, two police officers came to our house to tell my parents that the search was over. The look on their faces said it all. From the moment my parents realized that Denny was truly missing, they clung to the hope that he would be found alive.

The officer in charge, his name I can't recall, removed his hat and rested it against his chest. His gray, wispy hair stood erect and danced on top of his head like seaweed swooshing back and forth with the tide on the salty ocean floor. With his full face and bulbous red nose, he reminded me of Santa, a very sad Santa.

He cleared his throat and said, "John. Linda..."

Mom didn't let him finish his sentence. "You found Denny? Oh God, please tell me you found him."

It felt like eternity before he opened his mouth again to speak.

The night Denny disappeared, Mom had asked the same officer how many missing children cases he or anyone else in his department had ever worked. His answer had been none. Zero. Zilch. It was a loaded question, though there was no way Mom had meant it to be.

The police having no experience was a double-edged sword, a plus or minus depending on how you looked at it. A plus because no experience implied that that we resided in a reasonably safe town where nothing bad ever happened, so Denny temporarily losing his way wasn't altogether out of the question. It was a minus because the police department didn't have any experience in such matters, and maybe they didn't have the faintest clue how to track down a missing kid. The police in all the movies and primetime detective shows were always portrayed as *tough as nails cops* who had seen too much or had grown too callous to wear their emotions on their sleeves. After a long day's work, they went home, poured themselves a stiff drink and sat alone at their kitchen tables, drinking their sorrows away. Before turning in for the night, they'd creep into their kids' rooms and spend several minutes just staring at them and marveling over their ability to sleep so soundly because they didn't have a care in the world. Our guys weren't cool, calm or collected. They were visibly shaken.

Sad Santa started over. "John. Linda. We found Denny's body in the woods."

Mom went to sit down, but there was no chair. Dad caught her in mid-air.

Once she had somewhat collected her bearings she asked, "Well, where is he? I want to see him. I need to talk to my son and see that he's alright."

Dumbfounded, the two officers looked to Dad for help.

Dad cleared his throat several times, but when he spoke, his voice trembled. The burden of telling Mom had been foisted on him whether he liked it or not. "Linda, honey, Denny's not coming back. You can't talk to him."

"No, that's not true. There's been some kind of mistake, I'm sure of it," she said, sounding like a crazy lady. "John, tell him that it's not our son they found."

Dad couldn't say the words that she needed to hear because it was their son and he was dead out in the woods. My whole life I had believed that there wasn't anything broken that Dad couldn't fix. We all felt that way about him, but Mom more than anyone. No problem was too big for him to solve, until now. Mom grabbed hold of Dad's sleeve and tried pulling him toward the door.

"Our baby's still missing and we need to go find him because it's cold and he's hungry and tired and too scared to come home. Now do something, dammit! Why aren't you doing anything?" she asked, gnashing her teeth.

"Stop it! Stop it!" I screamed, trying to wedge myself between the two of them.

"Linda, please," Dad begged. "Please, listen to me. Denny's gone. He's dead."

Like the wicked witch from the movie *The Wizard of Oz*, she melted into a giant heap of nothingness onto the floor. It took both Dad and the officers to help her to her feet, but she was too weak to stand on her own. She leaned into Dad's body and buried her face in his chest, covering his sweatshirt with snot. I wanted somebody to console me, but nobody did. Through her tears she whispered to Dad in a voice loud enough for everyone else to hear, "Why? Why did we have to move to this, to this..." she couldn't finish. She was blaming Dad, which was ridiculous and unfair. Untangling herself from his strong hold, she ran to the kitchen and grabbed her coat that was hanging on the back of the kitchen chair. Dad followed her.

"Linda, where are you going?"

"To look for Denny. Damn those woods, and damn the move, and damn you!" Dad winced at her harsh words. "It was your idea to move out here to no-man's land! How could you let this happen?"

Once again, she melted. Dad was powerless against her condemnation and he too began crying. I hated the way she spoke to him. It wasn't fair of her to blame him. It was true that the move was his idea, but it wasn't like we were living in Siberia. We weren't exactly isolated, we had plenty of neighbors. I couldn't take it. I ran to Dad and wrapped my arms around his waist. He smelled of fabric softener and of Mom's perfume. I don't know how long we all stood in the kitchen crying, but Mom was the first one to stop. It was like someone had flipped a switch—crying, not crying.

"I want to see my son. Take me to him," she insisted.

The officers exchanged concerned glances before Sad Santa said, "As soon as the other officers are done taking pictures and taping off the area, his body will be brought out of the woods. It's quite a trek out to where he is."

Mom said that she didn't care if she had to walk a thousand miles. She needed to see for herself that the found child was indeed Denny.

"Linda, it's Denny. They're sure," said Dad, but Mom was already half way out the door.

I was left with David and Daniel, who at this point had no idea that Denny was even dead. Both had fallen into a deep sleep in front of the TV in the family room after lunch. They were the only ones able to eat anything. Casseroles and crockpots filled with bubbling stews and sloppy Joes lined the kitchen counter. We were running out of space in the refrigerator for all the food the neighbors sent over. After my parents left, only our neighbors and family and a few officers remained at the house. They gathered in the driveway and garage milling about, not sure of whether to stay or go. My aunts passed out Styrofoam cups of steaming coffee and hot chocolate and invited everyone to eat something before they left. Some of the neighbors fixed a plate, but mostly they just talked.

"I must've walked past that same spot at least a half a dozen times earlier in the morning," Mr. Schneider explained to a group of women who dabbed their eyes with the hankies provided by the ladies alter society from our church, "but didn't notice the flash of bright color until I was just about ready to call it quits for the day. I had to leave for work. The way I see it, the wet leaves stuck to that tree trunk like porridge to a pot, making it all but impossible to even notice that there was something there in the first place. An animal, maybe a dog, must've started rooting around in that very spot the minute we moved on to another stretch of the woods. I could only see a smidgen of his shirt but I knew it was him."

The police officers passed on the food, but they accepted the coffee and spoke in hushed whispers among themselves. I heard one of them comment on how peaceful Denny appeared. "Looked like a small critter hibernating in a den for the winter." He paused and took a long swig from his coffee before continuing. "Almost looked like he was just taking a little nap." His comment really got to me. I knew that he didn't mean any harm, but I didn't like that he compared my baby brother to a hibernating varmint. All I could think about was a picture in my science book of an Arctic squirrel sleeping underground with his body twisted in the shape of a doughnut and his fluffy tail wrapped around his skinny frame. The caption underneath it read: *This tiny mammal appears to be dead, but he's only sleeping. After a long hibernation, he will wake in early April.*

I wished the same could be true for Denny. I wished that we hadn't moved, but all the wishing in the world couldn't change the fact that Denny was dead.

25
What We Choose to Remember

My next visit with Ava came a week later. In between sessions, I spent a lot of time thinking. Not so much about what we discussed, but about Ava. She was what my doctor at the hospital called an impartial third party. My parents had their hands full dealing with my brothers and coping with their own grief. My girlfriends were sympathetic, but ill-equipped to give me any kind of guidance. Like everyone else at my school, they too seemed frightened of me. It felt good to talk without worrying that my words were further inflicting pain on the people I cared about. Because she wasn't personally vested, I knew that I didn't have to worry about what I said to Ava, or how I said it. I didn't hold back when it came time for the second session.

"You know, your comment about how I ended up in the hospital felt like—I don't know—like you were trying to make me fess up to something. You didn't even give me a chance to tell my side of the story. I thought it took months for shrinks to get to the bottom of things or to figure out how crazy someone was, but it seems like you had your mind made up about me before we even really got started."

"My job isn't to decide how crazy you are. As far as not letting you tell me your side of the story, it's important that we adhere to some guidelines. We must stick to the time allotted. Your time was up, but you're correct in your statement that I haven't heard your side of the story. Would you like to tell me about it?"

I expected more push back, but since she asked, I told her what I thought. "I haven't read the hospital notes, but I can only imagine how crazy they make me sound. I suppose if I had been Miss Klein, I would have been a little shaken up too, but I'm not sure that she's the most credible witness. She's very rigid you know."

"I've read the admission notes from the hospital and your gym teacher's version of what happened. Hers is very consistent with what the others at the school had to say, but you may proceed."

"It happened almost two weeks after Denny's funeral. My parents insisted that I go back to school. My other two brothers went back the day after the funeral. Everybody—my parents, the police and all the neighbors—knew about Will and me. My dad confronted Will's dad about the two of us a few days earlier. He forced me to go with him to Will's house. Once there, he turned into a crazed lunatic. He spewed obscenities and hurled accusations at the two of them that were totally unjustified. At first, Will's dad was sympathetic and apologetic. He assured my dad that if he had known about the two of us secretly dating, he would've encouraged Will and I to come clean, but his apology wasn't good enough for my dad who claimed that Will had somehow taken advantage of me or practically raped me. After several heated moments, Will's dad had heard enough. He told my dad to get off his property and to not come back or he'd call the police. Screaming and shoving followed. It was very scary and embarrassing. Eventually we left, but my dad had it in his head that Will was some kind of predator. It was awful. That first day back at school, I didn't see Will at all, but we weren't exactly on speaking terms anymore so I wasn't surprised. I figured he was just avoiding me. Half way through gym class, Shari approached me and asked if I had heard about Will. I had no idea what she was talking about. According to Shari Will had left the state and was living with his mom. She said that everybody was talking about it, even the secretaries in the office, but I didn't believe her. I was numb. Why had he left without saying goodbye? I knew why he couldn't come to the funeral, but why didn't he say goodbye? I had done nothing. He was the one who had hurt me. I asked Miss Klein if I could be excused because I wasn't feeling well. I'm pretty sure that the only reason she let me go was because she felt sorry for me. Ordinarily she would've told me or anyone else to go get stuffed. Anyway, I went to the locker room and splashed cold water on my face, but it didn't help. My heart pounded erratically like a jazz drum beat. I thought I was having a heart attack and tried to snap out of it by hopping in the locker room shower. I stood under one of the showerheads fully clothed and let the water rush down over me. You'd think that the cool water would have jarred my senses, but it didn't. I felt all fuzzy and dizzy, so I sat on the stall floor. Shari came into the locker room to check on me and freaked out when she saw me sitting there. I was so mad at her and remembered yelling at her to shut up because it really wasn't that big of a deal. The next thing I knew, Miss Klein was there. She turned the water off even after I asked her to keep it on. She wasn't listening to me, which really made me mad. When I tried turning it back on, she swatted my hands away from the faucet handles and told me no. "Daisy, honey. You've got to get out of the shower now. You're so thin and fragile as it is. You're going to make yourself even more sick."

More sick? What did she mean and why did she care? I remember thinking to myself. I kind of pushed her, but not hard, and turned the water back on. I remember Miss Klein screaming at Shari to go get help, but I told her that I didn't need help and that all I wanted was to be left alone. She didn't listen and started spouting off about how she didn't want me to get sick because the locker room was so cold and she begged me to let her help me out of my uniform so I didn't catch pneumonia. I responded with a stupid comment. I didn't even mean what I said and she blew everything out of proportion.

"What did you say to her, Daisy?" Ava asked.

If she read the report, then she already knew what I said. I didn't understand why it was so important that I say it, but I did. "I told her that I wanted to be left alone and that if I got pneumonia then maybe I'd get lucky and die, but I didn't mean it."

"And?" Ava asked.

"And what?" I replied

"What else did you say?"

"I said if the pneumonia didn't kill me, maybe I'd just kill myself. I said that I didn't have a reason to live, but again I didn't mean it. I was joking. You already know all of this. What's the point of all these questions?"

"And do you remember what happened next?"

What happened next was the basis for me sitting in her office rehashing the same old crap in the first place. It was all a big misunderstanding. "I've already explained all of this to that doctor in the hospital. Why are you beating a dead horse?" I was admitted into the hospital and placed on suicide watch for the next 24 hours and then I moved in permanently for a while. "Yeah, I woke up in the hospital all because I took a shower with my clothes on."

Ava opened my folder and began reading the hospital report aloud. It was accurate up to the part where I had zero recollection. Evidently, Miss Klein and the French teacher, Mademoiselle Renaux managed to coax me out of the shower. As they were drying me off, they said that my mood shifted from weepy and apologetic to hostile. I supposedly bolted from the locker room, past the front office and out the front doors of the school. The only part of their account that sounded vaguely familiar was the reference to the snow. The snow had already begun falling by the time I woke that morning. Ice crystals decorated my bus window, but they didn't completely obstruct my view. I remember thinking how the farmers' fields resembled giant slices of Texas Sheet Cake. Not the kind with thick chocolate walnut frosting, but the kind Mom made. Nobody but Mom liked the walnuts or the frosting itself, so she dusted her sheet cakes with powdered sugar. What I didn't remember was how the light, fluffy snow had turned into an icy mix around noon and turned the side streets into glistening sheets of glass. I didn't remember the bus nearly plowing me over either. The driver of that bus claimed that I darted out in front of him and froze in the middle of the street. He compared my deadpan eyes to that of a deer staring into the headlights of an oncoming car. It was his opinion that I wanted him to hit me. Ava finished reading the notes and placed them back into the folder and waited. She gave me the chance to refute the account, but I couldn't. I had no recollection of any of it. I had been hit by a bus and survived, but I couldn't remember any parts of that story.

"I don't know what to say. I don't remember anything beyond talking to Miss Klein in the shower," I admitted. It worried me that none of the bus driver's account rang a bell. "Why did the doctor in the hospital ever mention any of this? Maybe I am crazy if I can't remember everything that happened."

"You did talk about this with your doctor."

"I did?" I asked tearfully.

"Daisy, you're not crazy just because you can't recall every last detail of an event that took place during a highly stressful situation. Your mental faculties were skewed because of the trauma you endured. You've experienced a vast amount of change in a relatively brief period and it has taken its toll. It's extremely difficult for people to completely wipe out a bad memory. What you can recall is your brain's way of trying to help you avoid stress. Your psyche separated itself from part of that event as it was occurring to protect you. We call that a coping mechanism, but it's important that you move beyond the forgetting."

"If what you say is true, why can I recall absolutely everything leading up to and after Denny's death? I remember every conversation that Will and I ever had, but I can't remember everything that happened to me the day I snapped."

"You're just going to have to trust me with some of this stuff, okay?"

Strangely, I did trust her, though I barely knew her.

"Now, I need to ask," she said transitioning from one topic to the next, "Who is Will?"

There were still several minutes remaining in our session, but not enough time on the clock to tell her everything, so I stuck to the basics. I described how we met in eighth-grade gym class the school year before and how I behaved like such a dork that first day in Miss Klein's office. I told her some about the sneaking around we did because of my irrational parents and surprised myself by even hinting at the intimate side of our relationship. I didn't admit to anything too personal, but I shared with her that Will was my first kiss and that he probably would've been my first for a lot of things if I hadn't been such a prude. At first, talking about Will made me feel happy, but after a while I began feeling sad again. I missed him horribly and hated the way things had ended between the two of us. Just about the time when it would have made sense to touch on the subject of our breakup, my time was up. Ava concluded our session with an observation.

"As I listened to you talk about Will, I heard you make several self-deprecating comments. I'm assuming that he was responsible for ending the relationship, and that you've absorbed all the blame for him doing so. If you're agreeable, I'd like to talk more about Will the next time I see you."

I had planned on talking about Denny in my second session, but we didn't get around to it. During my next session, I told her all about Will.

26
The Light Under the Door

"Don't do it, Daisy. It's too risky," Kim had warned me.

"If your parents find out, you'll both be toast and you can forget about ever seeing Will again," Shari cautioned.

Neither one of my friends thought my decision to sneak out of the house was a good one. Even I thought it was a harebrained idea and probably too risky, but I didn't care. My desperation muddled my ability to think rationally. Sometime around Halloween, something or someone had been driving a wedge between the two of us. Anytime I hinted at the fact that something was wrong, he got defensive.

"Dang, how many times do I need to tell you that there's nothing wrong? Give it a rest already," he'd say.

"But I love you," I'd tell him, "You're not acting like you feel the same." At that point, if we were alone, I'd rest my head on his chest and turn my face up toward him in such a way that he had no choice but to kiss me. The kissing part was always nice, but when it was over, he went right back to being moody and I went back to worrying.

I didn't put up much of a fuss when he first told me about his plans for the night his dad was going to be out of town, but the more I thought about it, the angrier I got. Not at him, but at myself for being such a scaredy-cat all the time. Nobody I knew ever listened to his or her parents so why did I? I didn't tell Kim or Shari my ultimate plan. They wouldn't have approved. I had decided that I was going to go all the way with Will that night. For that to happen, I had to sneak out of the house. Dad announcing that he was leaving Saturday morning for his brother's cottage and wouldn't be returning until sometime Sunday was a gift and I felt like just this once, God was on my side. Getting around Mom would be a piece of cake because anytime Dad was out of town she retired early for the night. She'd say something like, "I'm crawling under the covers with a good book and not coming out until I've finished reading the entire thing." True to her word, she did just that, but passed out in less than an hour's time because she was fighting a wicked cold. Denny curled up next to her because he wasn't feeling the greatest either. David and Daniel were both over at friends' houses, so by nine o'clock, our house sat silent, like an empty office building at night. To be safe, I waited an hour before sneaking out my bedroom window. I probably could've just slipped out the front door without anyone hearing me, but my parent's room is on the front side of the house. Thankfully Gussy was at the lake with Dad, so I didn't have to worry about shushing him or the sound of his beating tail on the ground when I tried sneaking back in.

From the road it appeared that nobody was home. Not even Will's car, which he normally parked in the driveway, was there. A few days earlier Will had been rear-ended when exiting the mall parking lot, so his car was in the shop getting a new bumper. I assumed that Will had his buddies park their cars in the garage so it didn't look like he was having a party. Some of our neighbors were nosy. As I slinked down the long driveway toward his house, I began to have second thoughts but swallowed my fear and reminded myself why I was there in the first place. Our relationship needed saving. When I reached his front porch, I was surprised to find that the door was unlocked. As a matter of fact, whomever the last person was to enter or exit Will's house had failed to pull the door completely shut, so I was able to let myself in. I figured that nobody would hear my knock anyhow from all the way in the basement. Halfway down the steps, I ran into Shelley Hall, a girl from my speech class. She was new to our school and though I didn't know her very well, she seemed nice. "Hi Daisy! Everybody's downstairs. I'm grabbing a cassette from my purse, I'll be right back," she explained. I continued down the steps and rounded the corner to the main area of the basement. Leaning against the pool table with pool sticks in their hands were Denise and Ricky. Brian was hunched over the table in the middle of taking his shot.

Denise was surprised to see me, but her reaction wasn't catty. "Daisy, Hi! Where did you come from?"

"From home. The door was unlocked...I had no idea that so many people were here...Where's Will?' I asked.

I had to hand it to Ricky, he was fast on his feet. "Not sure, really. I think he might be in the bathroom." Just then, the door to the bathroom opened and out stepped Will's friend, Michael. Ricky quickly changed his story. "You know what? I think he might be in the backyard having a smoke. I'll go get him," he offered.

"That's alright. I can find him myself," I said.

Nobody, but Denise tried stopping me. "Daisy, don't!" she said. "Let it go, okay? Do yourself a favor and let it go."

For a millisecond, I considered following Denise's advice. I only suspected foul play, but if I snooped around, there was a good chance that my suspicions would be confirmed and then what? I decided that I couldn't live without knowing the truth.

A sliver of muted light along with the faint smell of Sandalwood seeped through the imperfections of Will's closed bedroom door. Ever since his stay in San Francisco, Will was all into Haight-Ashbury and everything associated with the counterculture movement. He bought a lava lamp, started wearing patchouli, and he developed a habit of burning incense while listening to bands like the Grateful Dead. Will was turning into a totally different person, somewhat of a hippie, but I didn't mind. I liked that he was different from all the rich preppy guys that I went to school with. When my reluctant knock didn't yield a response, I pressed my ear to the door and listened for any sound that would indicate who was in the room. I had just about convinced myself that maybe I was wrong about Will when I heard Stacy's muffled giggle and the sound of Will's brass bedframe squeaking. I should've left when I had the chance, but like a gawker standing on the side of the road, I couldn't look away. I had to see for myself, no matter how gruesome. I knocked once more, but with more urgency than before.

"Knock it off you guys and get the hell away from the door!" Will shouted. I knew his harsh words weren't directed at me, but I took offense and decided that I was done pussy footing around. In one swift whoosh, I flung open his bedroom door. In the center of his bed, bodies tangled like two fishing worms, were Will and Stacy. A sea of flesh flashed before me. Stacy's white legs jutted out from underneath Will's half clothed body as his hips moved rhythmically up and down. I gasped, catching Stacy's attention.

"Whose there?" she called. "Will, someone's in the room!" She reached around for the top sheet that was bunched up at the foot of the bed.

"God dammit!" Will yelled, freeing the two of them from the twisted sheet that Stacy had just covered them up with. He zipped up his jeans while searching for his t-shirt that was next to Stacy's jeans on the floor. He pulled his shirt over his head, all the while swearing. "What the hell is wrong with you dumb asses? You really need to..." He stopped ranting when he discovered that the dumb ass responsible for barging in on him wasn't one of his friends. Our eyes met, and for a moment I felt as if I were standing on the edge of a cliff debating whether to step off or to inch away slowly for more stable ground. The lump in my throat prevented me from speaking and the only sound I could muster was a pathetic little, "meh." I sounded like a bleating sheep, like a weakling.

Even in the dark, I could tell that Will was on the verge of tears. "I'm sorry, Daisy. Please, I feel terrible, don't hate me."

"Well, it's too late for that! How could you?" I asked.

"I don't know! I don't know! For days I've been racking my brain trying to find the best way to tell you, but I just couldn't find the words. I guess I thought that somehow you already knew and you'd break up with me. I don't know, but I do care about you, I really do. It's not you it's me. I don't know what's wrong with me."

I didn't feel the least bit sorry for him and I told him as much. "You don't care about me. All you care about is getting in girls' pants. I hate you, Will. You're just like the rest of them. You're just like your dad. You're a pig and I never want to speak to you again."

"Don't say that. It's not true. I love you."

I wanted to believe him, but I had too much pride.

"Telling him off felt good," I explained to Ava who hadn't so much as cleared her throat throughout the duration of my story. "But later, back home, I regretted saying it. It was over, but I didn't hate him. Not even a little bit."

"You didn't hate him. You loved him, but you were hurt. Sometimes hating feels easier than loving especially when you have no say in the matter," said Ava. Her empathetic words stirred in me a sense of gratitude I'd never felt before.

"Have you ever been in love?" I asked, glancing at her desk at one of the more recent portraits of her and her family, "I mean before your husband. When you were my age?" Though shorter and stockier, her husband reminded me of Fred Rogers from *Mr. Roger's Neighborhood*. He had kind, soulful eyes and a welcoming smile, much like Will's. I held my breath, hoping she'd answer my question. On more than one occasion she referenced her policy of refraining from disclosing personal information unless it held therapeutic value for her patients. "We're here to talk about you, not me," was her standard tag. To my surprise, she admitted that she had been in love once before.

"Well, what happened? How did it end?" I asked.

Considerable time passed before Ava answered my question. "Life sometimes forces your hand..." she began, but then paused. I figured she was debating about how much to tell me. "Oh, the details don't matter because the result was the same," she said. "Like you, I was left with a broken heart."

"Come on! Tell me," I begged.

Like Dad, I could tell that sitting behind the wheel was where Ava was most comfortable. Dad never let Mom drive. She wasn't a bad driver, but being a passenger made him uncomfortable. Ava was the same way. People put their trust in her all the time, but her putting her trust in someone was a different story. She slouched down in her chair and the poker face that looked back at me as I divulged my deepest and darkest secrets was replaced with an uncomfortable grimace, but I didn't back down.

"Well?" I asked, growing impatient. "Are you going to tell me or not?"

Ava nervously fingered the cuff of her silk sweater before inching the fabric up past her elbow. There, stamped on her arm, was a blurred number. It took a few seconds for me to register what it was I was looking at. I tried not to act too shocked, but the sight of it scared me. Ava bore the mark of a Holocaust survivor. For years I had been subjected to watching endless hours of public television because that's what Dad and my brothers liked to watch. They never grew tired of the black and white footage that revealed the horrors of the war, Nazi Germany and the Holocaust. All those subjects disturbed me, but also fascinated me at the same time. When it got to be too scary, I told myself that it wasn't real and was part of a long ago past. Like most children, I was naïve and believed that the tragedy of those times ended when the Allies defeated Germany. It never occurred to me that the survivors had to find a way to go on living. My interest in the subject wasn't really piqued until my parents, like millions of other Americans, became engrossed in a made for TV movie called, *Holocaust*. My parents let me watch it with them, but not my brothers. They were too young. I had nightmares afterwards for weeks, but once the initial shock wore off, I too wanted to be Jewish. It became somewhat of an obsession. I didn't want to stop being Catholic, but I wanted to be a Jew. To me, Jews seemed so much more devout and proud than the Catholics I went to church with. It irritated Dad to no end that every Christmas and Easter we had to arrive at Mass an hour early just to find a seat. He called those people who attended only twice a year *Chreasters,* a made-up word that many devout Catholics used to describe those who attended church only on Christmas and Easter. Jewish people seemed to embrace their faith in everything they did, not just at certain times of the year. They wore their Judaism proudly, or so it seemed to me then.

"You were in a concentration camp?" It was an obvious question, but I didn't know what else to say. I already knew that she was Jewish. My parents mentioned that fact before they broke the news that they were forcing me to go into therapy. After being released from the hospital, I was so happy to be out that I got pretty good at hiding how bad I was feeling. My parents hadn't been all that impressed with my doctor or his results, so they agreed to give me a chance at finding my footing on my own. I even spoke a couple times to Father Dan, which was pleasant enough, but really didn't help. Maybe they were playing on my fascination with Judaism by finding me a Jewish doctor. When I asked why they picked a Jewish woman and not a Catholic, Dad explained that she had come highly recommended and that her heritage had nothing whatsoever to do with her skills as a therapist. He then made some random comment about Einstein being Jewish.

"Yes, I was. Along with my entire family," Ava confirmed.

"But you survived. How was it that you and your family survived?"

Without blinking an eye, she said, "They didn't. Only I did."

I wanted to crawl inside myself for asking such an inconsiderate question. There were so many questions I wanted to ask her, but I was afraid I might say something stupid again. Asking her how many people were in her family felt like a safe question.

"In my immediate family, four, my mother, father, younger brother and myself. But let's not digress too much. You asked me if I had ever loved anyone other than my husband and my answer is yes. It's a rather strange coincidence, but I was almost exactly your age. My love's name was Heinrich. Much like your parents, my parents forbade me to date. They didn't even want me seeing Heinrich, though my father and his father taught together at the same university. My father was a serious, stern man, but very loving. He had high hopes for his children, and he expected my brother and me to excel in all areas that he deemed valuable— music, art and academics. There was no time for boys or frolicking. My brother was too young and didn't care for girls yet, but I was in love. Behind our parents' backs we carried on a great affair of the heart.

Heinrich's father was very wise, as were my aunt and uncle, and many of the other families we knew. They could see the political writing on the wall. Sadly, in addition to being wise and doting, my father was also too proud and stubborn, and he refused to leave his homeland, despite the rise of Hitler and the Nazi party. He was a patriotic citizen of Germany and didn't believe that it would ever get as bad as it did. Many families fled Germany, but mine stayed. My aunt and uncle managed to get to the United States. As for Heinrich's family, I had no idea where they went. His parents didn't burden him with any of the details surrounding their plans, but simply told him they were leaving and of course he told me everything he knew. Oh, we were foolish," she said, closing her eyes as she reflected on their innocence. "We spoke of running away together. Of taking to the woods to live as one with the wild animals who would surely take pity on us and shield us from the evils of our fellow man. Heinrich loved animals. He was a vegetarian at a time when very few people were. But our love wasn't meant to be. Heinrich's parents left Germany earlier than planned, and there was no time for him to get word to me. I never saw him again. I heard in one of the camps that the Nazis caught up with his family in the Netherlands." Not a single tear dripped down Ava's cheeks as she recounted the story about her family and first love, but my tears fell steadily. Again, she placed the box of tissues in my lap just as she had on my first visit.

"I'm sorry that I'm crying," I told her.

"You have no reason to apologize. It's a sad story," she reasoned.

"What happened to your parents and brother? Will you tell me about them?" I asked.

She shook her head. "I don't believe so. I've probably already told you too much, but you must know, I didn't tell you the story about Heinrich or my family to make you feel that your loss is somehow less traumatic, or to marginalize your experience. After the war, I came to the United States to live with my aunt and uncle. I met other survivors and some had stories far more harrowing than my own. I felt so guilty that I had survived and was living in a home with actual family. Many people lost every person who ever mattered to them, and they had no one to share their sorrow with. But I had an aunt and uncle and cousins, two boys who were far younger than I, to fawn over and give my heart to. They didn't replace my brother, but they were instrumental in teaching me that I was capable of loving again. If it wasn't for my cousins, David and Élan, I'm not sure that I would have given birth to my own children. A woman cannot be a fit mother if her heart is hardened by bitterness and hate. My Aunt Liora loved me as if she had been the one to labor with me for nearly a day, as my real mother had. And as for my Uncle Josef, my father's brother, he picked right up where my father left off. He made certain that I continued with the piano and kept my nose in the books. I was practically a full-grown woman by the time I reached them, but they babied me and tried to shelter me from all the ugliness in the world. As humans, we try to forget all the pain, but if we can't feel pain, then we cannot feel happiness."

"But I don't want to feel the pain anymore," I told her.

"Daisy, have you really let yourself feel it?" Ava asked. "I mean really feel all of it—the anger, the regret, the sadness and the shame? It's okay to feel everything. It's only when people fail to feel it all, love, sorrow, empathy and regret, that all human decency falls to the wayside. It's not healthy to get consumed with only one emotion. On the days when you feel pretty good, follow the flicker of light at the end of the tunnel, and you'll eventually find your way out. Sometimes we're only given a glimmer of what is good, but that flicker can be bright enough to sustain us. What other choice do we have?"

"But then what? What's waiting for me when I find my way out?" I asked.

"Life, Daisy, the rest of your life. But only if you're willing to embrace both the good and the bad. You can't have one without the other," Ava said again.

"But when will the pain stop?" I asked. "Will it always be there?"

Ava's eyes really were the windows to her soul, and in them I could see the truth, but I wanted to hear her say it. "Honestly?" she asked.

"Yes, of course" I pleaded, "Honestly. When will it stop?"

Her heavy, contemplative sigh was telling. "Never. It's part of you now, but with time, you will begin to heal, and slowly the pain will reside. Your heart will never be the same, but it will still work if you let it. I loved Heinrich, and when he left, my heart broke into a million little pieces. Later, when I got separated from my parents and witnessed first-hand the death of my baby brother, my heart broke again. My aunt and uncle taking me in, and then later meeting my husband and having my children, did wonders to help mend my heart. It's almost whole again, but not quite. I've accepted that there's a part of me that will always be broken. Think about all I would have missed out on if I had just thrown in the towel and wallowed in my sorrow. You lost your baby brother and a boy you loved within a 24- hour period. As humans, we experience so many wonderful, but different kinds of love, each one unique and specific. When one love disappears, another cannot replace it, but that love can attach itself to your heart and lead you to another place that is wonderfully unexpected. Love is love is love, and it is all good if we open ourselves up to take it in."

Denny died, but wasn't murdered. Somebody was with him when he took his last breath and tucked him away like nobody would miss him. Not knowing what he was doing or saying or feeling at the time of his death was probably worse than knowing. At least Ava knew the evil that robbed her of everyone she loved. Denny was the sweetest little boy in the world. There wasn't a malicious bone in his body, and the thought that someone may have been mean to him or hurt him in some way was too much for my heart to take. He was my brother and my parents' child. I wanted so badly to talk to Ava about Denny, but it didn't feel right after hearing about her family. It would have to wait until next time.

27
Can't Get It Out of My Head

Like an obnoxious jingle from a television ad or a snippet from a catchy song on the radio, the image of Ava's tattoo lodged itself into my brain. My fascination with the unsightly stamp grew at an alarming rate, much like the ivy that once blanketed the fence surrounding our old house in the city.

Mom had planted the invasive plant to disguise the rusty chain link barrier that separated our backyard from our neighbor's, but the ivy took over everything, choking out the light and causing nearby plant life to perish. Over time, Ava's tattoo became like that ivy. The image and what it represented consumed my every thought. In the middle of French class, while attempting to conjugate reflexive verbs, it occurred to me that my tendency to get undesirable images or thoughts stuck in my head was not really a new phenomenon, but an old issue that I had been struggling with for years. My preoccupation with the tattoo was reminiscent of the time when I got fixated on the lyrics of a song.

When I was a little kid, there was not much that I looked forward to more than the arrival of Saturday morning. Saturday cartoons and the sitcoms that aired throughout the day was the highlight of my existence. From early morning to mid-afternoon, I camped out in front of the television set along with my brothers to take in one show after another. Nothing, aside from Catechism, which my brothers and I were forced to attend September through April every Saturday morning for an hour, came between my Saturday ritual and me. But one unseasonably warm, spring afternoon,

Dad somehow convinced David and I to forgo *Fat Albert* and *Land of the Lost* to help him clean out the garage. Daniel and Denny were too little to help, so they stayed inside with Mom. David and I were gullible enough to believe Dad when he promised that it would be a lot of fun. Possibly it was the lure of ice cream afterward that really cinched the deal, but whatever the reason, I quickly regretted my choice. Mom was smart and wanted no part of the dust or the burden of deciding what should stay or go. She busied herself inside with light housework, which included baking bread from the starter that was passed on to her from a neighbor lady a few months earlier. It didn't matter that we already had multiple loaves of bread in the freezer, or that we had desserts coming out of our ears. Mom insisted on baking more. She had become obsessed with the starter that was being passed from person to person like a chain letter that no one would dare break. A smelly bowl of *Herman*, as it was oddly referred to, sat covered on our kitchen counter at all times waiting for Mom to feed it more flour, so it could ferment and grow.

The picture-perfect weather put Mom in a playful mood. "Hey, whattaya say I spin some tunes? Good music may just be the motivation you worker bees need to get that garage whipped into shape." The smell of baking bread and music wafted through the open windows of the house and tantalized our senses as we sorted, swept and purged. One of the albums on her playlist included The Beatles' *Sgt. Pepper's Lonely Hearts Club Band.* Everyone in my family loved *The Beatles,* but Mom more than anyone. She especially loved John Lennon because like her, he was a gentle spirit and musical.

I knew most of the songs on the album, the more popular ones that were played on the radio, but some of them I wasn't familiar with. One song in particular, *She's Leaving Home*, had a strange effect on me. I wasn't sure if it was the eerie sounding harp in the background or the paradoxical lyrics that triggered my mini-meltdown or what, but the song stirred in me emotions that I hadn't felt before. I couldn't explain it. Panic-stricken, I locked myself in the bathroom to try to sort it all out. I felt like I had lost all control. My mind and heart raced with gloom and doom thoughts. Mom must have heard me crying and stood outside the bathroom door trying to coax her way in or me out. "Daisy, what's wrong? Let me in. You're scaring me." I opened the door, but I had no words to describe what I was feeling.

"I don't know what's wrong with me. I just feel so weird inside," I cried. "That song, *She's Leaving Home,* it makes me sad. It's pretty, but it scares me. Why do I feel this way?" Not even Mom had any way of knowing what was wrong with me then, but she did her best to make me feel better. She threw her arms around me and squeezed me so hard that my back crackled and popped like crispy rice cereal.

"Oh honey, you needn't feel ashamed. That's what happens when your heart is as big and wholesome as yours. You're like your mother. You feel too much. Good music evokes feelings of happiness, but it can also make you feel sad and contemplative. You're getting older and experiencing what my mom used to call *growing pains.*"

Like always, her words soothed me at the time. But over the next few days that followed, as those same lyrics looped over and over in my head like a laugh track from a comedy show, her words did little to comfort me. Ava's ink stained flesh haunted me in the same way. I couldn't help it. I wanted desperately to rid myself of the image, but I found myself closing my eyes and reciting the series of numbers on her left forearm over and over again. I envisioned Ava concealing the tattoo throughout the winter, which in Michigan begins before Thanksgiving and stretches far past Easter, but wondered what she did during the spring and summer months when it was brutally hot and humid? When she wanted to sun herself at the beach or take a break from gardening and lean over her fence to visit with a neighbor? Did it bother her if people saw it? I couldn't exactly ask her. I didn't know her well enough. Perhaps it was as much a part of her as the tiny freckle above my lip or the strawberry birthmark Denny carried on the left side of his chest. Maybe she viewed it as a source of pride, a symbol of her strength and remarkable perseverance. But like that one line of lyrics, it was all I could think about. How could anyone do something so cruel to Ava who was so wonderful and wise? Like livestock in the fields waiting to be slaughtered, she'd been branded. Scrubbing it away with a little soap and water or slipping the painful reminder on and off her arm like the keepsake locket Mom wore around her neck, wasn't an option. In a way, both Mom's locket and Ava's tattoo symbolized loss.

From the moment Denny first batted his curled lashes and flashed his crooked smile, my parents were smitten with him. He was their golden child. To prove just how special he was, he was the only one to inherit

Mom's bouncy, loose curls and Dad's fair hair. Denny was a toe-head, just like Dad had been as a little boy.

My own hair, mousey brown and straight, was nothing special. The only part of me that resembled either of my parents then were my eyes, deep-set like Mom's and my nose—slightly upturned like Dad's.

Because my brothers and I understood how horrible they both would've felt about us knowing that he was their favorite, we kept our mouths shut.

By Denny's second birthday, his hair brushed the tops of his shoulders and curled around his face like a cherub from a Leonardo da Vinci painting. The thought of cutting his hair practically killed Mom, but for Dad, Denny's long hair had become a real bone of contention. Mom procrastinated cutting it and said things like, "Oh, the next time I take Daniel and David in for cut, I'll drag Denny along too," or "What does it matter how long it is? He's just a toddler and not in school yet. It's not like he's going to show up at kindergarten with hair like Rapunzel." The final straw was when a group of doting old women from our church mistook Denny for a little girl. Dad put his foot down and insisted that Denny get a *big boy haircut*. He, not Mom, took him to the barbershop. Dad left with a baby and returned with a son who'd never again be mistaken for a girl. He also came home with a ringlet of Denny's hair and a beautiful locket to keep it in. Mom wore the locket for practically a year before eventually taking if off. About a month or so after Denny's death, during my brief stint in the psych ward, the locket resurfaced.

"What are you wearing?" I asked. "Around your neck?"

"Isn't it beautiful? It's the locket Daddy gave me. Surely you remember it," she said, before taking it off and handing it to me.

If felt so light in my hand, but the weight of what it represented weighed heavy on my heart. I pressed the clasp to release the oval shaped case and pried apart the two halves. I wanted to pick up the small bundle of bound hair stashed inside it and press it to my nose to see if it still smelled of Denny's kiddie shampoo, but I didn't. It would've hurt too much if it smelled of nothing at all. *That you are dust, and unto dust you shall return.* Those were the words spoken at Denny's funeral. Denny was nothing but dust. The lock of his hair was all that was left to symbolize his physical presence on Earth. I snapped it shut and dropped it into Mom's lap. "Where's the locket holding my hair, or Daniel or David's hair? Why did you only think to save a lock of Denny's hair?"

"Honey, what do you mean?" she asked. Puzzled by my question, she looked to Dad for clarification.

"Don't look at him!" I yelled. "Answer my question."

Dad reared up from his seat. "Daisy, that's enough. Why are you trying to upset your mother?"

"No, Dad!" I fired back, "I'm not. I'm just asking a simple question. Gosh, why do you always take her side? You baby her just like you always babied Denny. Let her answer my question!"

Mom swallowed hard, but didn't cry, which was out of character for her. She wasn't much of a fighter, so most disagreements ended with her in tears. "I'm sorry if I've upset you. I stumbled across it the other day when I was going through my jewelry box. I suppose wearing it makes me feel closer to your brother. It's a comfort to me, I guess."

"Oh really? It just so happened that you were going through your jewelry box?" I demanded. "You can barely run a comb through your hair or brush your teeth, but you were looking for jewelry to put on? Give me a break!"

Mom didn't place the necklace back on. She slipped it into her purse. "Your Dad bought it for me because he knew I was having such a difficult time thinking about cutting Denny's lovely hair. You remember his hair, don't you?" I glared at her like she was stupid. "That's silly, of course you do," she said. "After Denny, your father and I decided that we wouldn't have any more children, which is a very difficult decision for women to come to terms with. It was hard for me to accept that there would be no more babies in our future," she finally admitted. "We hadn't planned on Denny, but after he was born I underwent a procedure to ensure that there wouldn't be any more babies. It was the worst decision I ever made, my biggest regret, and I fear that it's the reason why God took Denny and the reason why he's now making you suffer so terribly. You children are paying for the sins of your mother."

Dad found Mom's admission atrocious. "What the hell are you talking about, Linda? You can't possibly believe that. It's just not true." Dad couldn't stand for anyone, not even Mom herself, to imply that she was anything other than an ideal mother and wife. As for me, her candidness floored me. I had no idea that she had her tubes tied after Denny. It was hard for me to fathom that my uber-devout parents would ever go against the teachings of the church, but they had. All kinds of questions swirled in my head. Did Father Dan know what she had done? What about our old priest? Did she get permission from the church? Or did she just do it of her own accord and that's why she was riddled with so much guilt? The thought of her needing to prevent pregnancy because my parents were having sex sickened me. All I could think about were Stacy and Will and the night I barged in on them half-naked on Will's bed.

"Gosh! Gross! I didn't need to hear that," I shouted. Mom dropped her head in disgrace.

"It was a gift," said Dad, not touching either of our comments with a ten-foot pole. "Nothing more, nothing less. He had curly hair like your mother's. Why is it so hard for you to understand this?" He, not Mom was the one tearing up. "To be honest, I'm astonished by your behavior. Denny was our son. Your mother and I are in mourning and we're both doing the best we can."

"John, stop," Mom pleaded. "Daisy has the right to her feelings. We need to hear her out." Mom was willing to forgo her own feelings for the sake of mine and everybody else's. Normally I appreciated her selflessness, but in that moment, I wanted her to fight back. I wanted her to get mad and tell me to shut the hell up and to stop acting like a selfish little bitch, but she didn't or couldn't.

Saint Linda, I thought. "Did it ever occur to you how it made the rest of us feel that you had four children yet you only saved the hair belonging to one? Mom, you took Denny to the photographer every six months until he started school, but the rest of us had one lousy picture taken to commemorate our first birthdays. When the police asked for pictures of Denny you found a ton of just Denny, by himself. Denny sleeping, Denny at the park, Denny doing absolutely nothing that warranted a picture aside from the fact that he was your most prized possession and now the stupid locket. How many pictures do you have of just me lying around?" I asked. I was talking like a self-indulgent brat, but it felt good.

"You're right," said Mom, her voice brittle and croaky. "Please forgive me for being so careless. I had no idea that you felt that way. I know you probably don't believe this right now, but Daddy and I love all of you kids exactly the same. We've never loved one of you more or less than another and it kills me that you're hurting and there's nothing I can do or say to ease your suffering. If I could carry this cross for you, I would. I'd cloak all your unhappiness and depression and walk to the ends of the earth if it meant that you could be happy. I blame myself for everything, for all of this. I got too busy and stretched myself too thin and just wasn't paying attention. The music lessons, the scouts and the move were all too much. I'm a horrible mother. I wasn't minding the store and look what's happened?" The floodgates opened, which wasn't what I wanted. I had hurt her when my intention had been to show how she had hurt me.

"This is nobody's fault, dammit!" Dad cried. "It was an accident. Denny was sick and we didn't know it. Jesus! Nobody had any way of knowing."

I regretted my behavior. I wasn't angry with my parents, not really. Neither of them deserved the tongue-lashing. Truth was, I hadn't given that locket a second thought when dad first brought it home and if I had to put money on it, neither had Daniel nor David. I said what I said because I was so pissed about how awful my life was. My anger was ravenous. I felt like an insatiable character from a video game gobbling up everything in its path, but never feeling satisfied. It was exhausting bearing so much hostility, and no matter how hard I tried to express my feelings, my anger never subsided. There were so many things that pissed me off, but mostly I was just angry with myself. I was mad for believing that Will had actually cared about me and for being dumb enough to think that he and I could be like Mom and Dad—together forever. I should've known all along that he wasn't the guy for me. He was special, but not special enough and neither was I. "I think the two of you should leave," I said. "I'm really tired and I just don't feel like talking anymore."

Despite my bluntness and obvious desire to be left alone, Mom wasn't ready to leave. "But we just got here. Look," she said, reaching down into an oversized, holiday themed bag, "I've brought you a few things from home. This place is just so drab. Let's see... I've got your afghan that Grandma Nancy crocheted for you last Christmas, your fuzzy slippers, a few of your teen magazines, and oh yeah, a shoot from my Christmas cactus and..." Her eyes danced with excitement as she pulled from the bag a large, glossy box containing a 1,000-piece puzzle. "We can start working on it today if you'd like. We wouldn't have to talk. I know how you love puzzles. I would've gotten a bigger one, but I'm banking on the fact that you're getting out of here before the holidays. No point in starting something that we won't be able to finish, huh?"

In a blink of an eye, I committed yet another unforgiveable sin. I hurt Mom's feelings again. "I'm sorry, Mom. It's just... I'm not that into puzzles anymore. Maybe Daniel or David can do it with you."

Biting her lower lip, she said, "Well, that's okay, I guess, but I had no idea. When did you stop liking puzzles?" Mom and I had been doing puzzles for as long as I could remember.

"For a while," I admitted.

Mom placed the box back in the shopping bag to drag back home. Dad was disappointed in me. He couldn't look at me.

"Linda, I think it best that we go," he said. Mom stretched out her goodbye like I was heading off to war and she might not ever see me again, but Dad couldn't get away from me fast enough.

Later that day, my session with my patronizing psychiatrist was an epic failure. "So, how was your visit with your parents?" he asked.

I shrugged. "Okay, I guess."

"Why Okay? Did something happen? Identify your feelings. Okay is a lazy answer."

I wasn't in the mood for his introspective name-that-feeling game. "Nothing happened today that doesn't normally happen. It went exactly as I thought it would. I expressed my opinion and my mom got upset, which in turn caused my dad to get pissed off at me. That's pretty much how it always plays out with the two of them," I explained. "I guess I'm not allowed to grow up or have an opinion or ever express my dissatisfaction over anything. I'm expected to be their dutiful little daughter, nothing more, nothing less."

"Well, I'm not so sure I believe you," he said, raising his fuzzy, caterpillar like eyebrows questionably. "Your parents seem like two very reasonable people who have invested a lot of time and resources into making sure that their children's needs are being met. When you confronted them, did you have a two-way conversation or did you yell at them?"

"I'm not sure what you mean. I didn't confront anybody. We had a conversation."

"You're sure about that?" he said in an accusatory tone. "When your parents decided to extend your stay at the hospital, they did so to ensure that your depressive mood was stabilized, but also to provide you with the opportunity to sort through the enormous amount of anger that you're harboring. You don't make it very easy for people to want to be around you."

"I'm not harboring anything. What are you talking about?"

"Daisy, it's important that you stop lashing out. What else is bothering you? If you're not ready to stop blaming others and those people who just want to help you, then you're not ready to work on the real issues. What's the real reason you're so angry with your parents?"

Either way, he had it all wrong. I wasn't angry with my parents. I thought Mom showing up wearing the necklace without considering how it would make me feel was insensitive and so I told her. Didn't everybody want me to spill my guts? I was over it. "I'm not upset with my parents, but you're right in saying that I'm not ready to work on myself. There's nothing wrong with me. Why can't I just feel lousy? Is it a crime? I just want to be left alone for a while. Is that so wrong?"

"No, it's not a crime, but it's not healthy. You're choosing to confront your parents on issues that I'm not so sure you really care about. You can express just fine how you feel about insignificant things that happened years ago, but you can't talk to your parents or anyone else about what you're feeling right now. Anything that's too difficult or painful you avoid. You pick fights instead. You can't hide from your feelings. They have a way of catching up with you sooner or later. What are you feeling? Tell me what you're thinking!"

"You want to know how I'm feeling? You want me to be honest?" I asked.

"It's not about what I want. It's about what you need to do. You'll feel better if you get a few things off your chest," he said.

"Okay. I'll tell you how I'm feeling. I'd like to see a different doctor. I don't really like you and I don't believe that you really like me. I don't think that it's good for my recovery to have a doctor who doesn't like me. There," I said it, feeling better. "How's that for honesty?" I asked.

He didn't answer and I didn't get a new doctor.

28
Secrets

Ava's disclosure regarding her traumatic past really got me thinking about secrets and why most people keep them. A secret is generally thought of as information that remains unrevealed or information that is purposely kept from others. But it was my belief at the time that a new word needed to be invented to describe information that people kept to themselves or unknowingly filed in their subconscious because they had no clue of its importance or because they wanted to spare other people's feelings. Such was the case with our neighbor, Mr. Schneider.

Mr. Schneider lived next door to us in an old farmhouse that had been in his family for generations. Moving back to the farm, he once confided to my parents, was out of necessity and not desire. A fireman by profession, he had no interest in carrying on the family tradition, but he was compelled to move back to care for his elderly parents. When his mother passed and his father finally succumbed to the Multiple Sclerosis that he'd been battling for nearly a decade, Mr. Schneider never bothered moving back out. Nor had he bothered to get married or have children, which is probably the reason why he never got around to mentioning to my parents how frequently he saw me sneaking around all over the neighborhood with a boy who came from a dubious home.

When the police showed up at his door in the middle of a storm to ask permission to search for Denny in the abandoned buildings scattered across his acreage, he consented, no questions asked. He had grabbed his raincoat and high-powered flashlight and led the search. The gusting wind and icy rain made it practically unbearable to be outside, so Mom and the boys stayed back at the house while I tagged along with Dad to help look for him. For over an hour, we scoured the buildings from top to bottom, but found no sign of Denny. The police assured Dad that they'd take another look come morning, but in the meantime, there were other matters that needed their attention. Back at the house, my parents were instructed to find a couple of recent pictures of Denny. Mom knew exactly where to look and found five good close-up pictures of just Denny by himself. When Mom handed the stack of photographs over to the older police officer, Daniel ran to him and asked the question that everybody was thinking, but was too afraid to ask, "Do you think somebody kidnapped my brother? Is Denny really gone?" Mom didn't allow the officer to answer him. She clutched Daniel to her chest and assured him that the photographs were just a technicality.

"No, he hasn't been kidnapped. The pictures are for the police so they know what he looks like. He's not the only lost little boy in the world. When they find Denny," she said, putting an emphasis on the word *when*, "they just want to be certain that they have the right little boy. Your brother is temporarily misplaced, but he'll be home before you know it."

David's ears perked up in response to Mom's comment about Denny being misplaced. "Mom, should we pray to Saint Jude or Saint Anthony?" he asked tearfully. Mom clamped her hand over her mouth as if she didn't trust herself to speak. Dad answered David's question for her in a frail, timorous voice.

"It wouldn't hurt to pray to both, son," he said.

When the younger officer asked Dad to show him to the phone, the other officer sat Mom down and began quizzing her again. He jotted down a few comments before asking her a string of questions pertaining specifically to the woods behind our house.

"You know, it's not uncommon for kids, especially boys, to get the urge to go exploring uncharted land. They go off into the woods with their buddies or by themselves to see what they can find. Sometimes they take their BB guns and shoot at squirrels or rabbits or in the hollows of old trees. We all know how little boys can be. They're curious and rambunctious and not afraid of anything. Do you think Denny may have done just that—gone off into the woods and somehow got turned around? Has he ever ventured out to the woods by himself or with a friend? Is he allowed to go out there?"

Mom took offense to his line of questioning. "Of course, we don't let him go off into the woods by himself. He's seven years old. Sometimes he takes off to play at nearby friend's house without permission and he is scolded for his careless behavior when he gets home, but to my knowledge, he's never been out to the woods. Denny is permitted to ride his bike up and down our property line along the snowmobile and four-wheeler paths, but that's it. He knows to always check-in, but clearly, he doesn't always do that. We're not neglectful parents."

Mr. Schneider, who had returned to the house with us, had a different opinion on the matter. "Uh, I don't want to step on any toes here," he said, "but I've witnessed all of your children ducking in and out of those woods multiple times. Denny, never by himself, but always with Daisy and—" he chose his words carefully as he directed his attention towards me, "that friend of yours. That boy I always see you knocking around with." He didn't give the officer or my parents the chance to ask me the name of my friend before adding, "Come to think of it, I saw your friend walking in the field behind my house earlier this afternoon. Neither you nor your brother were with him. He was out there by himself."

Mr. Schneider's comments hung in the air like an undesirable stench.

The second officer had walked back into the room just in time to hear Mr. Schneider's comment. The officer asked, "Who's the friend your neighbor's referring to?"

Dad didn't let me answer. "Daisy, what the hell is Mr. Schneider talking about? Who did he see?"

Will didn't have anything to do with Denny, and I said as much. "He's referring to Will, but he wouldn't have anything to do with us not being able to find Denny. You don't think he was somehow responsible for Denny's disappearance, do you?"

Mom winced. "Don't use that word. Your brother hasn't disappeared and why are we talking about Will Banks? What does he have to do with you or Denny?

The cat was out of the bag. I had to fess up. "I'm sorry, but Will and I are more than just friends. We've been dating since last spring."

"What? How? What are you talking about? Did you know about this?" he asked Mom in a harsh, accusatory tone.

"Of course, I didn't!" she answered in an equally biting manner. Then she turned to me and asked, "How could you? What were you thinking?"

I wanted to disappear. My parent's faces were swathed in contempt for me. The officer who had been on the phone held up his hands and said, "Ok! Everybody needs to calm down and keep things in perspective. Flying off the handle isn't productive. Daisy, we need to know about Will and what you think he may have been doing in the field behind Mr. Schneider's house."

All eyes turned to me. My thoughts were swirling as I tried to digest all the accusations. I felt unsteady. It was like I was walking through a funhouse with distorted mirrors on a sloping floor. Nothing felt right or made sense. I needed time to think, but everybody was staring at me with squinty, condemning eyes. "Okay, just to clarify, Will and I are actually no longer dating. We broke up yesterday, so I haven't seen or talked to him all day. Mr. Schneider is telling the truth. Sometimes, to get some privacy or just to see each other, we'd take long walks in the woods or meet on one of the dirt roads with our bikes. Sometimes we'd let Denny tag along so he didn't rat us out, but you're all crazy if you think that Will would ever do anything to hurt Denny or has anything to do with him being missing."

"Denny's not missing!" Mom shouted, "Stop saying that!"

"So, you and Will were dating. Denny knows who Will is, so he wouldn't be afraid of Will if say, he ran into him somewhere. He trusted him, right?" Dad asked.

I understood what Dad was implying and I didn't like it, not one bit. "No, Denny would never be afraid of Will because he has no reason to be. What are you getting at?"

"He's not getting at anything," interrupted the officer. "Mr. Doyle, you need to leave the questions to us. Right now, all we know is that Mr. Schneider saw

Will at—what time did you say you saw him?" He asked Mr. Schneider.

"I didn't, but oh, geez, let me think—I guess it was after lunch sometime. A few hours after lunch, so around 3:00 or so," he estimated. "I didn't exactly make note of the time. I just remember seeing Will walking out of the woods and wondering where the other two were.

"Okay, and Mr. and Mrs. Doyle, you said you last saw Denny around the same time, right."

"Yes," Mom answered. "John had just returned from his brother's place. Denny was playing outside in the yard. He helped his dad carry in a few things from the car and went back outside to play."

For Denny's sake as well as for Will's, I had to talk about Will and the woods, which was totally humiliating. They wanted to know how many times we met, what we did out there and how often Denny went with us. I couldn't tell them the one thing that they really wanted to know, which was why Will was out there that day. I didn't have a clue. I told my parents, the police and Mr. Schneider everything else. When I was finished, the police seemed satisfied with my answers. Mom and Dad were mortified.

"You were smoking?" Mom asked.

"So, when are we going to question Will?" asked Dad.

The older police officer set Dad straight again. "Mr. Doyle, I appreciate your desire to help, but I've got to ask you to let us do our job. You may not question Will. Do you understand? He's a kid, and right now, we have no reason to suspect that he had anything to do with any of this. We'll handle it. You need to stay with your wife and family. We'll keep you updated. What's important now is finding your son. The longer he stays gone, the slimmer the chances of finding him becomes. For now, work on calling everyone you can think of. Like Mr. Schneider here, someone may have seen him, but didn't think anything of if it at the time. There's not a lot we can do with that storm out there, but we'll search for him first thing in the morning. Try to remain calm. It's still early and he may still show up on his own tonight."

But Denny never showed up.

29
Stormy Skies

Mom was never on time for anything anymore, which is why I pitched a fit when Dad announced that he was unable to take me to my next appointment with Ava. "I don't want Mom to take me. Why can't you just do it? No offense," I said to Mom, "but you'll be late or forget to pick me up altogether."

Like a shrinking violet, Mom assured me that she hadn't taken offense.

"Because I can't," Dad snapped. "Now stop! You're being ridiculous. Your mother's going to take you and that's final. You can't afford to miss any more school and I can't afford to miss any more work. Somebody's got to pay the bills around here," he said, eyeing the pile of unopened mail that cluttered the kitchen counter alongside the two bags of Chinese take-out that he had brought home for dinner. Prior to Denny's death, Mom had overseen the family finances and taking care of dinner, but after she missed mailing out a few important payments, Dad took over the checkbook. Coming home with dinner a couple of times a week was another new task he took on.

"But Dad," I complained, "she'll be late and you'll get billed for an entire session whether I'm there for all of it or not."

He refused to listen. "Let me worry about that. You're being difficult for the sake of being difficult. For weeks you've dragged your feet. You whined and carried on about not wanting or needing to see anyone and now, suddenly, you're griping over something that hasn't even happened yet. Trust me, Dr. Blume isn't going to turn you away if you're a few minutes late."

"Now she might have a point," Mom said after several minutes of listening to the two of us go back and forth. "Maybe you should just take her. I'd hate for her to be late." Dad blew off Mom's comment by pretending to be interested in the carton of chicken fried rice.

"Is that a mushroom or a piece of chicken?" he said, passing the carton of rice over to Mom to inspect. "Heaven forbid if it's a mushroom. You better get it out of there before David sees it. I specifically said no mushrooms in the fried rice."

"See!" I shouted, smashing my fortune cookie onto the counter, freeing the tiny sliver of paper that held my fate. "Even Mom knows that she won't be able to get me there on time. Ava has rules you know. I'm not her only patient. I can't just waltz in whenever I want."

"It's only chicken," said Mom handing it back to him.

Dad winked at her and called for the boys. While he waited for them to belly up to the table, he opened the bag of egg rolls. "Well, what's it going to be?" I asked. I hated when Dad purposely ignored me. "Hello—I'm talking to you. Can you hear me?"

Dad placed an egg roll on my plate along with a packet of duck sauce. "Enough! Your mother's taking you and that's that. You'll get there when you get there and if you're late, too bad. God knows we're breaking the bank for you to continue seeing her." His reference to how much my therapy was costing caught me off guard. I could feel my cheeks burn hot, but he didn't seem to notice. The old Dad would've never had spoken so harshly to me, but the stress of keeping it together for the sake of everyone else had really taken its toll. He bore the brunt of being the emotionally sound member of the family. I understood only too well that Denny's death proved to be the chink in his armor. The parents whom I once viewed as indestructible were falling apart before my very eyes, and I worried that, like me, they'd never be the same people they were before losing Denny. If I wasn't the same and they weren't the same, then who were we? My family had always been the normal family, as close to perfect as any one family could get, but in the blink of an eye, we were the family holding on by a shoestring. Dad put up a brave façade, but he was just as devastated as the rest of us.

Mom was taking me to my appointment and that was all there was to it.

Gray clouds, swollen with rain hung in the sky. Like the horizon, my mood grew murkier by the minute. Mom was more than fashionably late and I began to worry that she had forgotten me altogether. To avoid watching the clock, I ignored my better judgment and permitted my curiosity to drift in the direction of convulsive laughter that was coming from the bus parked in front of the school. I wanted to laugh and feel carefree too, but I didn't know how. Girls with high ponytails swaying from side to side and boys with their heads covered in bandanas sprinted across the lawn in their flashy track uniforms to catch the bus before the sky completely opened and the meet was officially called. Naturally, the sight of them made me think of Will, and how different everything would be if he were still in town. I had just about convinced myself that my life would be perfect, when reality came knocking. Absolutely nothing would be different if he were still around. Too much needed to be undone for things to be different. My inability to stop obsessing over all the "what-ifs" was the hurdle I couldn't clear. My mind buzzed with thoughts of "If only I had..." and regret hung like a noose around my neck. I feared that at any minute the chair would be kicked out from under me and I'd be left hanging in the town square like an outlaw from an old cowboy movie to be judged and ridiculed by angry spectators. A sign placed about my neck would list all my despicable crimes, and everyone would see what a horribly flawed person I really was.

Despite knowing that absolutely nothing would be different, I ran through my list of "what ifs" for the millionth time. *What if I had never become involved with Will in the first place? What if I hadn't planted the seed in Denny's impressionable head that the woods were somehow special or magical, a place like Narnia, a place where adults didn't go and children were free to do what they wanted with whom they wanted? What if Denny hadn't gone out into the woods that day, but instead remained home under my parents' watchful eyes? If he had stayed home and collapsed there, they could've rushed him to the hospital where he might have been saved. What if he had been resuscitated?* I wanted to be saved. What if Ava was my only hope?

My prayers for Mom to be on time went unanswered. I was pissed by the time she finally arrived. "You look hungry," Mom said, as I scooted across the front seat of the station wagon.

"What are you talking about? How does one look hungry?" I asked snottily. I didn't feel like pretending that I wasn't ticked. "What took you so long to get here? You're so late."

"Never mind, Daisy Mae," said Mom. "I'm here now and we've got plenty of time."

I hated when she called me Daisy Mae. It was so stupid. Why didn't she just call me Daisy Diana, which was equally as dumb? "We don't really," I said. "A hurricane is brewing and you know you can't see two feet in front of you when it's raining."

"Don't be so melodramatic. I can handle a little rain," she said. She knew that I was right, so she changed the subject. "So, did you eat all of your lunch? You barely touched your breakfast." Before I could come up with an acceptable excuse she added, "Pushing the food around on your plate isn't the same as eating, you know? That's the oldest trick in the book. That and slipping your food to Gus." I curled my lips, but held my tongue. I knew better than to poke a sleeping bear. She wouldn't let it go, though. "I think it might be a good idea if we talk to your pediatrician about your weight."

That got my attention. "I ate everything," I lied. "I ate my entire lunch. I even bought a brownie from off the snack cart if that makes you feel any better. Gosh! I hate when you act this way. You're such an alarmist."

"Okay, okay! Simmer down. I'm just worried that you're not taking care of yourself, but if you say you ate, then I believe you. I'm sorry."

"K," I said.

"But if you lose any more weight, I'm calling Dr. Li."

"Sheesh, you don't need to call Dr. Li. There are plenty of girls in my school who are way skinnier than I am," I assured her.

"Let's not fight," she said. "We'll just keep an eye on it. Okay?"

"Yes!" I agreed but only to silence her. Assuming that we had reached some kind of understanding, I switched on the radio and closed my eyes, but our truce was short lived. She had to have the last word.

"Okay, one more thing and then I'll stop badgering you. Tell me this, if you ate every last bite of your lunch then what all did I pack?"

I knew the brownie comment was taking it too far. She didn't believe me and I had no clue what she'd packed. All I knew was that she packed more food than any one person could possibly eat in a single sitting. Some days, when the guilt over wasting food was just too much to shoulder, I donated my lunch to Tom Clark, a boy whose locker was to the right of mine. He was a major jock, which meant he was always hungry. "Dang! Your mom packs a ton of shit," he'd commented on more than one occasion.

Mom was relentless. "Seriously?" I asked. "You want me to prove it? No way! You'll just have to take my word for it."

She didn't, but I kept my mouth shut from there on out. Arguing would've only put us even further behind schedule, so I didn't protest when she exited off I-94 and whipped into the nearest drive-thru to order me something to tide me over until I ate a real dinner. She must have really been worried about my weight loss. My family rarely ate at fast food restaurants. I choked down two chicken nuggets and nibbled on a few French fries, which pacified her for the time being. In addition to my depression, Mom was convinced that I was on the fast track to developing an eating disorder. It was true that I had lost some weight, but I wasn't deliberately starving myself or making myself throw up. I just didn't have much of an appetite. The death of the singer Karen Carpenter, who had died from heart failure caused by complications related to anorexia, was the basis of her obsession. She had loved the Carpenters and took the singer's death hard. Not quite as hard as she had John

Lennon's, but it had stayed with her for some time. From that moment forward, no slim-hipped girl, including me, was safe from Mom's scrutiny.

30
Skirting Around the Real Issues

On a dime, the weather went from bad to worse. A torrential downpour replaced the spring shower leaving sections of the expressway flooded. Mom was forced to travel at a snail's pace to avoid hydroplaning off the road. Though nearly an hour late, Ava was still at the office when we arrived.

"Be careful!" she called from the door. Mom and I held hands as we waded through ankle deep water across the parking lot. "By the looks of things, we might need to find ourselves a boat to get home. These old city sewers can't handle this much water."

I was so thankful to be out of the car and couldn't bear to think about the ride home.

"Ava, why were you waiting in the doorway?" I asked. "Were you watching the storm?"

"No," Ava said, holding a silver key ring out in front of her, "tonight is my late night. The receptionist left some time ago. Typically, she locks this outside door after the last patient of the day arrives. The only way in or out afterwards is if she or I unlock the door. I was in the process of checking the parking lot one last time for you before calling it a night myself." She then turned to Mom and said, "I hope the drive wasn't too stressful."

Mom stepped forward and introduced herself to Ava. "Hello, I'm Linda Doyle. We've spoken on the phone, but we haven't met."

"Of course," said Ava warmly, "What a pleasure it is to meet you." She held Mom's hand for several seconds after shaking it like the two of them were old friends. "Your hands feel like ice. Let me find something for the two of you to dry off with." She went into the lobby bathroom and came out with a stack of paper towels from the dispenser. "These will have to do," she said, handing each of us a few flimsy paper towels.

Mom dabbed at her face with the paper towel like she was blotting up a stain on the carpet. With her spindly fingers, she fluffed the hair that was plastered to the top of her head and unzipped and zipped her jacket as if she couldn't make up her mind whether to take it off or leave it on. "I must look a mess," she concluded. Mom was nervous. Her fidgeting hands were a dead giveaway. "Guess I picked the wrong day to vacuum out my car."

"What's that?" asked Ava.

"Oh, I'm just lamenting about how forgetful I am these days. I didn't remember to put my umbrella back under the driver's seat after I vacuumed out my car. The day just got away from me somehow. Sorry for rambling on and on. I guess I'm inarticulately trying to apologize for being so late."

"Oh," said Ava, waving off her apology, "Don't be so hard on yourself. Seems like I never have mine when I need it either. Hopefully you didn't wash the outside of your car."

"Pardon?" said Mom.

"Oh, it's silly, really. My husband claims that the only way to guarantee rain is to wash your car. He swears up and down that it rains every single time he takes the car through the carwash. I guess today would've been a lousy day to wash a car," said Ava.

"Oh yes," Mom agreed. "And by the way, I left a message for you with your receptionist. Did you get it?" she asked.

"Yes, I did, but we'll have to talk after Daisy's session if that's okay," Ava explained.

Her office was stuffy, which felt good to me, but Ava removed her sweater and draped it around her small shoulders like a preppy schoolgirl. "I'm a little warm, but you're probably chilled from the rain. I can make you some tea if you'd like. I'm still sipping on a mug from earlier. It's probably cold by now."

"Nah, I'm good," I said. "We should probably get started."

From where I sat, I had the perfect view of Ava's tattoo. Every time she raised and lowered her arm, it flashed before my eyes like a neon sign. It took every ounce of willpower I had not to allow my gaze to fix on it the entire time. I tried focusing on something else in the room. Sniffing the air, I said, "Hey—It smells good in here. Like flowers or something."

"Hmm," Ava said, confirming my observation. "I suppose it does. So, how are you feeling today, Daisy? How was school?"

Uninterested was my attitude toward school, and everything else for that matter, but I knew Ava would take issue with such an indecisive response. As far as I was concerned, school was the least of my worries. I didn't want to go, but since I had no say in the matter, I sucked it up and went. It wasn't as bad as it had been just after Denny's death. Most of the students and teachers no longer looked at me like I was some kind of freak show attraction. Mostly I felt invisible and indifferent. School was fine, or as fine as it was going to be for the time being. I wasn't socializing with Kim and Shari yet outside of school, but at least we were talking again. Most days we ate lunch together, but some days, when I felt like the walls were closing in on me, I'd skip lunch altogether and hide out in the library where I pretended to read. There was no food permitted in the library, which probably contributed to my recent weight loss. I eventually gave in and answered Ava's question. "School's the same old same old. I hate that place."

Ava frowned. "You hate it? Hate's a pretty powerful word."

"Yeah," I said. "I guess." Instead of elaborating on my feelings about school, I commented on the beautiful glass bowl that had recently been placed on her coffee table next to her two-sided clock. "Mm, what's this?" I asked, lifting the bowl to my face. It was filled with what looked like dried fruits, flowers and cinnamon sticks. "Can you eat it?"

"It's potpourri and no, you can't eat it," said Ava. "You'd get sick."

"Potpourri?" I'd never heard of it. I studied the contents of the bowl more carefully. "Oh, I get it. It's kind of like the stuff inside the little pillows that you put in your dresser drawers to keep your clothes smelling nice, right?"

"Yes, it's sort of like that," said Ava. "Those are called sachets." She leaned forward and fished out a shriveled-up piece of orange rind from the mix and held it to her nose. "My mother used to have bowls of this sitting out around the house when I was a girl. It wasn't quite as aromatic because she made hers from scratch with dried flowers and herbs, but it smelled quite lovely. I suppose it's easy enough to make, but I've never tried."

"Where did you get it?" I asked

"Last question," she said, giving me a curious stare. "My husband found it in a little boutique he stumbled upon while out in California for his last medical conference."

California? I wanted to ask. *Did he see Will?* Instead I said, "I like it. It smells a lot like you. Not that you smell like cinnamon or anything like that, but your perfume is similar. I like how you smell. What kind of perfume do you wear?"

She cocked a brow. "If there's time, which there probably won't be, I'll answer your questions later. Deal?" I nodded. "I'm sensing that there are more pressing issues that you'd like to discuss. You seem agitated."

"Oh yeah? Like how? How do you know?" I asked curiously.

"You're stalling. You've mastered the art of avoiding uncomfortable conversations." The doctor in the hospital had accused me of the same thing. He was right, but he was also an idiot.

"Okay! Gosh! Sorry that I'm curious about your life," I said, trying to make Ava feel guilty, but it didn't work. Ava wasn't a pushover. "So maybe we should just pick up from where we left off. You were telling me about how I'd be feeling better again—like really soon."

"Okay, good idea," Ava concurred. "Our last visit ended on what I believe to be a very positive note. You asked a scary question regarding your recovery and I provided you with a frank and equally scary answer. You'll never completely get over the loss of your brother, not entirely. I'm not going to lie to you. For some time, it will be difficult for you to think of Denny or Will without thinking of the other, but..."

Her words were like a fishing line and I was like the fish on the other end being yanked out of the water. They pulled me to my feet. "Great! That's not what I wanted to hear."

Ava titled her and said brusquely, "Sit down and let me finish, please. You can't look at your recovery as a now or never situation. You've got to look at it as a work in progress. You'll have good days and bad days. You'll always look back, but not for as long and not as often. You'll need to make a concerted effort to live in the here and now. Stop asking why and stop expecting the world to provide you with a suitable answer. Sometimes there is no suitable answer, and so you must forge a new path. What we're doing in therapy is no easy task, but there's no avoiding it."

Ava was right and I knew it, but sometimes I didn't feel like dealing with my feelings. I wanted nothing more than to wake up in the morning and think about stuff that used to matter to me, like Mom's blueberry pancakes or my pastel days-of-the-week underwear and which pair I'd be wearing that day. I would've said that I longed for the days when things were easy and carefree, but the truth of the matter is that I was never "foot loose and fancy free," as Mom liked to say. Even before Will and the death of Denny, I struggled to find balance with my emotions. "What does my Mom want to talk to you about?" I asked, not quite ready to talk about Will or Denny. Ava wasn't cross at me for changing the subject.

"Like most parents, your mother wants feedback about your progress," Ava explained.

Her explanation seemed reasonable enough, but Ava didn't know Mom. "Oh great, so this is the part where you tell her everything I ever told you, right?" I asked.

Ava shook her head. "No, no! What you and I talk about is confidential. I'd never reveal anything to your parents that we've talked about without your consent. I'll only share with her an overall summation of your progress and lay out for her your continued treatment plan, but nothing else. Your confidences are safe with me."

"You don't know her like I do. She'll push and push until you spill all my secrets. She has a way of getting people to talk. She's worse than the Gestapo," I said. I regretted my reference to the Nazi secret police as quickly as I said it and I told her so. "Aw crap, Ava. I'm sorry. That was a really stupid and insensitive thing to say, especially to someone like you."

"Why?" she questioned. "It's true. The Gestapo was relentless when interrogating their detainees and getting people to talk. Admittedly, mothers are equally as skilled because most will stop at nothing to protect their children, but I'm a pretty tough nut to crack. I can handle your mother, okay? You mustn't worry. So, what's on your mind today? Did something out of the ordinary happen?"

I did have a splitting headache, but there was more to it than that. I was fed up with feeling that my life was over while all the other freshmen were having the time of their lives. I was jealous, and tired of being a bystander. It sucked. "The car ride here was bad. My mom's a horrible driver. Not all the time, mostly when it's raining or snowing. She's just so nervous all the time. She's a worry wart."

"She's a parent," Ava corrected me.

"Yeah, well I'm not going to parent like she does if I ever have kids someday."

Ava's ears perked up. "Do you like children? Would you like to have some when you're older and married?"

I hadn't really thought about it before. "I suppose, but after the whole Denny thing, who knows?"

"You mean because he died?" asked Ava.

"Yeah and how he died," I said.

"Would you like to talk about your brother?"

I did, but I didn't. "You probably already know most of the story, don't you?"

"I know some, but I'd love to hear about your brother from you. We don't have to talk about his actual death if you're not ready."

I could feel the tears forming in my eyes. "I'm not sure if I'll ever be ready."

"It might help if you just let it out, Daisy. It'll hurt, but what do you have to lose at this point?"

I told her about Denny.

31
The Scream

"Denny's body was found in the woods. It wasn't left out on the cold ground for animals to mess with. It was stashed in the trunk of a fallen, rotten tree on a bed of crunchy leaves."

"Stashed?" Ava asked. "You mean hidden?"

"Yes, hidden. The police said that whoever was with him went to great lengths to make sure that his body was properly tended to before tucking him away. Whoever was with him did a decent job hiding him too. His shoes were tied and his shirt was smoothed out. It was tucked into his pants. My brother never tied his shoes, unless Dad was around to pester him. Dapper Dan was wasted on Denny."

"Dapper Dan?" Ava asked. "Who's he? His friend?"

"No! Seriously, you don't know who Dapper Dan is?" I asked. I was surprised since she had kids that she didn't know who he was. Ava shrugged, so I explained. "Well, he's a little cloth doll for boys—I had the girl version—Dressy Bessy, Dapper Dan's sister. Anyway, the dolls teach little kids how to zip, tie and button. Denny learned to do all those things for his doll, but when it came to dressing himself, he didn't bother zipping, tying or buttoning anything. All those things took time and Denny couldn't be bothered. He was perfectly fine with looking like a hobo."

"I understand," said Ava, "please continue."

"Well, aside from what he was wearing, he looked almost identical to how he looked at the funeral parlor. You know, in his coffin. His arms were folded across his chest and his hair was swept over to one side. For once he didn't look like the Shaggy D.A."

"The Shaggy who? I'm sorry, but I'm not following you." Sometimes talking to Ava was a pain. She wasn't up on American pop culture.

"Never mind about that. What I mean is that there were no bruises on his body. No injuries. The police said that his body showed zero signs that he had been struggling or was physically harmed in any way. Whoever was with him took care of him. He even had his rock in his hand."

"Rock? I don't get it. Was the rock some kind of clue?"

"No. At first the police were hopeful that maybe it was, but it wasn't. Will had given him that rock earlier in the summer. It was silly, but Denny carried it around with him everywhere. He called it his lucky rock. It was shaped like Michigan. When the police mentioned it to my parents, I knew right away what they were talking about and explained to them how it came to be in Denny's possession. They did find something else on Denny's body that I couldn't explain."

"And what was that?"

"They found a note. A note from Will was in the back pocket of Denny's jeans."

"Did the note hold any information that helped the police investigation? Was it important or relevant to the case?" Ava asked.

"The note was important, but only to me. That note was everything. It was the only proof I had that Will did still love me."

Ava maintained her impenetrable composure, but I could tell that she was having a difficult time following my choppy rendition of what happened to my brother.

My story didn't make any sense because I wasn't making sense. My thoughts were a scrambled mess. I did my best to explain. "The note had nothing to do with the case, but it was important to me. You see Will had passed the note to Denny to give to me, but I never saw it. Denny must've shoved it in his pocket and forgotten all about it. When Dad read it, he just went nuts."

"I'm sorry, Daisy, I'm confused. So, the note had nothing to do with Denny's death either?" I couldn't go on with my story because my brain suddenly started feeling all fuzzy. *Oh God, please don't let this happen now!* I thought. Sweat sprouted from my forehead. The left side of my face went numb, while squiggly flashes of light bounced in my peripheral vision. I covered my face with my hands as tears flooded my eyes. "What's happening to me? Make it stop! Please make it stop!" Suddenly I couldn't catch my breath. I was gasping for air.

Like a mother lioness, Ava leapt onto the couch and grabbed me by my shoulders and said firmly, "Listen to me. You're not going crazy and nothing bad is going to happen to you here in my office. I won't let it. I'm here, right next to you, but I need you to do something. Can you do something for me?" She asked, wiping the tears from my face. I nodded because I couldn't speak.

"Just close your eyes and concentrate on my voice. Pretend that you're a balloon and just let yourself float to the ceiling. It takes no effort."

I gasped in and out loudly and only one squeaky word came out, "Scared."

"I know. I know you are, but you're safe." In time, my breathing slowed down. "That's it," she said, urging me to continue to take healthy, healing breaths. "Feel the air filling your lungs and supplying your body with everything it needs. Breathe in and breathe out. Good. Keep doing what you're doing. You've got a handle on this breathing thing. You're in control." Squeezing my eyes shut even tighter, I focused on her soothing voice. "Are you ready to continue with your story?"

"I think so, but is it okay if I keep my eyes shut? These lights are hurting my eyes."

"Go ahead and keep them shut," said Ava, taking my hand and giving it a reassuring squeeze. Without asking her permission, I leaned into her and rested my head on her shoulder. She let go of my hand and wrapped both arms around me. Her hug was warm and calming, just like her Mother Earth smell. It was the first time anybody had touched me since the funeral and it felt so good. After Denny's Mass, I stood with my family in the receiving line to thank everyone who had come to pay their respects. I must have hugged over a hundred people that morning, but not for a single second did I feel consoled. I couldn't feel anything. The two people I wanted to embrace had left me and weren't coming back. Will and Denny's absence left a gaping hole in my heart.

With my eyes sealed, I continued my story. "The night Denny went missing, Mr. Schneider came back to our house after helping us search his property. He explained to the police that he had seen Will and me many times, and he had seen Will and me with Denny several times, and that he'd seen Will earlier in the day back behind his house. I'm not sure what questions the police asked Will later that night or the next day, but they must have been satisfied with his answers because they didn't question him again until after Denny's body had been found. In Denny's hand they found the rock and in his pocket a note from Will. The police naturally went back and questioned Will for a second time, but again they felt his explanation was legit. Will admitted to seeing Denny the day he went missing. That's when he passed him the note. He knew he couldn't call me or just stop by and he had a hunch that Denny would be outside playing and he was right."

"What did the note say?" asked Ava.

"Among other things that I'll never know, he asked me to meet him in the orchard behind Mr. Schneider's house at three o'clock, but because I never saw the note, I never knew that Will had been waiting there for over thirty minutes to talk to me. He knew better than to knock on the door. My parents would've let him in, but they wouldn't have left us alone and unsupervised. We needed to talk."

"So, you never actually read his note?" asked Ava.

"No, only Dad read it. To this day I can't believe that he did that. He didn't need to. It was such an invasion of my privacy. It was a note to me from Will, for my eyes only and had nothing to do with Denny. Even the police told him that. I felt so humiliated, but also ashamed for even caring about what the note said in the first place. Dad was so smug after he read it. Do you know what he said to me after handing it back to the police officer?"

"No, I don't. I'm sorry. That must have felt like a complete violation of your privacy," said Ava.

"He looked at me and said, 'He's a shit bird. You're better off without him.'"

When I finally opened my eyes again, Ava was staring at me.

"Daisy, what happened to your brother?"

I wished more than anything that I could tell her, but nobody, not even the police were one hundred percent certain about all that happened that day. The only concrete facts came from the autopsy. Denny died of natural causes related to an undiagnosed heart defect. It was something he was born with, but because he never displayed any of the telltale symptoms associated with having a heart defect, nobody caught it. "All we know for sure was that poor Denny's little heart gave out that day. He was playing in the woods and it just happened. The doctors said that he most likely didn't feel a thing. His death might have been prevented if only the doctors had known. My mom really lost it after hearing that. She beat herself up. She swore up and down that she should've known that he was sick and that she had missed all the signs. Denny was a picky eater. He usually wanted to skip eating altogether or ate very little at meals. He ate like a bird and was small for his age, but the doctors never expressed concern about his size so Mom never worried. But the sign that she kicked herself for missing the most was how Denny would go from 100 miles per hour to zero at the drop of a dime. He didn't fall asleep as much as he just collapsed. It was like he had narcolepsy or something. We all thought it was so funny at the time. Mom blamed herself, but I blamed me. It was my fault and nobody else's."

"How? How was it your fault? How could you have saved him? Are you a super-hero? Are you *Wonder Woman*? What do you think you could've done to prevent him from dying?" Ava asked.

"I don't know. Something."

"You can't possibly believe that. It's neither your mom's fault nor yours. Everything you just described could apply to any child. My own children were picky eaters and scrawny and like Denny, they played from sun up to sun down. My youngest would sometimes fall asleep at the dinner table. By the end of the day, he couldn't keep his eyes open long enough to eat sometimes, but neither he nor any of my other children had heart defects. And if they had, I wouldn't have known unless someone had told me. As for it being your fault, that's nonsense. You think because he went out to the woods with you and Will that you are somehow responsible? He was sick and nobody knew it—end of story! Why do you insist on taking the blame?"

"Why?" I couldn't believe that she had to ask. "Because somebody has to. It's got to be someone's fault and it's not Mom's. She's too good and things like this don't just happen for no good reason. God let Denny die because somebody did something wrong and that somebody was me. I was selfish and too wrapped up in my own wants to be appreciative of the life that I had."

"How so? What did you do that was so selfish? You don't seem like a selfish girl. Trust me, I've met many, many selfish girls over the years. All I ever hear from you are comments about how you disappointed this person or hurt that person, or how you should've done something differently. My goodness! It must be exhausting trying to be so perfect all of the time."

"I'll tell you what I did. I had a perfect family, a perfect boyfriend and an all-around perfect life, but I got too greedy and wanted too much and look what's happened! I'm being punished, and as a result, my entire family is being punished too."

Ava shook her head. "No! You're going to have to do better than that. If what you say is true, that God punishes people because they're selfish and do bad things, then why did God allow so many of my people and my entire family to be murdered? What sin did they commit? What were millions of people atoning for, and why on Earth would he send a sadistic mass murderer to execute his plan? Why were some spared and so many others taken?"

"I don't know! I don't know!" I cried. "I just know that everything in my life was going just fine when I was following all the rules and doing what the adults told me to do. It wasn't until I started growing up and met Will and started making decisions for myself that everything started to fall apart.

"You grew up? You're growing up and becoming an adult and Denny will never be able to? Is that what this is about?" Ava asked.

I didn't want to answer her questions. I was done. I jumped off the couch and ran to the door to leave, but Ava followed me.

She wedged her body between the door and me and said, "Sit down!"

"No! I don't want to!"

"Where are you running to?" You're at a crossroads. You're in a real pickle, aren't you? You won't allow yourself to move forward, but you can't move back either."

"I don't know! Just let me out! If you don't, I'll scream!" I threatened.

"Good! Go ahead," Ava encouraged. "I wish you would! You'll feel a lot better if you do."

"You're kidding me, right?" I asked.

"I'm not," she said coolly.

The actual scream lasted only a few seconds, but it felt amazing. Years of pent up emotions, fermenting since I was a little girl, spilled out of me in a cry that rivaled that of any scream queen from the grizzliest of horror films ever made. Within seconds, Mom was pounding on Ava's door.

"Daisy!" she called. "It's Mom. Are you okay? Dr. Blume, what's going on in there? Let me in."

Ava cracked her door open just wide enough to peek her head through. "Everything's okay," she assured her. "Daisy's fine. Trust me. Please return to the waiting room and I'll be with you shortly." Mom refused to leave until she heard it straight from the horse's mouth, the horse, of course, being me.

"I'm sorry I scared you, but I'm okay. Honest."

Ava led me back to the couch where we sat. "It feels good to lose control, doesn't it?" she asked. It did, but I wasn't sure how long the rush would last and I didn't want to ruin it by thinking about it too much. "It's therapeutic to relinquish some of that rage."

"Yeah. I suppose," I said weakly.

"Oh, come on," she urged. "Saying that it felt great, or that you feel better in this moment, isn't going to jinx you."

My eyes widened in disbelief. "I was just thinking that very thought. How did you know?"

"I know because I was once you. If happiness shined its sweet face on me one day, I was certain that sadness would greet me the next. When I first met my husband at the university, I thought he was just another simple, overindulged American. I resented his casual demeanor. *Why should anyone be so happy all the time?* I thought. He was relentless in his pursuit of me, but I barely gave him the time of day until we had a few classes together. One day, we were paired up to work on a project. It didn't take long for me to discover that he was quite likable. His positivity was like a magnet and I was drawn to it. Though also a Jew, he was American born, so I didn't believe that he was capable of truly understanding anything I had experienced. I was certain that there was no way he could relate to my pain. How could he? I never confided in him about my experiences during the war, and I rarely talked about my family. Initially, my response when he prodded me was to push him away.

Over a short period of time, we fell in love. I was so happy, but I lived in constant fear that it would all be taken away from me at a moment's notice. And one day, it nearly was. He broke up with me. I was stunned because it was so out of the blue. Naturally, I demanded to know his reasons. He wasn't honest at first. His excuse had been medical school. Having a girlfriend and going to school was just too much to balance, or so he said. After much prodding, I was finally able to get him to admit the real reason why he was ending our relationship. He said that he couldn't see it working out between the two of us in the long run. A son of a Rabbi, he'd marry only once and for life. He said that he couldn't share his life with me because I couldn't share my life with him. Naturally, I was confused. I was giving him everything I had. He was talking nonsense. Then he said something that changed my life, something that I must remind myself of daily. He said, 'If you can't share your pain with me, then you'll never be able to truly share happiness with me.' His words were so simple, but they were the truest words I'd ever heard. Only after days of mulling over what he had said could I bring myself to tell him everything, including the scariest part of all and do you know what that was?"

I had no idea, but I took a guess. "You told him about your brother and parents dying in the concentration camp? You told him that you loved someone else before him?"

"Yes. I did tell him about all those things, but that was easy. Admitting my shameful secret was an entirely different story."

"Huh? What do you mean? What could you have done that was so bad?

"You will understand, but most people wouldn't. It's so simple, but so complex to the person left holding the bag. There wasn't a day that went by that I didn't praise God for letting me live when so many, including my precious family, had died. I was spared, but why? What did I ever do to deserve such a gift? To ask for happiness on top of the gift of life felt greedy and excessive. I had been given more than my share. Real happiness was off the table for me, or so I had convinced myself—"

"Don't say that!" I said, interrupting her. "You deserve everything. You're wonderful and perfect and you've helped me so much."

"You're sweet, but I've said too much. It was unprofessional to share so much with you. Please pardon my lapse in judgment."

"It's okay. You didn't do anything wrong," I assured her. "Like I said, you're perfect."

Ava sighed. "I've got a newsflash for you. I'm not perfect. You're not perfect, and neither are your parents, and that's okay. You must let yourself off the hook. Life is messy. You'll find yourself against the ropes time and time again, but if you can't find a way to forgive yourself each time you mess up, you'll never be happy, no matter what anyone else tells you."

"What do you mean?"

"What I mean is that you're growing up and taking ownership of your life and that's scary because you're bound to make mistakes. It's scary when you discover that you have a mind of your own and don't always need adults, not even your parents, telling you what to feel and how to think at every turn. It may not seem like it now, but to make a decision and then later discover that you were terribly wrong is a blessing."

"Huh? How?"

"The world doesn't stop spinning so that you can transition from childhood to adulthood without any heartache. Bad things happen and they don't just happen to you. Your brother died and his death wasn't fair, but it happened. Will loved you as much as he could for his 16 years, but he wasn't any more to blame for his feelings than you were for yours. He grew up even faster than you did, and he wanted things that your heart, body and mind just weren't ready for. Instead of trying to assign blame, accept the fact that life sometimes deals out random and unexpected blows. You've got to forgive yourself for not having any control over either situation, and you must forgive yourself for growing up when Denny will never have that chance," she said.

I hadn't thought of any of it the way she explained it. She made it sound so simple. "But where do I start? How do I start?"

"You start by mourning Denny and accepting his death for what it was, an unexpected tragedy. Mourn the loss of Will, yes, but cherish the sweetness of your time together. Don't let regret cloud all that was good. Most importantly, forgive yourself for growing up and disappointing your parents. Be sad, but each day, try to find something to be happy about. Lean on those people who want to be there for you. Share your happiness and your pain with your friends and family. They need you to share as much as you need to share. And when you're done grieving, wipe away the tears from your eyes and give happiness a second try," said Ava.

"He will wipe away every tear from their eyes, and death shall be no more, neither shall there be mourning, nor crying, nor pain anymore, for the former things have passed away," I said, reciting the words on the front of Denny's prayer card.

"That's a nice sentiment," remarked Ava. "But do you actually believe it?"

Shrugging I said, "I suppose so."

"Well that's not good enough! Former hurts will heal and the pain will lessen over time, but only if you trust it will."

"Humph," I scoffed. "That'll take forever, and being this sad really sucks. I hate it."

"You're right, it does suck. Your recovery will be neither swift nor easy, but I promise, you will be happy again. Maybe not today or tomorrow, but happiness is an obtainable goal. You will defeat this depression, Daisy Doyle."

A soft giggle escaped from the smile that was taking shape on my face. My amusement at her words didn't go unnoticed. Ava was on to me. "What? You don't believe me? Why are you snickering?"

"No, no. I do," I assured her. "I guess it's not what you said, but how you said it that sounded kind of funny."

"Funny?" she pressed. "How so?"

I didn't know how to answer her questions without hurting her feelings. For starters, the word *suck* coming from her sounded more foreign to my ears than her accent itself. But even more funny was how she used my full name. It sounded like a smart-alecky comment Will would've made if he were talking to me. Certain my explanation would get lost in translation, I took the easy way out. "Daisy Doyle defeats depression has a nice ring to it, don't you think?"

"You might be onto something," she said.

For the next six months or so, Ava and I suited up each week to do battle. That's how she referred to my depression—as a battle. "Wars are not won in a day. Victory is obtained through strategic planning and careful execution. Some days will be productive and seem almost easy. Other days, you'll feel defeated and want to retreat, but you must stay the course."

Ava was right. My recovery was slow and sometimes inconsistent—a breakthrough one day and a breakdown the next. Ava was patient though. When we mutually agreed that I had safely transitioned from the crisis zone to the maintenance zone, my weekly sessions ended. I saw her on an as-needed basis only, which at first was a little unsettling because I worried that, like a bad habit, depression would find me again if I wasn't in her constant care. Ava was quick to squelch that fear. "It's quite possible that your depression may rally, but now you have the tools to fight it and to keep it at bay. I'm always just a phone call away if you need me."

The new me took a little getting used to. I wasn't the same person I had been before Denny's death or before meeting Will. Traces of my former self still existed, which made it difficult sometimes to find the version of myself that I was comfortable being. When I explained my identity dilemma to Ava she told me not to sweat it.

"You are like a mosaic, a piece of art created out of the remains of something else. Your life experiences are like the colored glass or stones used to create a new art form. Like an artist who must pick and choose which shards go together to form the most attractive pattern, you must pick and choose which life experiences you will use to create the best version of yourself. It is for you to decide who you want to be from this point forward."

Part Three

32
I Don't Want to Be Here
Fall 1987

I noticed Gus lumbering across the straw-colored field carrying an unusually long stick clenched between his teeth. He looked ridiculous, like a clumsy tightrope performer trying to cross a taut wire without falling. His determination to reach his destination, pulled at my heartstrings and I wanted to roll down my window and yell, "You can do it! You're almost there," but I was still too far away for him to hear me. It was the popping and crunching of the gravel underneath my car tires as I turned off the road and onto the driveway that finally captured his attention. Like a thief realizing that he's tripped an alarm, Gus froze in his tracks. I stopped my car in the middle of the driveway, but I didn't turn off the ignition. He stared at my idling car for several seconds before dropping his stick and lowering his body to the ground. With his forequarters in front of him and his hindquarters sticking up in the air, he looked like a jungle cat waiting to pounce. His pink spotted tongue spilled from his mouth and his fanlike tail began swishing back and forth like a geisha's fan. It screamed, *"My girl is home! She's come back!"* I wanted to share his enthusiasm, but I couldn't. I wished more than anything that I had been returning home for some purpose other than the actual reason. For the heck of it, I closed my eyes and, like a gullible child hovering over lit candles on a frosted birthday cake, I made a wish. I was cautious because I had come to accept, among other things that no amount of wishing could ever undo the past. Instead of wasting a wish on something that could never be, I wished for something more practical. *When this is all over,* I thought, *let me shed the straightjacket that binds me to my sorrow, and slip into something billowy and light. Let me try on a flowing, flouncy getup and experience what it is to move with the ease of a dancer. Let me find peace and sashay my way through the rest of my life without a care in the world. Let me dance on life's stage with the whimsical free spirit and bohemian boldness of a rock star.*

I opened my eyes and reminded myself that wishes were for kids and hopeful saps, and that it was time to suck it up and face the music. It was time to turn the final page of the greatest love story ever told. The story of Mom and I was nearing its end. And just when I believed that my thoughts couldn't have sunk any further, I spied Gus belly crawling across the grass toward my car like a soldier planning a sneak attack. He was such a sweet boy. For his sake, I turned off my engine and got out of the car. He stopped when he saw me and just like in the movies, our eyes locked. I nodded, giving him the go ahead to stand, but it took him forever to get up on all fours. "C'mon, you can do it," I said encouragingly. "You can do anything, boy. You're a king, aren't ya boy? King Gus." I looked away so I didn't embarrass him and recalled how he got the silly nickname in the first place.

It had all started with Denny's holiday program. He had landed the lead role, which wasn't much of a part at all, but it was a big deal for a kid his age. Mom was asked to play the piano, which in hindsight is probably the reason Denny was given the primo part in the first place. He wasn't much of a singer, but he did possess an undeniable stage presence. Mom ran lines with him like he was preparing for a Broadway audition and it paid off. His performance was top notch. He ate up the praise and attention from the audience, which is probably why he went around singing and listening to Christmas music 24/7 for several months after the performance. We tolerated the music during the actual holiday season, but by the time March arrived, even Mom had had enough. She hid the Christmas albums in the basement and spun some lame story about shipping the albums off to Santa in the North Pole for him to rub out all the scratches. Her story worked, but it did little to discourage his singing. He sang constantly. Oddly, his favorite Christmas songs weren't *Frosty the Snowman* or *Rudolph the Red Nosed Reindeer*, like every other normal kid, but songs we sang at church during Advent and Christmas. His personal favorite was, *Hark! The Herald Angels Sing*. The fact that he didn't know most of the lyrics, or the lyrics to any of the songs for that matter, was kind of cute in the beginning, but then it got super annoying. He made them up as he went along, but rarely did they make sense. Any time anyone tried correcting him, he'd get mad and go on singing his version of the song. "*Peace on earth and mercy mild,*" became— "*piece of earth and mercy wild,*" when Denny sang it, and, "*Oh what fun it is to ride in a one-horse open sleigh,*" became—"*Omar Farms he likes to ride in a horse pulling his sleigh.*" Eventually Denny got the hint that his singing was getting on everybody's nerves, so he took to serenading Gus. He'd lure him into his room with slices of salami or bologna and then bolt the door. When the lunchmeat was gone, so was Gus' interest in Denny's performances. He'd scratch and whine at the door for someone to let him out. It was at that time that Denny innocently started referring to Gus as the Newborn King. He'd sing, *"Hark the herald angels sing our dog Gus the newborn king."*

Mom blew a nut when she heard it. "Denny, you can't call Gus the Newborn King," she explained. "Baby Jesus is the Newborn King. It's sacrilegious and disrespectful to Jesus to call the dog that. Do you understand that it hurts Jesus when you call him that?"

"No," Denny admitted. "Why can't they both be called that? Gus is a newborn. He's still a puppy and I pick him to be the King."

"He's not a puppy," Mom argued. "Look how big he is."

"Uh-huh. He is too!" insisted Denny. "The vet said he's a puppy until he turns three." As usual, Denny didn't know what he was talking about.

"Still," Mom pointed out, "he's not very king-like."

Denny was too little to truly understand, but after being told at least a hundred times to stop calling him that, he settled on just referring to him as a king. "Would it hurt Jesus' feelings if I call him King Gus?" he asked.

"Well, I suppose that would be okay, but it's awfully silly. Gus is only a dog."

"Not to me he's not," said Denny. From then on, the nickname became a standing joke. Denny would sometimes pretend that Gus was the king of his make-believe kingdom and that he was Gus' loyal subject. He'd tie his already stinky blanket around Gus' neck and place one of his many crumpled *Burger King* crowns atop his block-shaped head. "Stand for your king," he'd say before parading Gus into the room. Denny sounded so bossy, but the rest of us played along because of how cute Gussy looked. If Dad happened to be home, he'd say something like, "King my butt! Don't put your blanket on that stinking dog. His Highness smells like he's been bathing in ditch water again."

I took a knee before calling to him. "C'mon, Gussy! Come here boy!" Like a greyhound from the starting box, Gus was off the second he heard his name. His hip dysplasia had become so bad that he couldn't really run, at least, not like he did before. He hopped like a bunny. I managed to stay on my feet as he dive-bombed into me. He smelled awful, like he'd been rolling around on a dead animal carcass, but I didn't care. I buried my face into the side of his neck and whispered sweet nothings into his stinky ear. "I've missed you. You're such a good boy and still so handsome. I love you, Gussy!" Too excited to let me love on him for too long, he busted out of my arms and scampered off to locate one of his many tennis balls or chew toys that he'd stashed in the yard.

The front door opened and Dad poked his head out. "There you are," he called from the open doorway, "how was your drive? I was getting worried. Didn't have any car trouble, did you?"

33
David and Daniel

Like Gus, I wanted to run to the familiar voice, but I couldn't. My inner child longed to jump into his strong arms where it was safe, but the skeptic in me knew that there was no such thing as a safe place, not really. I knew that heartache was like a slobbering bloodhound. It tracks you down no matter how big of a lead you think you may have on it. Lying to him was easier than admitting that I'd rather be anywhere but home. "The drive was fine. I've made the trip before. You shouldn't have worried."

"I know, I know. I'm sorry, but that's what us Dads do. We worry."

"Well, don't," I said, "I'm a big girl and I can take care of myself."

"Awe, Daisy, I know you can." He stepped down onto the porch. "I'm sorry to be such a worry wart. I'm just so glad that you're home, that's all. I love you, sweetie."

I wanted to say, *I love you too, Daddy. I'm sorry for ripping your head off*, but the words got stuck in my throat. It broke my heart to see him look so lost. He appeared soft and small, not at all like the strong Spartan that he used to be. For the first time ever, he looked his age. His normally thick hair was noticeably more sparse, and was graying around his temples. I was certain that every girl found her dad handsome, but mine really was. Everybody, even some of my friends' moms, commented on how good-looking he was. I even noticed women from our church checking him out during Mass. I've often wondered over the years if it ever bothered Mom that so many women were attracted to her husband. It was a morbid thought, but I wondered how many women would be beating down his door to date him after Mom died. Because my feelings were too raw to say anything that could make either of us feel any better, I changed the subject.

"Are the boys here? I have something for them." I looked around the yard for them as if at any minute one of them would come running by with a loaded squirt gun or a water balloon to throw at me.

"Oh, you know teenagers. David's still sleeping and Daniel's glued to his Nintendo. That's all they do. Sleep, eat and play video games. They're eating us out of house and home. Speaking of eating, are you hungry?"

"Nah, I stopped and got something on the road." I hadn't eaten anything since breakfast the day before, but I didn't dare tell him that.

"So, was your drive home uneventful? Car holding up okay?" he asked a second time.

"Something's wrong with my radio," I decided to tell him. I'm not sure why because I didn't really care about the radio. "It doesn't work. I had to drive the entire way home in silence. I don't know what's wrong with it."

"Ugh, really?" he said, rubbing the stubble on his chin. "Oh well. Guess it could be worse. At least it's not the brakes or the transmission. You can drive without a radio. Could be a blown fuse or just something with the antenna. We'll get it looked at before you head back to school."

I couldn't believe we were talking about a broken radio when Mom was inside on her deathbed. Everything about being home felt surreal. I wanted to scream at the universe, "How can this be happening again?" but I had learned a valuable lesson after Denny's death. The universe was too vast to care about someone as insignificant as me. I knew that we'd all have to find a way to move on after Mom passed whether we were ready to or not, especially Dad. David and Daniel were basically still kids and would need him. I'd need him too, but just as it was with Denny's death, I felt guilty for needing something that Dad was incapable of giving—a mother's love.

Dad shifted his weight like he was standing on hot coals and asked, "Hey, Dais, so what's it going to be? I'm freezing my butt off here. Are you going to pull your car up onto the apron or what? You can't leave it parked in the middle of the driveway. I can move it if you want." It was a simple question, but I felt like I had brain freeze. "Oh, just give me your keys. I'll move it," he said. As he walked out even further onto the porch, something slipped from out of the kangaroo pouch he created using the bottom of his sweatshirt. "Shit!" he yelled. He lifted his foot off the ground and rubbed his big toe. Only then did I notice that he wasn't wearing any shoes.

"Was that a potato?" I asked.

"Yeah, but it felt like a bowling ball. I'm trying to make some potato soup. Your mother loves potato soup. It won't be as good as hers, but it'll be okay."

"So, she's still eating? That's a good sign, huh?"

Dad shook his head. "I'm not sure why I'm making the soup. She won't eat it, but making soup is something she would do at a time like this."

"That sounds nice," I said. "I'll eat some for her."

Dad nodded his head and smiled. "She'll like that. She likes when you eat,"

"Go inside before you freeze to death," I told him. "I'll grab my bags and move my car after I toss the ball around a while with Gus. I'll be in in a couple."

Dad turned and went back inside. He left the potato perched on the top step like a bird on a wire.

Once inside, I noticed for the first time that my fingers and toes felt like ice. I sat down in front of the fireplace to warm them. "Daisy, you're here," Daniel said, bursting into the living room like a Tasmanian devil. He tried bending over to hug me, but he was either too tall or I was too short and my head got wedged in his armpit. I stood and he squeezed me like he hadn't seen me in years even though I had just been home two weeks earlier. He smelled like he'd just bathed in cheap cologne.

"Mmm, you smell good," I said. He didn't really, but I suspected his recent interest in girls had prompted him to give more thought to his hygiene and appearance. Some idiot, most likely David, had probably told him that girls liked dudes who smelled good.

"No school today?" I asked. He didn't answer my question. Instead, he mumbled something into my ear, but it just sounded like a bunch of gibberish. "I can't understand you. What are you trying to tell me?"

His body tensed. "I said that I hate God! God sucks ass!"

My kneejerk reaction, as the wiser, older sister was to tell him that he shouldn't say such things, especially considering that it was obvious that God hadn't exactly taken a shine to our family, but since I shared his sentiments, I didn't give him a hard time. "Don't waste your time," I told him. "Hate's a senseless emotion. You think that hating someone is going to make you feel better, but it doesn't. All it does is force you to relive over and over the hurt that someone has caused you. Take it from me, all that hate just makes you feel worse.

If you really want to stick it to someone, forget about 'em."

Daniel stopped hugging me. "Whatever! He sucks and I'm tired of His shit."

My heart broke for Daniel, but I knew there was really nothing I could say or do to change his mind. My attempt to lighten the mood with a little flattery fell flat.

"Not to change the subject or anything, but your hair's looking pretty sweet. You don't look like a miniature G.I. Joe anymore with that short buzz cut shit."

"Meh, I dunno. What difference does it make? I guess it's cool that Dad's not on my ass all the time to cut it anymore," he said.

Daniel's crappy mood was all consuming so I said again, "It's nice. You look good and don't go getting all, '*I don't give a crap about anything*', because I know for a fact that you do."

"It's alright," he said, probably just to get me off his back.

"It's better than alright dude. I swear you've grown a couple of inches since the last time I saw you. Are you on steroids or something?"

"I'm gonna need some steroids if I'm going to make the top team come spring. Dad thinks that I'm going to be taller than he is, and maybe even David, which is one thing I got going for me, I guess."

"You've got a lot going for you. Don't be so hard on yourself."

"Thanks, Daisy. I'm glad you're home."

"Me too," I told him, and for the first time, I meant it. "Where's David, by the way? Where's Dad? I've got something for you guys."

"David's in the shower and I think Dad's in Denny's room checking in on Mom."

"Denny's room? What's she doing in there?" I asked. Daniel shrugged.

My parents probably hadn't planned on turning Denny's bedroom into some sort of shrine, but that's basically what it had become. His room was exactly as he left it when he died years earlier. Right after his death, my parents walked around in a total haze. We all did. Once the initial shock subsided, they were so dead set on trying to salvage what was left of our shattered family, that sorting through his room was put on the back burner. It wasn't a priority.

For a while, his room became almost like a confessional for all of us. I couldn't speak for what the others in my family did or said when they went into his room, I just know that from time to time, I'd hear his bedroom door open or close, and I'd walk by and see light, or hear the soft mumblings of a one-sided conversation coming from the other side of it.

The night of Denny's funeral, I slipped into his room when everyone else was finally asleep. Nobody was sleeping much at the time, but I wasn't sleeping at all. My hypersomnia came later. I didn't really need to sneak in there because it wasn't like my parents had banned any of us from going into his room, but I didn't want anybody else in there with me. I figured that I'd have a better chance at seeing him or sensing his presence if I went in alone. Because he hadn't been dead long, I thought maybe I could coax him into revealing himself to me. I asked him what heaven was like and if he missed us. I said things like, *Flicker the light on and off if you can hear me* or *communicate with me through Gus.* Poor Gus had slept outside his bedroom door for months waiting for him to come back. I had hoped that, just maybe, Gus would whimper and look at Denny's picture or stare into my eyes and convey some kind of secret message that Denny was trying to send me. Of course, I didn't see him or feel him or receive a communication through Gus, but I smelled him. His room smelled like him for several months after he died, and I was so thankful for that. But after three or four months, his room smelled like nothing and I gave up trying to contact him from beyond the grave.

"Oh wait," Daniel said, after a second or so, "Hospice brought in the bed last week. Last Monday I think. Mom can't sleep with Dad anymore. Too many seizures. I don't see the point in any of it because Dad hasn't slept in the same bed with her for a while now anyway. But the nurse said that Mom would be more comfortable in a hospital bed. Most nights Dad sleeps in the chair next to her bed. And to answer your question, it was her idea to put the bed in Denny's room. I guess it makes sense that she wants to be in there. Maybe having all his stuff around her makes her feel closer to him or something. Don't you think?"

"I'm sure it does," I assured him.

"Dad worried that it might upset her too much to be in his room, but from what I can tell, it hasn't. She doesn't say much, but the few times I've sat in with her I've noticed her smiling in her sleep."

"She smiles?"

"Yeah, weird huh? Hey, maybe Denny's telling her some of his stupid knock-knock jokes. Remember those?" Daniel asked.

"How could I forget? Those were painful. Do you remember his favorite?"

Daniel chewed on the inside of his bottom lip as he tried to remember. Smirking he said, "Okay, okay—here you go! Knock, knock."

I played along. "Who's there?"

"King Tut," he answered, contorting his upper body to resemble one of those hieroglyphs of an ancient Egyptian you see in pictures of murals taken from inside a pyramid or sarcophagus.

"King Tut—" I started to say, but Daniel was an eager beaver and delivered the punch line before cue.

"King tut-key fried chicken! Get it, King tut-key fried chicken," he said, repeating the line as if saying it twice made it extra funny. Laughter bubbled up from deep in his gut and erupted from the pit of his stomach like a fizzy burp. It was unrestrained and contagious. I don't think either one of us ever found Denny's joke particularly funny, but we threw our arms around each other and laughed and slapped our knees like it was the most hilarious thing we'd ever heard. Snot shot from Daniel's nose and he used the bottom of his shirt to wipe it.

I pushed him away from me. "Ooh, gross! You sicko!"

"Well, I guess some of them were kind of funny," said Daniel.

"Not really, but God, it feels good to laugh. It really feels good," I said.

David, who slipped into the room without either of us realizing it, insisted on knowing what we're laughing about. "What's so funny? What feels good?" He was wearing basketball shorts and nothing else. His skin was soft and pink. I shivered just looking at him.

"Jesus, David. Ever hear of clothes?" I asked.

Unlike Daniel, he didn't hug me. He greeted me with a pillow to my head. "Hey, what's up, Sis?" With his wet slicked-back hair he looked like a 1920s gangster.

"Nada. What's up with you, Al Capone?"

He got my reference and grinned. "Eh, not much. I finally got to sleep in a little bit this morning. You just get home?"

"A couple of minutes ago."

He was trying to play it cool, but I could tell by his high-pitched, quivery voice that he was scared shitless, just like everybody else. "Have you seen Mom? Have you had a chance to talk with Dad?"

"Why? What's up?"

"Brace yourself. That's what's up. Mom's a freaking zombie. She's all doped up."

Daniel flew from off the couch and got up in David's face. "Why don't you shut your big, stupid mouth, David?"

"What? She is!" David argued.

"No, she's not. Don't make her sound like she's a freak. She's on a lot of medication and it makes her sleepy and sometimes she's out of it. A zombie is someone who rises from the dead, and then comes back to life and goes around killing people. That's not Mom," said Daniel.

David knew that he'd gone too far with his comments. "Sorry, dude. I'm not trying to be a jerk. I'm just trying to give her the heads-up. Somebody's got to warn her. Mom's going to die soon. She barely speaks, and when she does, it makes zero sense half the time. She's not Mom anymore. Daisy hasn't been home in a couple of weeks and Mom's gone downhill fast."

"Yeah, I know, but don't say it like that. She's not a zombie. She's our Mom."

David placed his hand on Daniel's shoulder as a sort of peace offering, but Daniel shrugged it off. "Dude, I'm sorry. I just didn't know how much Daisy knew. I'm sorry, man. I am."

Daniel didn't stay mad long. "K, just don't do it anymore."

"I appreciate the heads up," I told David, "but to answer your question, Dad phoned me last night." Last night wasn't really accurate, so I started over. "He called me very early this morning. I suppose it was actually more like in the middle of the night, but yeah, he called me."

"So, he called and you know what's what?"

"Yeah, he called. He was wide-awake like me, and he was afraid that if he did eventually fall asleep that he might not catch me in the morning before I left for class. He filled me in. Basically, he told me that Mom went back into the hospital for a few days, but that he didn't tell me because he didn't want me to worry, which really ticks me off, and that the doctors decided that the only humane thing to do was to send her home to die. He explained that Grandma and Grandpa and all of her brothers and sisters and friends had basically said goodbye to her at the hospital and—" David interrupted me.

"Yeah, about saying goodbye. Is it gross that I don't want to say goodbye to my own mother?"

"Gross? That's an interesting choice of words. I'm not even sure I know what you mean by that."

"Shitty. Weird. Selfish. Choose a word, Daisy. I don't know why I said gross, but my point is, I don't want to say goodbye. And it's weird because after Denny, I was so pissed that I never got the chance to say goodbye, or tell him how much I loved him, and then, after we found out how he died, I was so glad that I wasn't there to witness his death. I wouldn't have wanted to see him in the hospital attached to a bunch of tubes. Sometimes, out of the blue, I think about how really messed up it was that Denny just up and died the way he did without any warning. Now with Mom, I don't know which is worse. I was so wigged out by his death and told myself that it was all just a bad dream. The crazy thing is, I let myself believe it. Sometimes I'd wake up in the middle of the night and go to his room and open the door and expect to see him passed out on his floor or singing to the dog. And then by the time reality really sunk in, you lost your shit, and I was so afraid that I might lose mine, that I fought like hell not to. I figured Mom and Dad couldn't take another crisis. I suffered in silence and now with Mom, I'm feeling everything all over again and I don't want to feel anything all!" David cried.

I gave David a rueful smile and apologized even though I knew he wasn't looking for an apology. There was no malice behind his comments. He was right. I had hijacked our family's grief. "I'm sorry. I know that what I'm about to say will sound incredibly stupid, but I promise that I'm being honest. I was jealous of how quickly the two of you seemed to rebound after Denny's death. I knew that you were both horribly sad too, but you guys went back to school right away and went back to doing everything you had done before, like Denny's death was just a bump in the road. Maybe I'm remembering things wrong. I was so out of it. Denny's death combined with Will leaving and changing schools and the move triggered an emotional avalanche inside me. It was like there was an enormous monster lurking in the shadows, and I was the only one who could see it, and it was after me. It wanted to eat me or kill me. I know that you're not trying to make me feel like a total shit. I never really stopped to think about how you guys were doing, but now, looking back, I hate myself for how I behaved, and for how weak I was. I was so messed up that I could only see how his death and all of it impacted me."

"Don't," said David. "That's not what this is about. I'm not blaming anyone for how I dealt with Denny's death. Mom and Dad were great. They were there for me. I'm just saying that I don't think that I'll tell her goodbye and I don't want the two of you judging me."

"We'd never do that," said Daniel, "Not in a million years."

"Thanks, I guess, but there's more."

"We're listening," I said. "Talk to us."

David took a contemplative breath. "I just want her to die already. I don't want to say goodbye to my own mother and that's selfish and awful. I'm worried that there's something wrong with me? Do you think there is? Am I fucked up or what?"

"Hey, watch your mouth," Dad said, breezing into the room, clearly in search of something he'd misplaced. He pushed around the throw pillows and shoved his hands down into the cracks of the couch cushions.

"Looking for something?" I asked. He didn't answer me. "Dad, what are you looking for?" I asked again.

"There you are," he said to the tiny green notebook lying on the floor next to his chair.

"What's that?" I asked.

"I use it to keep track of stuff for your mom. You know, when she takes her pain medicine and how much liquid she takes in and who I need to call and blah, blah, blah."

David swiped the few stray tears from his cheek and asked, "Can I help with anything, Dad?"

"Thanks, bud. Can you go downstairs and toss a few more logs into the stove and then put the clothes that are in the washing machine into the dryer and bring up the dry clothes on top of the dryer?"

"Okay. Anything else?" David asked.

"Yeah, put some real clothes on your back, will you? You're making me cold."

"What about me?" Daniel asked, standing tall and straight like a soldier reporting for duty. "What can I do?"

"Hmm. You can either finish peeling the potatoes or clean the bathroom."

"Potatoes," Daniel answered swiftly. He didn't need to think about it.

"I can do something," I offered. "Anything other than cleaning the bathroom, that is."

Dad held up a finger. "Just a sec." He opened his notebook and wrote something down. When he finished, he looked up and said, "You can give me a hug."

"Seriously. What do you need me to do?"

"I am being serious. I really need a hug right now."

Wrapping my arms around him I said, "I'm sorry, Daddy. I thought you were kidding. Of course, I'll hug you."

He hugged me so tightly that I felt like he was giving me a chiropractic adjustment. As he was letting go I asked, "Would now be an okay time to see Mom?"

"You don't need to ask. She'd love that, but you better hurry. She just took her meds."

"Will you come with me?"

"Awe, don't be scared. It's just Mom, and there's nothing to be afraid of."

"I know, but I am," I admitted.

Dad took my hand and led me down the hallway. The door to her room was already cracked open, so he nudged it a little wider, just wide enough for me to slip in, and then took a step back. "You don't need me."

34
Mama Bird

I waited too long. She was already asleep, so I leaned over her bed and pressed my lips to her cool forehead. Her eyes popped open, but then slowly blinked back shut. Like the wings of a butterfly, her lids fluttered for several more seconds before she finally managed to keep them open for good. She was out of it and I was afraid that she didn't know who I was. "Mom, it's me. Daisy. I've come to see you."

With a little more coaxing, she emerged from her sleepy stupor. Though her eyes were heavy from the pain medication, I could still see in them a love that was reserved exclusively for me.

I wanted to crawl into the bed with her or better still—peel back her blankets and rest my head on her warm stomach like I did when I was a little girl and she was pregnant with each of my brothers, but I was too afraid that I'd crush her.

"Give your mother a hug," she finally said. "I won't break."

"Mom," I said, hugging her as tightly as I could without hurting her. "He can't have you! He's already got Denny."

"Oh honey, you need to be brave. It's time. It's time."

"Says who? It's not fair."

"Says me," she said softly. Tears fill her eyes. "Please don't be mad at me. I'm tired."

I gazed deep into her eyes and lied through my teeth. "Mommy, don't say that. I could never be mad at you." I could tell by the way the light faded from her eyes that she didn't believe me. She knew me too well. The last thing I wanted to do was to upset her, so I started over. "Dad's making potato soup for lunch. I can get us some when it's ready."

"Okay, maybe after I take a little nap. I suddenly feel so sleepy." Desperate to soak up as much love as I could before she fell back to sleep, I gave into my impulse and stripped back her blankets and rested my head atop her soft stomach. The space was warm and safe, like a bird's nest. "I love you, mama bird," I said.

"And I love you, baby bird."

"I really do wish that you were a bird," I admitted, not caring how stupid I sounded.

Mom perked back up. "A bird? Why on earth do you wish I were a bird? Why not an animal that's bigger and stronger? Why not a lioness or an ox?"

"Because they can't go wherever they want. Lions are fast, but only for short periods of time. Oxen are tough, but slow and stupid. If you were a bird then I could be your egg and after a couple of weeks, I'd hatch and the two of us could fly away together someplace safe, someplace away from your cancer and death and sadness."

"Mmm," she said, "I like the sounds of that, but what about Dad? What about David and Daniel? Would they be eggs too?"

"Not Dad. He'd be an eagle or a hawk because he's fast and strong. He'd be our protector, but David and Daniel would be eggs too. We'd be a family of birds and anytime things got bad or we wanted a change of scenery, we could just fly the coop."

Tears slipped once more from her squinty eyes. "You've always been my little dreamer, haven't you?"

I nodded and rubbed my face on the folds of her silky, soft nightgown. "This little bird is tired. I haven't been sleeping much lately."

"Then you must close your eyes and rest." With the tip of her index finger, she began tracing tiny circles on my back just like she had done when I was a little girl and couldn't sleep.

"That feels nice," I said.

After a several minutes, she rested her entire hand on my back. "Look at me a second," she said. "I need to tell you something."

"Do I have to? It feels so good here."

"Just for a minute. C'mon now," she insisted. I sat up and she brushed the hair from my eyes and touched my face with her warm hand. "I'm not afraid to die. I know the paradise that awaits me, but you know what does scare me?"

"No. Tell me."

"I'm afraid that a day will come when you won't remember how much I loved you." She pulled my hand towards her chest and placed it on her heart. "There may come a day when you can't feel it as easily or as strongly as you do now, but when that happens, you must close your eyes and think of me and this very moment. Keep our love alive, by always keeping me in your heart. Your heart is one of my favorite places to be."

"I won't. I could never forget," I vowed.

"Good. Now you've got to promise me one more thing."

"Anything," I pledged.

"When I'm gone, I need you to be brave."

"Don't say that," I told her.

"Daisy," she pleaded, "Please listen. You were so brave after Denny, and I need you to be that brave again."

"Brave? What are you talking about? I fell apart after Denny."

"You did, but then you put yourself back together again, and that takes a lot of courage. I'm depending on you to be brave for the others."

"That's not fair. Why do I have to be the one to be brave?"

"Because you do. That's just the way it is."

"I'll try, but I don't know if I can do it a second time."

"You can and you will," she promised me.

I wanted to believe her, but I wasn't as confident as she was. I rested my head back on the bird's nest, and she resumed making circles, but not for long. When her finger stopped whirling across my back, I knew that she'd dozed off again.

I stood and stretched and noticed for the first time the collection of potted plants and flowers decorating the dresser across from the bed. In the center of each bouquet between the flowers, the baby's breath, ivy, and fern were hand written cards attached to plastic pitchforks. Most of the names on the cards I recognized, but there were a few that I didn't. The prettiest bouquet, the one made up of gold and rust colored chrysanthemums, caught my eye. Next to daisies, chrysanthemums were Mom's favorite flower. Out of curiosity, I checked the card to see who they were from. It was signed simply—*Nelson B.* The name rang a bell, but I couldn't attach the name to a face. My brain had turned to a pile of mush. I heard footsteps in the hallway and poked my head out the door to see who it was. It was Dad. "Hey, who's Nelson B?" I asked. "Is that someone you work with?"

Dad shook his head in disgust upon opening the linen closet. The stack of sloppily folded towels and sheets, clearly the handiwork of either David or Daniel, resembled the Leaning Tower of Pisa. "No, but give me a hand with this would you?" He handed me the stack of towels he was holding in order to refold and restack what had already been put away.

"Nelson B," I said when he was done. "Who's he? He sent Mom a gorgeous bouquet of chrysanthemums, but I can't remember who he is."

"Oh, you probably wouldn't remember him," Dad casually replied, "He was a former student of your mother's."

Out of nowhere, an image of the strange little man's face popped into my head. "Oh yes I do. Mr. Boyd, the guy from the bar! The one who looked like a beady-eyed rodent? The guy you thought was a weirdo."

"That's him, but for the record, I didn't think he was a weirdo. Why do you have to say such unkind things about the guy?"

"Yeah you did, but whatever. I guess I didn't know that he and Mom were so tight."

"They're not," he snapped. "Can't the lonely bastard send flowers to your dying mother?"

"Geez! Okay! I'm sorry for bringing it up. I was just curious."

Dad promptly extended the olive branch. "No, I'm the one that should apologize. I've got a short fuse these days. I'm exhausted."

"I know you are. Why don't you go lay down for a little bit? I can sit with Mom for a while."

Reluctantly, he took me up on my offer. "You sure? I won't sleep long. Just a catnap."

"Sleep as long as you need to. She's in good hands. I'll wake you if I need you."

Back in Denny's room, I checked in on Mom and was relieved to find her still sleeping. In hindsight, I probably should've sat down next to her bed and took in her smell and memorized every line on her face and the shape of her neck and what not, but I felt too antsy to sit. I wanted to kick myself for not remembering my backpack. I was already behind on my reading for my American Literature and World Religion classes and the thought of playing catch-up once I got back to school left me with a sinking feeling. I walked over to Denny's desk in search of a distraction. His desk, gleaming and solid with antiquity, had always been one of my favorite pieces of furniture that Mom had refurbished. She brought it home for Denny about a month before he was born. Dad had been less than thrilled with Mom's find at the time. But after Denny's death, his desk, along with all the other things left behind in his room, were the only tangible parts of him that remained. Like silly souvenirs people drag home from their vacations, the countless photographs of Denny and the random collection of things preserved in his room were the only evidence any of us had that we once journeyed through life with him.

When he laid eyes on that desk all those years back, Dad couldn't hide his displeasure. "What in the hell is it, and more importantly, how on Earth did you get that monstrosity into your car in the first place? You better not have had anything to do with lifting it."

"It's a desk," Mom explained. "It's for the baby."

"For the baby?" Dad asked. "I thought you were done nesting."

"I am, but the baby's going to need a desk."

"Yeah, in about ten years. We don't have room for that," Dad had pointed out.

"We'll find the room. It was the strangest thing, really. I was driving home from the grocery store and for some reason turned a block sooner than I needed to and I saw it just sitting in the middle of someone's yard. I parked the car and went up to the door and knocked. An older gentleman answered. I asked him if the desk was for sale. He told me that he wasn't selling it, but that he was hauling it off to the dump. Can you believe that? He was getting rid of it!"

"Well, yeah," said Dad. "I can. It looks like something that belongs in the junkyard."

Mom ignored his snarky comment and continued with her story. "Anyway, he explained how he was moving into one of those sad assisted living places and couldn't take it with him. That just broke my heart. I couldn't very well let him discard something so beautiful. I had to take it. I really believe that it was meant to be part of our family." Dad didn't buy her hokey story, but Mom didn't give up. "And for the record, Mr. Crabby Pants, I didn't have anything to do with getting it in the back of the station wagon. The nice man and his son did all the heavy lifting. They were so sweet. I sensed that they were relieved that it was going to a new home."

Dad smiled. "Hmm, or maybe they were just relieved that they didn't have to make another trip to the dump."

It took months for Mom to restore the piece to its former glory, but when Denny turned one and was old enough to move out of my parent's room and into his own bedroom, the desk was hauled up from out of the basement for him. The desk, still as beautiful as ever, was coated with a fuzzy layer of dust.

I picked up the framed picture of Mom and Denny, taken just moments after his birth, and traced a tiny heart in the bottom left hand corner of the glass before swiping the rest of it clean with my finger. Aside from the picture, Denny's rusty harmonica, and the shiny black Uncle Sam's 3-Coin Bank that Dad bought him for his seventh birthday, everything else on his desk was junk. I tried opening the top drawer just in case there was anything of sentimental value inside the desk, but I couldn't. It was stuck. The drawer underneath slid open easily, but there was nothing in it but comic books. I left it open and reached my hand up behind the stuck drawer and felt around for whatever was causing the logjam. The culprit was a blue spiral notebook. Like the name on the card attached to the chrysanthemums, there was something about the notebook that made me think that I'd seen it before. There were several other notebooks in various colors and sizes buried underneath it, but the blue one stood out. I opened it.

The first several pages had Denny's favorite comic strips glued onto them—*Beetle Baily, Family Circus* and *Peanuts.* Page after page of Denny's drawings and watercolor paintings followed. The pictures represented all the things he loved most, dinosaurs, castles, army tanks, muscle cars and pictures of Gus. In some of them, I could tell where either Mom or Dad had to help him. Mom was great at drawing people and animals, but Dad was better at drawing things like three-dimensional figures and buildings or cars. Toward the middle of the notebook, I found a page tagged with a paperclip. On it was a picture of Denny and Gus—both wearing toothy grins and standing in the doorway of a tree house. No part of the picture was drawn to scale. Gus stood about a half inch taller than Denny, and the ladder leading up to the tree house stopped mid-trunk. For several pages that followed, there were different variations of the same tree house. About five pages in, a tree house, completely drawn to scale, appeared. The work was too good to be Mom or Dad's handiwork. It looked professionally done—like an architect's blue prints. At the bottom of the page in neat, boxy print was a note that read, *"Denny, what do you think? How do you like all of my additions?"* Next to the question was Denny's written response. *"The picture is missing one thing. See next page."* I turned the page. Once again there was a picture of Denny and Gus, but standing with them was a third person. The third person was a man, a short, squat man with beady eyes. Underneath the picture, in Denny's chicken scratch handwriting were the words *Me, Gus and Mr. B.* There was no mistaking it. The man in Denny's picture was Mr. Boyd. The same Mr. Boyd who sent Mom the flowers. It struck me as odd, but I told myself not to dwell on it. I closed the blue notebook and picked up the next one in the stack, but before I could get all the way through it, it occurred to me—the reason why I recognized the blue spiral notebook in the first place. I needed to tell someone what I had discovered, but I didn't have it all pieced together yet, and I wasn't even sure what it was that I thought I knew.

I grabbed the notebook, went to my bedroom and changed into some running clothes. Driving over to Mr. Boyd's house would've been faster, but I didn't want to risk waking Dad. I slipped the notebook down the front of my sweatpants and pulled on one of the three Michigan State sweatshirts I had purchased for Dad and the boys and hurried down to David's bedroom. His door was open. He sat on the edge of his bed doing dumbbell curls with twenty-pound weights.

"Hey, what's up?" he asked, eyeing my outfit.

"Nothing really, but I need you to do me a huge favor. I really need to go for a run. Dad's napping and I promised him that I'd sit with Mom for a while, but I feel like I'm gonna jump out of my skin if I don't do something with all this pent-up energy. Can you sit with her a bit? I hate to ask because I just got home, but I really need you to do me this favor. What do you say?"

David put down his weight. I could tell that he was a little freaked out by my erratic behavior, but there wasn't time to explain. "Well, I can, but you're acting a little weird. Is something wrong? I mean something more than just needing a run or the fact that Mom is dying?"

"Oh, yeah, I mean, no. No, nothing's wrong. I'm fine. Really, I am. Being home is just messing with my head a little bit. Running clears the cobwebs for me and mellows my anxiety. I probably need to go back on something, but with everything else that's going on, I didn't want to worry Dad or Mom."

"K," he said, "See ya in a few."

"Yep, in a few," I promised.

35
The Notebook

As soon as I got outside, I pulled the notebook out from under my sweatshirt and took off running. I was out of shape, but I felt good once I found my stride. Only when I envisioned myself talking to him did I consider the danger that might have been waiting for me. Just because Denny died of natural causes didn't mean that Mr. Boyd hadn't been up to no-good. I was certain that it was he who was with Denny when he died, but I couldn't figure out why he didn't come forward and just admit to the police that he had been with him. Maybe he was some kind of pervert or serial killer and he didn't want to tip off the police. I should've told David where I was going, but it was too late. It also occurred to me that he might not even be home because it was a Friday afternoon and he was probably still at work. I wasn't even sure exactly where he lived, but I knew that he lived in one of the houses on the private road off the main dirt road. I knew that it wasn't going to be too difficult to figure out. I cleared the woods and was a stone's throw away from someone's back yard. For once, luck was on my side because out of nowhere, Mr. Boyd came from around the side of the house pushing a wheelbarrow. He was dressed in tan coveralls and rubbery looking gardening boots. He placed his shovel and rake in his wheelbarrow and steered it over to his tool shed, but before he could put away all his equipment, the alarm on his watch started beeping. He shut it off and walked to the patio door and disappeared inside the house. I moved quickly because I knew that he'd be coming back out, but before going around to the front of his house to ring the doorbell like a civilized person, I stopped at the tool shed to find something that could serve as a weapon just in case he came after me. The only thing small enough to fit into the pocket of my sweatpants was a box cutter. Clutching the notebook to my chest, I ran around to the front of the house. I rang the doorbell but didn't hear it ding, so I knocked. There were no glass panels on either side of the door for me to look inside his house. I pressed my ear to the door, but I didn't detect any movement. I knocked a second and third time and waited. After the fourth knock, the door flew open. An oven mitt concealed Mr. Boyd's right hand, and he had a look of confusion and irritation on his face.

"Oh, uh, hello there," he said in a frazzled tone. "I was in the middle of pulling my supper out of the oven. Is something the matter? Your knock sounded urgent."

"Oh, sorry, no. I tried ringing the doorbell." I explained.

His face softened. His mouth relaxed. "My doorbell hasn't worked for years. I rarely get visitors, so I never got around to fixing it." I cleared my throat to start explaining the purpose of my visit, but he beat me to the punch. "I'm sorry, but how may I help you?" He stared at me curiously, like he was trying hard to attach a name to my face. His lips pursed like the information was on the tip of his tongue, but he couldn't quite spit it out. When his eyes widened and he released a nervous cough, I knew that he'd figured out who I was, but he continued with the charade of pretending not to recognize me. I played along.

"Mr. Boyd, it's me, Daisy Doyle. You used to take piano lessons from my mom."

The color drained from his face. "Of course, Daisy. How are you? Is everything okay? Your mom hasn't passed, has she?"

I shook my head. "No, not yet, but soon I'm afraid."

He lowered his eyes and shook his head remorsefully. "What a pity. I'm so sorry to hear that. I really am. Your mother is a wonderful woman. So kind and generous."

"Thank you," I said.

"So, what can I help you with?" he asked, eyeing the notebook that was still pressed to my chest. "Are you doing some sort of fundraiser?"

"No, nothing like that. Can I come in for a minute Mr. Boyd?" As soon as I asked the question, I second-guessed my request because I realized that I'd be better off standing on the porch where someone might have a better chance of noticing me.

"Certainly. Come in." There was no foyer, so we stepped directly into his living room. "Would you like to sit down?"

"Oh, no. This won't take long," I assured him.

"Okay, suit yourself." He removed the oven mitt and placed it on the console table next to the door and gave me his full attention. Everything in his house looked super old, including the mahogany Steinway piano sitting in the corner next to the fireplace. Mom would've loved it. He noticed me admiring it. "She's a beauty, isn't she? Belonged to my mother." I smiled, but I caught myself nervously twirling my hair. "Well then. I know that you didn't come all the way over here to see my piano, so to what do I owe the pleasure of your visit?"

I held up the notebook so he could see it. "What's that you've got there?" he inquired.

"A notebook. It belonged to my brother, Denny."

"I'm sorry, but I'm confused. What did you say you needed?"

"Soon after my brother died, you stopped by our house looking for some old piano books that you had lent my mom. She was asleep, so I told you to go into the music room and look around for them yourself. You were taking forever, so I decided to go help you look for them. You had already found your books, but you were getting ready to lift this blue notebook off the side table next to the piano. I knew that the notebook belonged to Denny, but I thought for some reason that you had somehow mistaken it as yours. Do you remember that?"

He pulled at his collar. "No, I'm sorry. I guess I don't. I remember going for my mother's books, but don't recall the notebook. I regretted coming over. Your brother had just died. I guess I just wanted to check in on her. I felt so bad."

He was lying. His right eye was twitching and his neck was red and splotchy like he was suffering from a bad case of sun poisoning. I opened the notebook to the page with the tree house and the picture of him, Denny and Gus. "You drew this, didn't you?"

He stammered. "That's a child's drawing."

"Not the people, the tree house. There's no way Denny drew that."

He looked at the picture more closely. "Indeed, I did, but I don't see your point."

I didn't hold back. "You were the one out in the woods with Denny when he died. The two of you were probably scouting out a place for his tree house. That, or you had already started the construction. You hid his body. Why? Were you messing with my brother? Are you some kind of sicko child molester?"

He took a step toward me. "No, nothing like that. Your brother was my friend."

I pulled out the box cutter and pushed the lever to release the blade, but nothing came out. I prayed that he hadn't noticed. "His friend? Why would a grown man be friends with a seven-year-old boy? Don't come any closer or I'll slice you up. Where's your phone? I'm going to call the police!"

"I'm not going to hurt you, and I didn't hurt your brother either. I promise. There's no need to call the police."

"Then why didn't you come forward? How come you didn't contact them? My mom's dying because of you. She couldn't get past losing Denny and not knowing what happened to him out in those woods."

"I didn't come forward right away. I guess I worried how it would look, but your mom knows, and so does your dad. They know because I told them."

"You're lying. If they know, then why aren't you in jail?"

Mr. Boyd's eyes glistened with tears. "I didn't do anything wrong. Put the box cutter away so we can talk. I won't hurt you. I could never hurt you or your brother. Please let me explain."

Oddly, I believed him, but I didn't want to take any chances. "Okay, but where's your phone. If you try anything, I'm calling the police."

"It's in the kitchen. Follow me," he said.

I followed him into the kitchen and traded a large carving knife sitting next to a cutting board for my bladeless box cutter. He pointed to the phone and I walked over and stood next to it. "Okay, start talking," I told him, "and if you try anything funny, just remember I've got this knife."

"I'm not going to try anything funny."

"Then go ahead," I repeated. "Start talking."

"Do you remember the time when I ran into you and your folks at the bar?" he asked.

"Yeah, what of it?" I asked gruffly, trying not to sound as petrified as I felt, standing in the kitchen with the man who was the last person to see my brother alive. He was just as scared. His voice shook and trembled like an unsteady hand.

"I—uh—shared a lot of personal information that night. Mostly about my little brother and parents. I told you all about how I'd been married for a short period of time, but what I didn't mention is that my wife and I had a child. A son. He passed away in his sleep when he was only a few months old. A specific cause of death couldn't be determined even after the autopsy. The best explanation the doctor could give us was that our boy died of something called crib death. Not having an exact reason for why he died was almost as hard to accept as his actual death. The randomness of it all caused something inside my wife to snap, and she slipped into a terrible depression. I begged her to go talk to someone, but she refused. Eventually her depression led to a suicide attempt, and her doctor convinced me to admit her to a mental hospital. I didn't want to, but he said it was absolutely the right thing to do. She got better, but when they finally released her, she didn't come home. She met and fell in love with another patient during the course of her stay. She left me. I'd lost everything that ever mattered to me in this world—my little brother, my parents, my child and my wife. I had no one."

"So, what does any of that have to do with Denny?" I asked.

"When I started taking lessons and met Denny, I felt like just maybe I was being given a second chance. In Denny I saw my brother, and I imagined that just maybe my own son would've been like him. Your little brother was creative, curious and imaginative, just as I had been when I was a kid. Sometimes when I showed up for my lessons, he was waiting for me. We'd talk and he'd show me pictures of his castles and cars, and other pictures that he had drawn in his notebooks. He knew I was an engineer. Once he shared with me that he wanted to build a tree house. I told him all about the one that my brother and I had built in the woods behind our house when the two of us were boys, before my brother died. Denny showed me his plans and asked for my help designing his tree house. He wanted it to be a surprise for you and David and Daniel. I assumed your parents knew. On the day he died, I had expected him to come out to the woods with your dad, but he came alone. Only when I asked him if anybody knew about our plans did he tell me that he was keeping it a secret from everybody. Like I said, he wanted it to be a surprise. Against my better judgment, I proceeded with our plan and showed him the tree. It was the same tree my brother and I had used to build our tree house years earlier. The rungs hammered into the trunk were still there. Denny climbed up the tree and stood on one of the branches and—"

Suddenly, as if someone has pulled the plug to the television from its outlet, Mr. Boyd went silent and his head flopped to his chest like someone had snapped his neck.

"And what? What happened next?" I already knew the, *what happened next,* but I wanted specifics. I wanted to know how he looked or if he gave any indication that he was in the throes of dying. I needed to know if he saw my brother's soul leaving his tiny body like a fledgling hesitantly fleeing the nest for the first time, or did he just close his eyes and was gone. "Answer me!" I yelled. "I have a right to know!"

Mr. Boyd lifted his chin and continued. "At first I thought he was just horsing around. He clutched his heart almost like he was overwrought with excitement and then he fell out of the tree. I administered CPR, but he was already dead. He was probably already dead even before he hit the ground. I panicked because I knew how his death would look. Everybody in the area knows about my brother and my wife and son. I am well aware that most people find me a little odd, so I cleaned up his body and carried it into the woods and hid it. It was a cowardly thing, but I didn't know what else to do. When you got sick and I heard rumors that your parents had to admit you to the hospital, I went to your parents and came clean. Your dad was furious and wanted to kill me. I didn't blame him. I'd considered killing myself, but your mom believed me and convinced your dad not to go to the police."

"I don't believe you. Why wouldn't they go to the police? They hardly knew you!"

He shrugged. "I know, I know. I would've gone to the police if I was in their shoes, but they didn't because of your mother. I knew your mother for only a brief time, but she was like no other person I'd ever met before. She was pure of heart and so easy to talk to. She was an angel. I guess you'd say that we had become friends. She believed me about Denny and found it in her heart to forgive me. I don't know how, but she did and in time, so did your dad. Please believe me."

The knife suddenly felt ugly in my hand. I set it down on the counter and slouched down onto the kitchen floor. Tears didn't come. For years I believed that knowing exactly what happened to Denny would somehow make me feel better but it didn't. There really was nobody to blame. I had so badly wanted to finger someone for the heinous act committed against my brother and my entire family.

I felt comforted knowing that Mr. Boyd had been with him when he died, and relieved to know that nobody had wanted to bring any harm to my brother. Mr. Boyd's intentions had been pure and Ava had been right. It had been Denny's time to go. I thought back to all the conversations I had with Ava about choices and choosing to be happy and choosing to remember the bad in order to remember the good. My parents had made a choice when they decided not to contact the police about Mr. Boyd. They had chosen forgiveness over vengeance.

Mr. Boyd walked past me over to the phone, picked it up and dialed. "John. Daisy's here at my house," I heard him murmur into the phone. After that, I stopped listening. A couple minutes later, Dad was standing in Mr. Boyd's kitchen.

"You okay?" he asked.

"I think so."

We didn't talk on the car ride home. The next day, early in the morning, Mom passed.

36
Truth

Mom's wake wasn't at all how I imagined it would be. For starters, there were tears, but not the beat one's breast kind. "I want people to celebrate my life, not mourn my death. Keep it light," were her only instructions, so we did our best to do just that.

In her honor, I wore my defunct sorority sister dress. Grandma thought my look was over the top and highly inappropriate. "You look like a beauty pageant contestant. You're at a funeral home for crying out loud," she complained, but I felt like I'd finally found the perfect occasion to wear it. David, Daniel and I took turns playing the piano. We didn't play churchy songs— no *Amazing Grace* or *Here I Am Lord*—we played songs that she liked. Only when David played *Beautiful Boy* by John Lennon did the tears flow easily and unabashedly. When he finished, there wasn't a dry eye in the place.

Family and friends came in droves to pay their respects, including Mr. Boyd, who talked almost exclusively with David and Daniel. I wasn't sure how I'd feel if I ever saw him again, but witnessing his interaction with my brothers, my heart filled with relief, because he was exactly what Mom claimed that he was, a sweet, harmless hermit.

Moments before it was time to leave for the wake, Dad pulled me aside and said, "I know that it's a lot to ask, but let's keep what you've learned about Mr. Boyd between the two of us. Maybe someday I'll tell your brothers, but now is not the time."

"Secrets are bad," I told him. "They have a right to know."

319

"And normally I would agree, but that man has suffered enough and so have your brothers. We all have. Besides, that's the way your mother wanted it. We can talk about this subject more when the dust settles a bit, but for now, we need to give your mom the send-off she wanted and deserves. Today is about honoring your mother."

I knew that he was right, so I let it go.

Ava also made an appearance. Dad was surprised to see her, but I wasn't. She had entered my life for a reason and was just as much a part of me as Will, Denny, Mom and the rest of my family. True to her word, she was present to share in my pain, just as she'd been there to share in my triumphs over the years.

"How are you holding up?" she asked, dabbing her eyes with her hanky.

I respond in jest by saying, "Remember, you mustn't dab your eyes with that hanky if you've used it to blow your nose."

"Huh?" she asked, ignoring my subtle grin. My comment was in reference to the comment that she had made to me during my first visit with her when she scolded me for wiping my eyes with the same snotty tissue I had used to blow my nose, but it went right over her head. "Oh, you're right," she said, pulling out a clean tissue from her purse. She blew her nose and waited for me to answer.

"Honestly? Not so hot. It sucks, but what choice do I have?"

"You don't. You've got to go through it and not around it," she said, encouragingly.

I knew only too well that what she preached was the gospel truth. "Well, you'll be relieved to know that I'm feeling every excruciating emotion associated with having my mother snatched unfairly away from me and I feel like total crap."

Ava swiped her hand across her forehead and hummed a sigh of relief. "Thank goodness. If you'd told me otherwise, I'd be worried." We visited for a while, but before she left she said, "Stop by and see me before you head back to school if you can spare the time."

"I'm two steps ahead of you," I told her. "I've already made an appointment."

At 6:40 the funeral home director announced that the family was going to begin praying the rosary in twenty minutes. His pronouncement prompted all the non-Catholics to begin saying their goodbyes. I decided that it was the perfect time to visit the restroom. Like a misshapen water balloon, I felt my full bladder swishing around in my lower abdomen. After relieving myself, I sat in the abandoned lounge area to enjoy a few minutes of uninterrupted silence. It felt good not to speak or listen. Later, as I was making my way out of the bathroom, I ran into Miss Klein. Seeing her was bittersweet. I had been so wrong about her back when I first met her. She, more than any other staff member at my school, went out of her way to keep an eye on me those first couple of months after I was released from the hospital and was struggling to find my sanity. I never properly thanked her for having my back, but when I tried telling her everything that I should've said back in the day, I lost it and began sobbing like an inconsolable baby. She cried too, but in her true no-nonsense fashion, she gained her composure pretty quickly and said, "Now look what you've gone and made me do, Doyle. If you were wearing the proper footwear, I'd make you run laps, but since you're not, you'd better dry up them eyes of yours and go call on your old friend, Will Banks."

"Will?" I asked. "What do you mean? Is he here?" My eyes perused the room for his blond head and white, flashy smile.

Miss Klein also looked around. "Well, he was. I just finished speaking with him a few minutes ago."

Since he was nowhere in sight, I bombarded her with a slew of questions. "Well how's he doing? When did he get back in town? Is he just visiting?"

"He got into town yesterday. I'm not sure of his plans, but after we spoke, I saw him talking with your dad. Maybe he knows where Will scooted off too."

My eyes darted in the direction of the door, but Will wasn't there. I noticed Dad sitting by himself next to Mom's casket sipping on a cup of coffee. He looked worn-out, but he smiled when he saw me and motioned me over with his eyes. I promised Miss Klein that I'd be right back and made my way over to Dad to drill him about Will.

He initiated our conversation. "There's something I need to tell you."

I could tell he meant business so I sat down next to him. "Okay, I'm listening."

He didn't beat around the bush. "It's about Will."

"What's wrong? Is he okay?" I asked impatiently.

"Will's fine, but I need you to know that I misjudged him all of those years back."

I felt myself scowling. "And you know that after having a five-minute conversation with him? Miss Klein saw you talking to him."

"Just listen," Dad pleaded. "I spoke with him longer than that, but nah, I've always suspected that he was an okay kid."

"Could've fooled me, but whatever," I said jerking my chin. "What did he want? I want to know everything. I hope you were nice to him."

He ignored my last two remarks. "He made his peace and I made mine."

"What does that mean? *Made his peace?* He didn't do anything wrong."

"I didn't mean it like that. He felt like he owed me an explanation about what happened between the two of you. He basically reiterated all the same sentiments he wrote in the note that he had given Denny to give to you, but this time around, he expressed himself a little more eloquently. He seems like a caring, mature young man."

"I wouldn't know what was in the note," I reminded him. "I never read it, remember?"

"I know that, and that's why I need you to hear me out. It was wrong of me to keep it from you. I apologized to Will and now I need to apologize to you."

"No, you don't," I told him. "I understand. I'm not stupid. I get now why you didn't give me the note."

"Please let me explain, Daisy. I need to get something off my chest. I wish now that I had told your mother."

"Okay, Daddy."

He drew in a deep breath and said, "I knew before the police showed up that night to look for your brother that he was already dead."

His admission surprised me. "But how? How did you know that Denny was already dead?"

"Sometimes I question if what I'm about to tell you really happened or if it's just a figment of my imagination. At times I remember very little from around the time of his death and the year that followed, but other times, I'm consumed with all the feelings associated with his death as if it occurred yesterday. Do you know what I mean?"

"I do, Daddy, and it's understandable."

"Thanks, but I'm not sure how to say what I'm about to say without sounding crazy."

"Sometimes it's easier to say something difficult if you close your eyes," I told him. "That's what I did sometimes with Ava."

Dad's eyes remained open, but his face took on a faraway expression. "I'd give anything to have one more chance to call your brother in for dinner, but at the time I resented having to get up from the table to go look for him. Can you imagine?" he asked. I didn't answer him because I knew that he was only trying to make a point. "I stood at the garage door and called his name five or six times, but when he didn't come, I stomped off into the back yard. Out of nowhere, I was greeted by a gust of warm air, which was odd considering the sun was nearly down and I could feel and smell the impending storm swirling around in the damp, chilled air. The warmth of that air enclosed me, and for a few seconds I was filled with an overwhelming sense of calmness and serenity. Almost as quickly as the weird sensation attached itself to me, it was gone, but before it could completely disperse, I heard in it the faint whisper of Denny's voice calling my name. At the time, I shrugged it off as a weird auditory hallucination, but later, when the police showed up and we began looking for him, I knew that what I had felt was Denny's soul exiting this world."

"Oh, Daddy," I said, "I totally believe you because I also knew that Denny was dead, only I didn't know how I knew." I leaned in closer to him before elaborating. Like Dad, I had a tough time believing that what I was going to tell him was based in reality.

"The night of Denny's funeral, I went to his bedroom and prayed for him to make an appearance or to give me a signal that he was somehow still with us even though he was dead, but I never got one. But now, after hearing your story, I wonder if maybe he had tried contacting me. Not the night of his funeral but on the actual day he died—at the time of his death. I knew when the police told us that they were going to find him that they wouldn't. I knew he was already gone. I don't know why or how, but I did."

Dad smiled at me, but it wasn't a forced smile. It was a happy smile. "He loved you. The two of you shared a special bond. You were like his second mother and he adored you."

A comfortable pause followed. Finally, I asked, "Can I ask you just one more thing?"

Dad stared meaningfully in the direction of Mom's casket before turning his attention back to me. "Of course. Ask away. I don't want any more secrets between us."

"Why didn't you tell Mom about Denny? She of all people would've believed you. Mom was totally into all that spiritual mumbo jumbo. She saw signs in everything, even when they weren't there. Remember how anytime she smelled something floral she'd insist that it was the Holy Mother? She could've been standing right next to a rose bush, but she didn't care. To her it was a divine message, a visit from Mary."

"She sure did. She argued that everything happens for a reason—the good, the bad—all of it. That's why I never told her. It would've killed her knowing that Denny sought me out, but not her, or maybe he did, who knows? Maybe she went to her grave with a similar secret."

As much as I wanted to continue talking about Dad's spiritual encounter with Denny, it was killing me not knowing about Will, so I changed the subject. "So, can we get back to Will and the note?"

Dad nodded. "The moment I read his note, I wished I hadn't."

"You did? Why? Was it embarrassing?"

"Because truth is a funny thing. We go to great lengths to seek it out, but once we find it, we often regret it because we realize that there are some things we're better off not knowing. When I read his note, it became painfully obvious to me that a part of you that had once belonged to me now belonged to him. You weren't my little girl anymore, and that was a hard pill to swallow. I had lost you and Denny practically at the same time. I needed to assign blame to someone for Denny's death, and Will was an easy target. He was a safe person to be mad at."

"You didn't lose me. I was always there. I just grew up some."

"I realize that now. I guess I just wanted to stop time because I couldn't handle any more changes. Your depression scared me and I was worried that the you I had always known was gone forever, like your brother."

"I'm sorry I put you and Mom through so much. I didn't mean to."

"I know you didn't. You couldn't help it," he said before reaching into his suit coat and pulling out a folded piece of lined paper. "Here, take it. This belongs to you. I should've given it to you years ago. My opinion of Will doesn't matter. I should've trusted you more. You could never give your heart to someone not worthy of possessing it."

My hands shook as I tried unfolding it. "If you don't mind, I'm going to step outside for a minute and read this before the rosary starts."

Dad grabbed the note from my hand, refolded it, and handed it back to me. "I do mind. There's no time for that. Will left about fifteen minutes ago. He's staying at his dad's place in the new subdivision just north of town, but I don't know for how long. It's the only house still under construction."

"What are you saying? I can't leave Mom's wake. What about the rosary? What will people say? Why didn't he stick around to talk to me?"

"I don't care what people think and he probably didn't stick around because he lost his courage and regretted coming. He could've left for several reasons, but what matters is that he came in the first place. And as far as ditching the rosary, you know what your mom would say—."

I answered, "Life is too short to dwell on the little things."

"Exactly, so go talk to Will."

"But what will I say? So much time has gone by."

Dad handed me the keys to his car. "You'll think of something on the way I'm sure. Now go, before Father Dan sees you. Most of his flock isn't sticking around for the rosary."

37
The Only Question That Really Matters

The driveway hadn't been poured, so I parked my car on the shoulder of the road next to what I presumed was Will's dad's car. Like a pirate walking the plank, I slogged across the two-by-fours leading to his front porch and prayed that Will and not his dad answered the door. I hadn't seen either of them since before Will left town. In the lifestyle section of the newspaper about a year before Mom got sick, I stumbled upon a wedding announcement for Will's dad. There had been no mention of Will in any part of the article, but it did reference the fact that the bride's two young daughters and son were part of the wedding party.

The unfinished house looked abandoned, which made me worry that maybe Will wasn't there. I forged ahead because I knew there was only one way to find out. I knocked on the front door and waited. I told myself that if he didn't answer, I'd take it as a sign that the two of us were truly not meant to be. The door opened, and I temporarily stopped breathing. Will looked exactly as I remembered but only taller and even more handsome. He was surprised to see me, which I found a little annoying since he had just crashed my mom's wake. "Daisy. Hey—how are you?"

"Well, I've been better."

"Do you want to come in?" he asked, opening the door wider.

I peeked around him. "Your dad here?"

"No. He's letting me crash here for a few days while I'm in town. I'm not really ready for the whole *Brady Bunch* thing."

"Hmm? What's that supposed to mean?"

Will looked embarrassed. "Oh yeah. You wouldn't know. My dad got remarried. I've got two step-sisters and a step-brother," he explained.

"Actually, I do know. I read about his wedding in the paper. Were you there?"

"Nah, I didn't go. I was pissed at him at the time," Will admitted. He stepped out of the way and asked again, "So are you coming in or what?"

I looked at my wrist to check the time but realized I wasn't wearing a watch. "For a minute I suppose." I followed him into a large, open space. There was an enormous chandelier hanging down from the raised ceiling, and the only furniture was an open sofa bed.

"Do you want to sit down?" he asked, pointing to the unmade bed. I flicked my eyebrows up as if to say, *you're kidding me, right?* But because there were no other seating options, I plunked down onto the edge of the bed. He sat down next to me. "Daisy, I've missed you," he said without a moment's pause. "I think about you all the time."

His frankness caught me off guard, but only for a second. "Hmph! You sure do have a funny way of showing it. I hardly think about you at all."

My bitchy comment didn't deter him from spilling his guts. "There were so many times I wanted to call you or write to you, but I figured there probably wasn't any point."

I found his choice of words galling. "There wasn't any point? What the hell's wrong with you? You broke my heart! You were my best friend and I needed you, but you left and I was left alone to mourn Denny and to get over your sorry ass all by myself!"

"I know. Take it easy. You didn't let me finish. I didn't call or write because you said that you hated me. Your dad wanted to kill me. I didn't know what to say. I was a loser and I thought it was better for everyone if I just left. After a while, I felt like too much time had passed to try to make amends."

"That's a load of crap and you know it. Be honest. It was better for you to leave because you were a spineless cheat. Why did you even bother coming back here Will? I'm so over you," I lied.

"Well, I'm not over you. It occurred to me the other day, when I was on the phone with my dad and he mentioned that your mom had passed, that I wasn't happy living in California anymore. Right around the time your brother died and all that shit was going down between the two of us, my mom went off the rails. She begged me to come live with her. My Dad didn't like the idea, but I wore him down. At first, I liked it. But after a while, I felt homesick for my friends and my grandparents and you, but I felt obligated to stay. I was all she had."

"But you were all I had," I told him.

"I know, and I'm sorry, but I'm here now. My mom's met this new guy and he seems to make her happy. They're planning on getting married. I don't know what to do. I hate the thought of leaving Stanford, but I'm ready to come home. I'm ready to give us another try and—"

"Wait! You go to school where?" I asked.

"Stanford. Does that surprise you?"

"Yeah, it kind of does," I admitted.

Will didn't hide the fact that I had offended him. "What's that supposed to mean? You think I'm too dumb to get into Stanford? Where do you go to school? Harvard?"

"No, Michigan State. C'mon, where else would I go?"

"Figures," he said smugly. "Well if I move back, I ain't going to State. I'll be in Ann Arbor. I'll be a Wolverine."

"Ooh! 'You ain't gonna be at Michigan State,' huh? Nice grammar."

"Dammit Daisy, I didn't come back to fight with you!" he snapped.

"Then what did you come back for? I wish you'd stayed away." Will looked dejected and I knew that I was hurting him and it broke my heart.

"I came back because I wanted to be here for you."

"Well, I don't need you. I gave up on you a long time ago."

Things weren't going at all how I had hoped. I felt like a pushover for leaving my family and running back to him after everything he'd put me through.

"I think I ought to leave. I don't know why I came in the first place. We ended a long time ago and I've moved on."

"Daisy, don't. I don't want you to leave. Please stay and hear me out," he begged.

"Why should I? I didn't want you to have sex with Stacy, but you did. I didn't want you to leave, but you did. I didn't want you to shit all over my feelings, but you did. So how does it feel to want?" I started to leave, but he reached for me. "Don't touch me," I yelled.

He backed off, but he didn't back down. "Just hear what I have to say and then you can go."

"Why should I? I need to get back to my family. If you had something worth saying, then you would've said it by now. I'm leaving."

Will was silent. He stared at me like he had a wad of bread stuck in his throat and needed a drink of water to wash it down. I waited for him to say something that would change my mind, but he just stood there. "Okay," I said, throwing my hands up in the air. "Well, it's been real. Good luck with your move and Michigan and everything else. Thanks, I guess, for making an appearance at my Mom's wake." I didn't really want to leave, but I was afraid that he was never going to say what I needed to hear. "Good bye, Will."

I made it all the way to the door before he yelled, "I didn't sleep with Stacy. You walked in before we had sex. It doesn't make what I did do with her okay, but we never actually did it. I was 16 and stupid. I wanted to have sex with you in the worst way, but you didn't want to be with me. I don't know what to say other than I'm sorry."

I turned to face him. "I'm sorry, but that's just not good enough."

"Well then, how about this?" He said, kneeling on one knee like he was going to propose.

"What are you doing? Are you crazy? Get off the floor." His grand gesture, though gushingly romantic, was a little over the top, even for me.

"Uh-uh, not until you hear me out. I messed up. Stacy meant nothing to me. Honestly, I didn't even like her because I was so into you. I'm not blaming you, but you made me feel like there was something wrong with me because I wanted to be with you. I really did want to be with you and not just in a sexual way, like, all the time. You're the only girl, or person that's ever really mattered to me. I know my timing couldn't be worse, and that I'm probably too late, but I love you. I still love you." He stood and then asked the only question that really mattered. "Is that good enough?"

Was it good enough? I contemplated his question. It was, but I didn't know about the next day or the day after that. Like a weather vane that changes its direction on the whim of the wind, I knew that some unforeseeable event could come along and move my life in a totally different direction, so I decided to take a chance and said the only thing that made sense at that precise moment, "Follow me."

Will trailed behind me back to the room with the sofa bed. I slipped off my shoes, slid down onto the mattress, and tapped the empty space beside me. Will joined me. Though fully clothed, our shared silence and proximity created a certain intimacy that I'd never felt with another living soul. There had been other boys after Will but nobody serious. Will took with him my heart the day he left for San Francisco, and I wanted it back. After a bit Will drifted off to sleep. The large room felt chilly and yet, too small to contain all the love I was feeling, so I nestled into the crook of his arm. The space, like Mom's soft stomach, was a safe nest. And though it was the most perfect place to be, I realized that I was no longer a fragile egg. "It's good enough," I whispered softly. Will stirred, but he didn't waken. The faint smile on his sweet, sleepy face told me that he heard me. And for the first time, in a long, long time, I didn't worry about what tomorrow would bring.

CPSIA information can be obtained
at www.ICGtesting.com
Printed in the USA
LVHW112056031218
599058LV00005B/122/P